I0565130

The Night People

A Novel About the Paranormal

by

C. LEE

for my dad

TABLE OF CONTENTS

CHAPTER ONE

This is a story about greed, obsession, and madness. I will refer to myself as "Joey", but that's not my real name. I'm also not using the actual names of the other people in this story, or I will use their nicknames. I come from a small town in the Appalachians. I will not be any more specific than that.

My family is from the old country. We settled here in the early 1800s, and we have been here ever since. For generations, the men either farmed or worked in the mines. We have recently gotten away from those professions and now almost everyone does construction and other forms of skilled labor. I was the only one in my family to graduate from high school since everyone else gave up when they were around sixteen. A couple of my relatives quit showing up a few weeks before their sixteenth birthday, and the principal was perfectly okay with it. His attitude was they had learned all they were going to learn anyway, and he and the other teachers were enjoying the peace and quiet. Some of my relatives got their GEDs and went to trade school. Others went ahead and joined the workforce. No one ever needed a job with a pension since the men in my family work until they die.

We each own a home on plots of land that have been passed down through the family for generations. Not far from our collected properties is a small mountain town where almost everything closes around five o'clock in the evening and nothing is ever open on Sundays. It consists of a main street and a couple of side streets. Each of the storefronts contains some sort of business vital to the existence of the people who live in the area, so there is rarely a reason to leave. At the end of the street is a non-denominational church that has been there for decades. Everyone attends on Sunday mornings because they don't want to be the one who gets talked about. This is not the kind of place people move to, but occasionally someone will leave. Although most of the people here are decent enough, the social dynamic in this place can be kind of tricky.

I'll try to explain.

If you allow yourself to become too involved in other people's lives, they will become too involved in yours. But if you stay away completely, they will wonder why you don't want anything to do with them and turn vindictive. That's when the speculation starts. And lies, no matter how outrageous, can become collectively accepted as the truth. You never want that since the actual truth becomes meaningless and the false truth becomes gospel.

But I believe the main collective quirk of this town is people can become overly sensitive, and thus, potentially violent if they believe their intelligence, or their honor, has been insulted in any way. For example, in the fifth grade, everyone in my class got into a huge fight over the famous NASCAR driver and owner, Junior Johnson. It started when Jack Hawkins swore his granddaddy was the one who had first taught Mr. Johnson how to drive.

No one believed him for a second. Jack and his entire family are known for telling ridiculous stories that couldn't possibly be true, and we all started laughing hysterically. Truthfully, we were laughing so hard we were crying.

But Jack wasn't trying to be funny, and he took it personally. To doubt his words meant we were doubting the credibility of his grandfather. So, with his family's honor at stake (and I use that term loosely), a huge fight broke out as he started beating people up. Almost the entire room got involved, including a few of the girls. None of Jack's close friends believed him either, but they were willing to back him up since they knew better than to cross him. The teacher was out taking a smoke and well out of earshot.

I was one of only four kids in our class who had not repeated a grade or two or three, so nearly everyone was bigger and meaner than me. (And yes, that includes every one of the girls.) Jack was supposed to be in the ninth grade, and he was big for his age anyway, so he was much stronger than the rest of us. He looked like a full-grown man compared to those of us who were in the right grade.

I was planning to stay off to the side where it was safe. But when Jack started beating the fool out of a friend of mine, I got involved as best I could. The fight ended several seconds later when one of the girls started crying and begging Jack and his friends to stop. Someone should have tried to find a teacher when the trouble first started, but we were just kids, and no one wanted to be a snitch.

The devastation in our little classroom was unspeakable. I came away with a bloody nose and a black eye, but I got off easy compared to some of the others. When the teacher finally came back, she let out a high-pitched scream that must have been heard for a mile. The other teachers came running and they also started screaming. Once they had all gotten over the initial shock, Jack and his friends were led out of the room and the teachers started bandaging everyone. There wasn't any kind of school nurse at the time, but that changed when the mothers started volunteering in shifts. They were given first aid training and they all pitched in for bandages and other supplies when needed. And yes, this incident is what started that little volunteer program.

This all happened on a Friday and by Monday I had recovered well enough to go back. But my parents kept me home over the entire next week for my protection—even though the troublemakers were no longer there. Several of the other kids stayed home as well. Our teacher was fired, and the principal taught our class for the rest of the year. He had no trouble from those of us who were still in there.

Jack and his friends were sent to juvenile hall, and his time in there did nothing to reform him. Years later he was sent to state prison for indecent exposure in the middle of a grocery store, but that's another story and I don't like telling it. One day he got in an argument with one of his cellmates and busted the guy's head wide open. At this point, I guess he will die in prison.

But Jack is an example of the kind of person you will find here. Up until then, he wasn't such a bad guy. All it took to send him to the dark side was to challenge his credibility or the credibility of anyone in his family. That's hard to avoid in this town since people here love to take the facts and twist them around.

Case in point, NASCAR legend Robert Glenn Johnson, Jr., otherwise known as Junior Johnson, is from Wilkes County, North Carolina which is hundreds of miles from here. Jack's family is not from that area, so I do not believe his grandfather ever knew Mr. Johnson when he was learning how to drive, much less taught him how to drive. However, "Johnson" is one of the most common surnames in America, and "Junior" is one of the most common nicknames—making it plausible Jack's grandfather knew someone who went by that name. It just wasn't the same "Junior Johnson" who became famous. Maybe his grandfather told Jack about a friend with the same name and Jack was confused, or maybe his grandfather was getting on in years and was confused about the Junior Johnson he used to know and the one who became famous. But regardless, Jack was furious when we didn't believe him, and we paid the price.

***

I graduated from high school on a Friday night and by Monday morning I was starting my new job as a custodian at a junior college about fifteen minutes up the interstate. I had no idea how the job fell in my lap.

One day, late in the spring semester of my senior year, my high school guidance counselor said a man from the nearby junior college had called and wanted to meet with me. I told her I wasn't planning to attend college, but she told me it was about a job.

That afternoon after school I drove over and learned they had an opening for a custodian. I had never given any thought to doing custodial work, but it was inside and that appealed to me right off. I visited with the head custodian for a few minutes and then he told me I was hired.

Sure, it's disgusting work at times. During exams, someone will typically puke their guts out right in the middle of class. The instructor calls me to the rescue with my mop and bucket while the rest of the class waits outside. I believe the women do it because of anxiety and I suspect it happens to the young men because they had a little too much before class to take the edge off. But outside of that, my job consists of simple mopping, vacuuming, dusting, and emptying trash cans. I arrive every day at three in the afternoon, and I clock out at midnight.

It only takes me and the other members of the custodial staff about three or four hours of intense work to complete our assigned regular duties. We then goof off for the rest of the shift. By then the students and faculty have gone home so we nearly have the place to ourselves, except for anyone who is hanging around in the library. One evening the college president, Dr. Seavers, dropped in around 10:00 pm to pick up an important fax in his office he did not want anyone else to see, and there we were playing cards in the middle of the cafeteria. (This was before colleges started using email.) I thought we were getting fired, but it didn't seem to faze him. He just smiled, said hello, and kept right on walking. My supervisor later explained President Seavers didn't care what we did during the last part of our shifts, providing the place was spotless when he came in the next morning. Dr. Seavers was also happy to have someone else in the building with him whenever he needed to work late–even if we were just goofing off.

Every night I get home around 12:30 and I go to sleep at six or seven the next morning. I then wake up around 2:00 pm and get ready for work. It's the perfect schedule for early morning hunting during deer season. I also hunt turkey, possum, ducks, and quail. I guess I came by it naturally since everyone in my family loves to hunt and fish. My grandmother first showed me how to fire a rifle, field dress a deer, and clean the gun afterward when I was only twelve.

During deer hunting season, I go out to my favorite stand on my family's property sometime around four a.m. and sometimes I get a nice-sized deer right around dawn. On the weekends I keep the same schedule, but at three o'clock I go out to the stand for an afternoon hunt instead of going to work.

Although I'm mainly a morning hunter because of my work schedule, I also love afternoon hunting as well. Right at sunset, when it's still light and the tree shadows are gone, is my best time for picking up a sizable deer. I easily have enough venison in my freezer to last for months once hunting season is over. Until recently, I thought I would spend the rest of my working life with this routine, which was fine with me. However, my extended family resented me since they all had physically demanding jobs and were often working under dangerous conditions. I also didn't have the financial burden of a wife and kids. I dated some in high school, but I never had a steady girlfriend. The local women later lost all interest in me when I started working as a janitor–which to me didn't seem right. But being single gave me the flexibility to have this kind of life with little stress or responsibilities.

Another thing that aggravates the rest of my extended family is the college shuts down for two weeks during Christmas and for a week every March for spring break. When some of my relatives heard I would not be working the week after Christmas, they asked me to help with a tough construction job they were doing. Even though it was out in the freezing cold, they assumed I would jump at the chance for some work since they were under the impression I would be missing two weeks' pay.

They were disgusted and appalled when I told them I was still getting paid even though I wasn't going to be at work. (It's called holiday pay.) And worse yet, I told them I had plans to compete in a hunting competition over a thousand miles away. No one outside of my immediate family has spoken to me since. I don't know if they ever found out I won the competition, but I believe it's just as well they didn't.

CHAPTER TWO

About three months later, I arrived at work one afternoon and clocked in just like always. But when I walked into the custodian's area, I noticed my supervisor was sitting at our small break table with a solemn look on his face. Something was wrong. He asked me to sit down with him, and with a tear in his eye, he informed me Dr. Seavers had requested a private meeting with me in his office.

It was always bad when the president called you into his office alone. He would have allowed my immediate supervisor to tell me if it had been good news. But a closed-door meeting with the head man either meant you were getting fired or your job was being eliminated. Depending on the physical size of the person being let go, the strength and conditioning instructor (who is very muscular) might be there as well.

The walk of shame to the other end of the building was excruciating as my mind raced as to what might be wrong. It was rare for someone to lose their job due to downsizing, and there was always plenty of warning before that happened. No, if I was about to lose my job, then I was being fired. But why? Did I inadvertently make someone mad? Did I mess something up? Or maybe I was being accused of something I didn't do.

I was shaking when I walked into his reception area. Mrs. Banks, his secretary, had a confused look on her face as she sent me into his office. That was not a good sign since she was usually very cordial.

But my fear faded away when I walked into Dr. Seavers' office. He was smiling and happy to see me. There was another man in the office with him. "Hello Joey, I would like to introduce you to Mr. Burt Russell. He has traveled a long way to meet you," he said.

Although I am using false names, with Mr. Burt Russell I am using the name he gave us at the time. I would later learn this was not his real name. And the next morning the similarity to his fake name and the name of a famous actor and hunter would lead to a huge misunderstanding where I almost got killed.

Mr. Russell was a big man—well over six feet tall, broad-shouldered, and barrel-chested. He spoke with an old-world accent, but I couldn't tell you which one. He had a long beard and mustache, which appeared to cover some ugly burn marks on the left side of his face. He wore slacks, a suit jacket, and a button-down shirt that was open at the collar. His neck was so big I believe he would have suffocated himself if he had tried to button it up and wear a tie. He had an eye patch over his left eye. He smiled, but it was a forced smile. There was something off about this guy.

"Mr. Joey, I have come a long way to meet you. You are a hunter. Yes?"

He spoke with a deep and booming voice. I nervously nodded in response. The giant gargantuan then leaned over and looked me right in the eye. His breath was horrendous.

"I heard about your performance at the hunting competition recently. I represent an organization, and we need you and your expertise. We want to offer you the opportunity of a lifetime," he said.

"What kind of opportunity?" I asked.

"My employers are conservationists," said the giant brute. "Their goal is to preserve and protect endangered species, and we need an experienced hunter and tracker like yourself. We want to locate and tag a specific animal that has been extremely difficult for us to find. I fear the poor creatures will die out completely if we are not successful in our efforts."

My first assumption was he needed me to find an animal in the area, but that didn't make sense since the only endangered species around here were small aquatic animals. That situation had already been dealt with by denying some building permits along the river.

I responded, "Sir, I only hunt the local game, and those animals are not endangered."

"No," he responded with a laugh. "You will not be hunting anything that lives around here. But you will be looking for a specific animal where your unique hunting expertise is needed."

"What kind of animal will I be hunting?" I asked.

"I'm not at liberty to say at this time," he said.

"Where will I be going?" I asked.

He shook his head, and replied, "I am not at liberty to tell you that either."

"Do I need to bring my rifle and a few boxes of rounds?"

"No. You will be using a tranquilizer gun, and we will provide that. You won't be killing anything," he responded.

"Do I need to bring my camo?"

"Bring whatever clothes you believe you will need."

"Well, how do I know what kind of clothes I'll need if you won't tell me where I'm going or what I'm supposed to hunt?"

Mr. Russell's good eye started twitching ever so slightly, as Dr. Seavers took over the conversation.

"Joey, the animal conservation foundation this man represents works to preserve rare and endangered species. They are endowed by several governments and large corporations, and they have offered to pay you very handsomely for your efforts. They've also offered a sizable donation to our little college if you agree to help them."

And there was the rub. I was beginning to suspect Dr. Seavers had a vested interest in this. But I was not high on the idea of going off somewhere with someone I didn't know, for any amount of money. I was ready to start my assigned mopping and cleaning of the building so I could be ready for the poker game.

But I needed to be careful about how I backed out of this. It was never a good idea to disappoint Dr. Seavers. About ten years prior one of the instructors didn't get tenure and had to look for another job because he wouldn't go out with Dr. Seaver's daughter–who looks just like her father and has a face that could stop a clock.

Dr. Seavers continued, "You would be gone for about three to four weeks, but it won't count towards your vacation leave. If your family calls and asks where you are, I will tell them you were doing such a good job I let you stay in my beach house for a short vacation. But it's my understanding you don't talk to your family much anyway."

This was true. My father and grandfather had never approved of me sleeping all day, and I didn't understand why. I worked second shift, and a lot of second shift people sleep during the day before they go to work. Besides, it's not like I didn't have a job. We had a big fight about it and afterward, we just checked in with each other every couple of months or so. I was sure I could slip away for a few weeks without them ever knowing. But I still didn't think much about this idea. Then they told me about the money.

"Joey, Mr. Russell's foundation is willing to pay you a million dollars if you agree to go on this expedition. If you are successful in helping them catch one of these animals, they will give you an additional ten million dollars–but that's not all. If you agree to go on this trip, they are going to donate five million dollars to the college whether you are successful or not."

There was the rub; I shouldn't have been surprised Seavers had an ulterior motive here. But the mere mention of all that money caused my common sense to leave me and I happily responded, "Okay, I'm in. When do we leave?"

With a big greedy smile on his face, Mr. Russell said, "We will come to pick you up at your home tomorrow at midnight. Make sure you are alone."

He then stood up, walked over to me, and got in my face as he said, "You will tell no one of this in the meantime or the offer will be withdrawn. Do you understand?"

Leaving in the middle of the night? And I couldn't tell anyone where I was going? That didn't sound right, but I was too nervous to ask why that was necessary. I asked Mr. Russell if I would be able to call my family while I was on the trip. He was quiet for a second and then he nodded without saying a word.

"Well, I guess I'll see you tomorrow at midnight," I said. "But what about the..."

I never got to finish my question.

"Wait...hold on a second," interrupted Dr. Seavers. He was looking at the bottom of his office door as if he had seen movement. He threw the door open, and there was Mrs. Banks looking guilty as sin. Our collected assumption was she had been listening. Dr. Seavers looked mortified, and Mr. Russell turned bright red. Seriously, he looked like his head was about to explode.

"Josie, what are you doing?" snapped Dr. Seavers. And Mrs. Banks quickly responded, "Oh, I'm sorry sir. I was dusting this here door frame with this here paper towel." She was wiping furiously around the door as she said this.

Dr. Seavers pointed out that dusting door frames was my job. She looked down at the floor and went back to her desk. I thought the whole thing was hilarious, but I managed to contain my laughter.

Mr. Russell was not amused. He abruptly ended the meeting and stormed out of the office. "See you tomorrow," I yelled to him, but he didn't turn around or even acknowledge I had said anything. Dr. Seavers and I stood there looking at each other. "Maybe this isn't going to happen after all," I said. But Dr. Seavers just shrugged and said, "I wouldn't worry. They seemed to be very interested in you. Take the night off and start getting ready. I'll pick up your mail while you're gone, and I can keep an eye on your place. I'll also clear everything with your supervisor. Even if you don't find one of those animals, with all that money I doubt you will still want to work here anyway."

I left his office and went straight to the parking lot. I decided to take the long way outside back to my truck. It would have been shorter to walk through the building, but I didn't want to see any of my co-workers since I knew they would be asking questions. As I drove home, I thought about that strange conversation and wondered where I might be going. He didn't ask if I had a passport, so I assumed I would not be leaving the country.

But what if something happened to me during the trip? Could I count on these people to do the right thing if I got killed or something? My parents and grandparents would die of worry if I left and was never heard from again.

In those days I would read and listen to music all night until my bedtime just before dawn. And if the weather was good, I would sometimes go night fishing. But I didn't do any of that when I got home. For hours I just sat in my den drinking coffee and looking at the walls in silence. It was a three-bedroom rancher my grandfather had built for me when I graduated high school and started working. He had enlisted the help of various family members who knew how to install plumbing and do electrical work. He did the rest of it himself. He also deeded a few acres of land with it. As I thought about that I began to feel bad for not talking to him as much as I used to.

Sunlight began to slowly edge through my windows, but I still didn't feel like going to sleep. Maybe I was just too full of adrenaline or maybe it was the full pot of coffee I had put away throughout the night. I guess it was a little of both.

Around eight o'clock I got in my truck and drove into town. I should have stayed home and started packing. But I had a lot on my mind, so I walked around for a while as I waited for everything to open. About ten o'clock I decided to stop by the local diner and get some breakfast. During the day several of the retired folks and the unemployable gathered there to swap stories and gossip. I found a table near the door and picked up a menu as I contemplated which plate of cholesterol to order. Then, after about a minute, I noticed the entire room was staring at me…and smiling.

CHAPTER THREE

Well, I can't say the entire room was smiling. One of the old mountain men sat in the back with a nervous, almost frightened, look on his face. We all called him "Buzz".

But everyone else was grinning from ear to ear. I nodded and kind of smiled back. Looking back on it, I wish I had just gotten up and left. That's usually the best thing when a whole room of people are all acting weird. But instead, I broke eye contact and went back to the menu.

Just as I was about to ask for a waitress, Old Man Doggett crept up to my booth and sat down across from me. He had grown up with my grandfather, but they weren't close. Mr. Doggett had never given me anything other than a slight nod when he saw me around town, but most of the time he just kept walking without making eye contact. He didn't seem to think much of me, and the feeling was mutual.

I put the menu down and waited for him to speak. He wanted something. The rest of the restaurant remained silent as they closely watched our conversation. And I mean the **entire** restaurant: the customers, the cook, the waitresses, the cashier–everybody.

I finally got tired of waiting so I went ahead and asked, "Mr. Doggett, is there something I can do for you?"

"Joey, there's something I need to tell you....I just wanted you to know that I have always had the utmost respect for you and your entire family."

"Thank you, sir," I responded, not knowing what else to say. As he said this the rest of the room began to slowly nod in agreement.

Mr. Doggett continued, "I don't know if your grandfather ever told you this, but I once saved his life when we were kids."

My grandfather had never said anything nice about any of the Doggetts. I knew he was lying, but I let him keep talking.

"You know that your grandfather is missing a toe? Right?" he asked.

"Yes, he lost it to gangrene when he was about ten. He has always insisted we wear shoes and socks when we go outside and that we always keep our feet clean."

Doggett perked up and responded, "Yes, I'm glad you know about that because I am the one who told him that his toe was infected with gangrene. His parents might not have sent for the doctor to get it cut off if I hadn't warned him in time. And you know what else? You wouldn't even be here if your grandfather had died."

I have heard the cautionary tale of my grandfather's lost toe many times. I won't tell it now, but not once did he ever mention this fool. But I continued to humor him.

"Thank you, sir," I politely replied.

We sat there awkwardly looking at each other for a few more seconds. I got the impression he wanted to say something else, but he instead got up and went back to his seat. Before I could go back to the menu, Mr. Smith came over and took Doggett's place.

Mr. Smith talked for about thirty minutes, but I will just give you the summary. He told me about losing his good-paying job with the local factory, and how his wife left him for another man after he was let go. He had lived with his mother ever since.

I didn't want to argue with him, but there was way more to his story. His divorce was all his fault. About ten years prior he had married a college-educated woman who sold real estate. He was big with muscles, and she was movie star beautiful. They were a striking-looking couple when they first got married. But within the first year of their marriage, Mr. Smith lost his job with the factory when he up and quit over a disagreement about copier toner. Thereafter he didn't even try to look for another job as he quickly gained about fifty pounds. His arms lost all their definition because he quit working out and stopped dying his hair. Strangers began to think he and his wife were father and daughter. She eventually left him and moved away to take a job out west. We later heard she married the CEO of her company who happened to be a multi-millionaire.

We all suspected Smith had wanted to get fired so he could just sit around at home while she worked and paid the bills. But I couldn't help but feel sorry for him even though he had brought the whole thing on himself. I continued to listen while he whined about how unfair his life was. But at the end of his sad story, he made a point of telling me that despite all his problems, he was still a dang good hunter.

That came out of left field. What reason could he have for making me aware he was still a good hunter? Up to that point, his pitiful hard luck story had had nothing to do with hunting. He finally went back to his seat. But before I could call for a waitress, someone else sat down at my table.

And that's how it went for the next three hours as each person in the diner took turns telling me all about their financial and personal problems. And it was always followed by, "I want you to know that through it all I am still a darn good hunter, and I never miss." Or if they weren't good at hunting and just needed money, they concluded by telling me they were going to die if they didn't get some financial assistance soon.

It was painfully obvious the entire room knew something about my meeting with Mr. Russell. But how? It hadn't even been a full twenty-four hours. Would Dr. Seavers say anything? I guess it's possible he might let it slip, but I couldn't see him saying anything to this pack of idiots. Dr. Seavers lived in an upscale area thirty miles in the other direction. He knew about the people in this town, and he never came here.

Then there was Mrs. Banks. It was logical to assume she was the culprit. Her home was just outside of town. At the time I assumed she must have said something to somebody. And telling one person around here is all it would take. What was I going to say to Mr. Russell at midnight? The secret was out, but it wasn't my fault. That would be my only defense.

I had not been all that hungry when I walked in three hours earlier, but as Mrs. Bueller was finishing up her rather graphic story about needing hemorrhoid surgery, the pain of hunger still managed to hit me—and rightly so. I had not eaten for several hours. But no one was interested in ordering or cooking food, since there were five more people I hadn't heard from.

Mr. Doggett tried to break back in line because he had forgotten to tell me how badly he needed a new hip, but he was firmly told he had already had his turn.

This was going nowhere, so decided to leave. I got up and said to the room, "Well, I hope everything works out for everyone, but I need to go so I can get ready for work."

I stood up, and so did everyone else, except for Buzz who kept his seat. I could tell he was seriously concerned about my situation. As I took a half step away from my table Mr. Doggett stopped me and said, "Hold on boy. You ain't going nowhere until we get this worked out."

I played stupid. "Get what worked out?" I asked as I began to shake a little. Mr. Doggett looked at the room and said, "Okay, we might as well get this in the open. We don't seem to be getting through to him. You know how his family is." Doggett turned towards me and slowly muttered, "We all know you secretly met with Kurt Russell the famous actor yesterday and that he has recruited you for a big game hunt to some far-flung place. We also know he is paying you some serious money to do this and there might be openings for more hunters. Heck, I think I just saw Goldie Hawn go jogging by about an hour ago. There is no denying it. I know you've got connections."

A few miles away there was a bed and breakfast located near some good places to fish and hike. We sometimes saw some of their clientele curiously wandering through town from time to time. And yes, sometimes they liked to jog in the morning. They stood out since they were the only ones around here who did that. Doggett might well have seen some beautiful and unfamiliar blonde woman jog past the window earlier in the conversation, but I seriously doubt it was Goldie Hawn.

My plan now was to tell Mr. Russell that even though the locals were telling wild tales about what I might be doing, no one seemed to know the precise truth. I was also going to stress to him I had no idea how they found out about any of it. I guess Mrs. Banks didn't quite hear everything we were talking about in Dr. Seavers' office after all. That made sense. She was hard of hearing and the door was closed.

But before I could come up with something to tell Mr. Russell, I first needed to get out of the diner from hell. The only thing I could think of was to politely deny everything and go to my truck. It seemed like a good idea at the time.

CHAPTER FOUR

I began by saying, "Okay, you don't understand. You see….", but I was quickly interrupted.

"No boy. We understand. We understand everything. You're getting a million to go and ten million if you are successful," snapped Doggett.

Well, they sure got that part right. Some were becoming furious, and others were beginning to cry. I again made eye contact with Buzz as he emphatically nodded towards the door. I should have followed his advice and left right then without saying anything else, but I was so mad that I shouted, "There is no way Kurt Russell and Goldie Hawn would ever come to this crummy little town, not on purpose."

That's when Mr. Bailey spoke up and shouted, "Okay look here you selfish rotten liar, my wife was at the beauty parlor this morning and she heard the whole thing while she was getting her roots touched up. You want to keep the money and leave us all high and dry. We also know you don't even need the money that bad. You've got that job with the college where you only work half the time and the free house your grandpappy gave you. You have no idea what real suffering is, but you are about to find out."

I was madder than I had ever been in my life. I got in Mr. Bailey's face and screamed, "Your bleach-blonde wife doesn't know what she is talking about. She never does."

And with that one statement, I had thoughtlessly committed the ultimate sin. I had just disrespected the man's wife by questioning her credibility in front of half the town. It no longer mattered she was way out of line for spreading false news about my personal business. It also didn't matter Mr. Bailey was half my size. He was ready to fight and so was everyone else. Individually none of these people were much of a threat, but together they were a grade A mob.

I know I shouldn't have said this either, but as I ran out the door I screamed, "You can all just stick it for all I care." Somebody yelled, "Get him!", and the chase was on.

I had never run for my life before. Let me tell you. It sucks. It really does. I hit the sidewalk and was heading towards my truck as I fumbled for my keys, but I never got there. The cook and his entire platoon of fat waitresses cut me off as they ran out their back door, down the alley, and out in the street. He had a meat cleaver and each of his heifers had grabbed a steak knife. There was now an angry mob in front of me and an angry mob behind me. I ran across the street and up towards the church.

As they chased me through town, there happened to be two out-of-town yuppies peacefully standing next to their BMW taking pictures and looking at a map. Whatever impressions they might have had about our quaint little town were likely shattered when I ran by screaming, "Call the sheriff. These maniacs are trying to kill me." But the yuppies just stood there looking horrified as I, and a parade of furious locals, raced past them.

My first idea had been to run into the church to see if the pastor could calm these people down. Surely these people wouldn't kill me in a House of God, would they? But the door to the church was locked, which meant the pastor wasn't there. I had to keep running.

I ran about half a mile outside of town before I stopped to catch my breath. I was hoping everyone would give up the chase, but I could still hear them screaming and cussing. I decided to leave the road and run west through the woods. I knew that move would probably eliminate several of the older folks and the ones who were out of shape. I then heard a shot ring out and a bullet hit the ground about two feet away from me. One of the women screamed, "Don't kill him. He's our only hope."

Finally, a voice of reason. If these people were counting on me to solve all their life problems, it didn't make sense to kill me dead right there. However, anger and greed can make people lose their minds.

I deliberately led everyone to a steep gully with a creek running through it. It was about thirty feet wide with boulders all the way across. I had been climbing down there and skipping across those giant rocks since I was a kid. I had no problem getting across the water and climbing up the bank on the other side. I didn't think anyone in this group would be able to easily follow me across this kind of terrain. But if someone had a gun, I needed to get out of sight as quickly as possible.

Once I made it up to the other side, I had to make a quick decision. I could go left and run about two miles to my home. But I would be a sitting duck in there. Even if I did get there before everyone else and lock myself in, I wouldn't be safe with my giant windows. They would have no problem shooting them out and coming in after me. And with the mood these people were in, I had no doubt they would do something like that.

In the other direction, about four miles away, was a place on my grandfather's property where they would never get to me, even if they knew I was in there. Back during the Cold War one of my extended relatives built a massive underground shelter in a small cave that could easily hold twenty or thirty people. The property and the responsibility for maintaining it had been passed to my grandfather since his house was just up from it. It was fully stocked for emergency purposes and this qualified.

I ran as hard as I could for the next several minutes and whenever I stopped to catch my breath, I swore I could hear someone coming up behind me. But when I turned around, no one was there. I would then start running again.

I finally reached the shelter just when I thought my heart was about to explode. I had trouble opening the big metal door since I was using a new and unused key with an old lock, but I was thankfully able to get the heavy door to open. I was so scared I wanted to climb in there and never come out.

Most underground shelters are a small, buried room, not much bigger than a walk-in closet. But this one was a cinder block cavernous home completely underground. It had originally been stocked with numerous cots and blankets so everyone would have a place to sleep during a nuclear holocaust. My grandfather later decided to make it comfortable for several people needing shelter from a tornadic storm. There were several battery-powered lamps, six different sitting areas with couches and easy chairs, a bathroom connected to a septic tank, and running water sourced from an underground spring. There was no kitchen or a way to cook, but it had a pantry full of non-perishable food. My mom, aunts, and grandmother swapped out the food about once every year. I helped myself to some candy bars and water as I plopped down on a couch to collect my thoughts.

I didn't mean to make all those people mad by being so guarded with the truth, but there was no way I could explain what was happening since I was sworn to secrecy. I was exhausted after my long and frantic run, and I had not slept since the day before. So even though I didn't want to fall asleep, I nonetheless did.

CHAPTER FIVE

I immediately woke up when I heard the creak of that giant steel door as it slowly opened. My battery-powered lantern had died. In the darkness, I heard a nervous voice call out, "Joey, are you in there boy?" It was my grandfather. Here in the mountains people sometimes call their fathers "Pap." In my family, this was what we all called our grandfather.

"Yeah Pap, I'm here. Is anyone with you?" I asked.

"Yes, your daddy is here with me. Are you okay? Are you hurt?"

"I'm okay. I was asleep."

Dad and Pap walked up to me in the darkness and they both gave me a giant bear hug for several seconds. I almost couldn't breathe. Pap explained they had been looking for me for several hours, and this was the last possible place they could think of to look. All afternoon they had been terrified they were going to find my dead body in the woods.

They both agreed I had done the right thing by coming to this place. It was our family plan that if any kind of emergency happened, and it was no longer safe to be at home or in town, we would all meet there if we could. I think Pap had always anticipated that one day the entire town would go nuts and start acting like maniacs.

Dad and I sat down on a couch while Pap turned on another battery-powered lantern, which he put on a coffee table in front of us. He got comfortable in an easy chair, and they both brought me up to speed on what had been happening.

I assumed the mob was behind me the entire time, but this was not so. They stopped pursuing me after I left the road since they were all too frail or out of shape to follow me quickly over rough terrain. It was no surprise to learn Doggett was the fool who had fired at me.

And speaking of that idiot Doggett, Pap clarified his actual participation in the gangrene story. Pap's parents were the first to notice his toe was infected and it was probably gangrene. They were also aware it would need to be amputated if that was the case. The plan was to take Pap to the doctor, but at the time he was out of town. This was back before medical care was readily available in rural areas, and all they could do was wait and pray until the doctor's return. In the meantime, they obviously didn't want to tell Pap about it since he was only ten. But Pap's mother was so beside herself with worry she told Doggett's mother about it in confidence and asked her to pray. I don't know how much praying old lady Doggett did, but she sure did some talking. She told everyone at church and everyone in her family about it, including her obnoxious son. He was about fifteen at the time, and immature. He took it upon himself to tell my grandfather he was about to lose his toe, and he didn't do it in a sensitive manner. He also pointed out to him he might still die anyway. Those next few days were the longest of my Pap's life while he sat around crying and scared out of his mind. My great-grandparents never had anything to do with the Doggetts after that.

"I made sure the police picked up Doggett for trying to kill you," Pap growled. "He's in the jail with all the others."

"Others went to jail? For what?" I asked.

Dad and Pap took turns as they gently told me the rest of it, and it was all bad. The people in the diner were furious I had gotten away. When they made it back to town, it was decided the best way to retaliate was by attacking my truck. The police were able to ascertain who had done what since there were plenty of witnesses nervously watching from upstairs windows. First, the cook and the waitresses took their cutting utensils and slashed all four tires and the spare. Mrs. Bueller, the old lady with the hemorrhoids, then bashed out my windows with a tire iron. Once they got the door open, the fat waitresses cut up my seats. Everyone else keyed the paint and scratched in words I don't want to repeat.

I was getting sick to my stomach listening to all this, but it got worse. A few people in the mob surmised I had gone home, so they decided to meet me there to further their point. (I don't believe they knew about our shelter since we didn't discuss it outside the family.) When I didn't come to the door, they figured I might be in there hiding.

Someone in the group then got the bright idea to smoke me out. Later, after the police arrived, there were differing reports as to who specifically had started the blaze. Everybody was blaming everybody else and this time there were no innocent bystanders secretly watching from a safe vantage point. But fortunately, someone had the good sense to call the Sheriff's Office and tell them there was an angry mob heading to my home.

The arsonists were all collected by the Sheriff and his deputies. But it was too late to save anything once the Fire Department finally got there. Doggett had not made the trip to my house. He went home after he took the shot at me, and the police picked him up there.

CHAPTER SIX

I had just lost everything I owned and for no good reason. It was also a safe bet Mr. Russell was going to leave me behind when he arrived to pick me up and found a deserted burned-up home, so that opportunity was probably lost.

I was so overwhelmed I started crying like a baby right there. After about a minute I started getting embarrassed Dad and Pap were seeing me like this. These men were tough, and they had raised me to be the same. But when I looked up, I saw they had tears in their eyes too.

Dad got up and ran a washcloth under some water. He handed it to me and told me to wipe my face. I tried to hand it back to him and he told me to just hold it on my forehead.

Pap got up and said, "I am going to run up to the house and tell your ma and grandma where you are. I also need to let the police know we found you. I should have done that first thing. I want you both to stay here while I'm gone. Joey, I'm not sure it's safe for you to be outside just yet."

"Pa, you still got your gun?", Dad asked.

"Yes, I do," he responded. "Do you still have yours?"

"Yeah, I've got it right here." Dad got out his .357 and put it on the table. While Pap was gone, Dad and I had a discussion of our own. Earlier in the day he had heard what he called "a cock and bull story" about Ted Nugent wanting me to go hunt elephants with him in Africa and Mr. Nugent was secretly staying somewhere in town. He also said there were some idiots roaming the streets and knocking on doors with record albums and electric guitars in the hope they could find him and get them signed. The owner of the bed and breakfast almost never got them out of his yard.

We then talked about what had transpired in the diner after our infamous meeting. There were a couple of people in there who had asked for help but did not participate in the chase, the demolition of my truck, or the burning of my home. So, they had not broken the law in that respect. But they did give the police a very distorted account of what had happened by leaving out just enough details to make it look like the whole thing was my fault. According to them, everyone in the diner had politely asked me for some much-needed financial help for some serious personal problems, and I responded by saying, "You can all just stick it for all I care."

I told Dad my side of it, and I told him *everything*–Dr. Seavers, Burt Russell, the Deal, and then the diner. Dad sat there listening, his eyes getting bigger and bigger. He was furious when I had finished, but not at me.

"Why can't people just mind their own business around here? And where does Seavers get off pressuring you into a ridiculous deal like that? How could he expect you to leave town with a total stranger?"

Dad then looked at me and asked, "You weren't going to run off and not tell us, were you?"

I was trying to come up with something to say, but then we heard the big metal door creak open. Pap was back, and he was not alone. Buzz was with him. Pap looked at me and said, "Joey, this man needs to speak to you."

CHAPTER SEVEN

Buzz sat down in one of the easy chairs. Pap offered him a candy bar and some water, and he graciously accepted.

I now need to tell you about Buzz. Just because a man lives in the mountains doesn't necessarily make him a true "mountain man", but Buzz was the real deal. As you may suspect, I am not referring to him with a made-up name for the purposes of this story. He really was known as "Buzz". He lived in a small one-room cabin on an old logging road that was rarely used anymore. He didn't own the property; he just had an arrangement with the owner. His little cabin had no electricity, and his water source was a small spring that ran a few feet from his front door. He made his living by picking flowers that only grow in the mountains and he sold them to florists. When he wasn't picking flowers, he would do odd jobs for people around town.

Buzz was mechanically inclined, and he was offered a job with a local auto repair shop. He would have made a lot more money and he could have moved into a much nicer place since the owner was willing to let him live in a small one-bedroom apartment over the garage. It wasn't much, but it was way nicer than living in an old cabin with an outhouse. Buzz was interested in the offer until the owner handed him a W2 form and said he couldn't pay his salary in cash. Buzz turned him down flat without saying why.

That was another one of his quirks. Whenever he had completed an odd job and it was time to pay him, he always refused a check and insisted on being paid in cash. If his temporary employers had any supplies on hand that he needed, he was okay if they wanted to pay him with that—which was most of the time. When he did use money, he paid with old crumpled-up bills. I had never been to his cabin, but I heard it consisted of a single bed, a wood-burning stove, a couple of kerosene lanterns, and a small table. He had some books and a small battery-powered radio, which was all he had in the way of entertainment. His closet was an old beat-up backpack.

About once a month he would indulge himself with a meal at the diner. He always sat by himself, but if you spoke to him, he would speak to you. I had some interesting discussions with him about hunting, and I learned something new every time. But if no one spoke to him, he would keep to himself and not enter any of the conversations.

It was fortunate he had decided to come into town and get a meal at the diner that morning. Pap explained Buzz was the one who had called the police when things started getting out of hand. After the quick phone call, Buzz wanted to be sure I was okay, and he tracked me to the shelter.

"Hold on," I said. "You tracked me here?"

"I sure did. I almost lost your trail when you crossed that creek, but I did finally pick it up on the other side," he responded with a smile.

"I found this place right before sundown. I was going to knock, but I heard someone nearby, so I disappeared.

When I saw your father and grandfather coming down the hill, I knew they would find you here and I felt I should leave you all alone for a few minutes. When your grandfather came out, I decided to let him know I was around."

Pap chimed in and said, "He appeared out of nowhere and about scared me to death. I'm glad I didn't shoot him."

"Yeah, me too," snapped Buzz.

Buzz looked at me and said, "Be glad you didn't go off on that hunting trip Joey. Get comfortable and I will tell you why."

And for the next several hours he proceeded to tell us a story I will never forget. Truthfully, this book isn't about me. It's about Buzz.

CHAPTER EIGHT

Everyone has called me "Buzz" since the day I first arrived here in town. I got the nickname the first time I saw Jim the barber and asked him to give me a buzzcut. He laughed and said, "Okay, Buzz." When he was done, he asked my name, and I told him "Buzz" would be fine. His little barbershop was full of locals at the time, and they have all called me "Buzz" ever since, which was fine with me. Buzz had been my family nickname when I was a kid and I used it when I was in college. In hindsight, I guess it was foolish to ever let anyone call me "Buzz" again. But it had been so many years that I didn't see the harm.

I am originally from the Deep South. My parents were older when I came along. They had given up on ever having children, but when mom thought she was going through the first stages of menopause, it turned out to be me. I was always their treasure, and I had the kind of childhood you could only have in the South.

The weather was good most of the year and my dad took me hunting and fishing all the time. My mother taught me how to prepare the game when we brought it home. We also went camping throughout the year–rain or shine. During those trips, my parents would teach me all kinds of things about survival in the woods. I guess the most useful thing they taught me was how to track animals, which we would sometimes do for hours over several miles.

My parents sent me to college after I finished high school. They were practical people and they encouraged me to choose a sensible major. The college I was attending had an excellent business program, so I decided to get a degree in business administration.

The first three years were great. I did well in my classes, and I made straight As. I made friends easily since I was always able to help everyone with their homework and I knew how to work on their cars. I would do the repair free of charge if they bought the parts. I was also able to explain how the local mechanic was ripping them off. I nearly put that crook out of business.

I would visit my folks every now and then on a weekend and I always went home for the holidays. They would have some kind of exciting hunting or fishing trip planned, and we always had the best time. Those would be the happiest days of my life.

It all changed the summer after my junior year. I stayed home during the summer break and worked as a lifeguard at the local pool. I knew my parents were getting on in years, but they both seemed healthy, and I had fully expected them to be around long enough for me to finish college, get a job, and then settle down with some nice girl as I started a family. But I was wrong.

Dad passed away suddenly one morning while I was at work. My supervisor took over for me and I drove home to find my mother in tears. We later learned he had had an aneurysm. Mom wasn't the same after that. Over the next month, I noticed she didn't eat much, and slept most of the time. She eventually just stayed in her room and rarely got out of bed. Looking back on it, I was a fool for not getting her some help.

One afternoon I came home from work and found she had passed away sometime during the day. I didn't ask for an autopsy. She had died of a broken heart.

Even though my folks left me enough money to finish school, I thought about taking a semester or two off. I could get a job in town and then hang around the house while I figured out my next step. But I knew there was a strong chance I would never finish if I did that. Plus, I knew my parents would want me to graduate.

I had some tough to make decisions before I could go back. First, I had to decide what I should do with the old home and the fifty acres of property that went with it. There was no way I could maintain it if I was off at school, and it wasn't wise to just let it sit uninhabited.

It wasn't an easy decision, but I decided that selling it was the best option. I could then put my family heirlooms and keepsakes in storage while I finished school. After graduation, I would find a job somewhere and put all their things in my new home. And selling the home and property would give me an enormous amount of seed money to get started in life.

I then got a call from one of my cousins. He had lost his job about a year prior, and his house had been foreclosed.

His wife, however, had just found a good job in my area and they wanted to rent the house while I was away at college.

He was my mother's sister's son and Dad had never thought much of him or his father. I should have known better, but my judgment was flawed due to my grief and immaturity. And not knowing what else to do, I agreed to let him live in the house.

The agreement sounded okay at first. He promised to take care of the place and he was also willing to pay a generous amount of rent. They were planning to buy a house once their finances had stabilized and would probably need to stay in my place for about a year. That gave me plenty of time to finish school.

We also had an understanding that my old room would remain undisturbed while I was gone, and I could stay with them during the holidays and the occasional weekend. True, it wasn't going to be the same without my parents, but the house would still be there and at least there would be family waiting for me.

He requested we have a lease drawn up. I asked why and he said it was required for him to have a lease so he could buy rental insurance. I went along with him, but I shouldn't have. I would later learn a lease is not necessary for buying rental insurance.

There was an attorney in town who had grown up with my father. He had always helped my parents with legal issues, and he helped me settle their estate when they died. He had warned me to never sign anything without letting him look at it, but my cousin and his wife put me on the spot. They got especially offended when I asked if I could at least read over the agreement. That should have been a warning, but I foolishly caved in.

I went back to college in mid-August, and on the same day, my cousin, his wife, and her two kids from her two previous marriages moved into my house. I noticed they didn't bring a lot of personal stuff with them.

After the first two weeks of school, I decided I wanted to go home for the long Labor Day weekend, but my cousin and his wife asked me not to visit right away since the kids were still settling in and it wasn't a good time for company. That seemed selfish to me. After all, it was my house, and I was letting them live there. But I let it slide.

Then, a month later, I got the call. It was right around midnight. My family home had just burned to the ground and there was nothing left. My cousin was not the one who called. It was a neighbor who I had asked to keep an eye on the place. He confirmed that my cousin and his family were safe. He also told me they didn't seem to be too broken up about it while they stood outside and watched it burn. To him, it looked like they were almost celebrating.

It was a good thing my roommate was away, and I had the room to myself because I don't think I have ever cried so hard in my life. I didn't even cry that hard at each of my parents' funerals.

I called my insurance agent the next morning and got some more bad news. I no longer owned the property and my policy had been canceled. I called our family attorney, and he was able to sort it out.

Without realizing it, I had signed the deed to the property over to my cousin and his wife when I signed their papers. They immediately opened a new homeowner's policy with another insurance company, and then they intentionally burned the place down to get the settlement.

The insurance investigators had no problem in determining how the blaze had started, and my cousin's wife broke under questioning. I believe the insurance investigators also spoke to my neighbor as well. She and my cousin went to prison, and I have no idea what happened to her kids.

There were several family heirlooms in my home that were valuable. At first, I suspected my cousin and his wife had sold them. But now I believe the items were distributed to various family members before he torched the place since my other cousins refused to let me in their homes after that. It was a good thing I had brought a couple of family pictures with me, or I never would have been able to look at my parents ever again.

Fortunately, my parents' vehicles were safe. They were stored in a private garage in town, and I had title to them. Mom had a 1954 Ford Fairlane, and Dad had a 1950 Ford truck. They were both in perfect condition. (My attorney friend had helped get the titles transferred to me.) My parents bought me a Ford Falcon when I started college, so I didn't need transportation. I also had my mother's antique gold jewelry. Our attorney had advised me to put the jewelry in a safe deposit box at my bank, and I'm glad he did, or they would have stolen that too.

I hated to do this, but the only practical thing to do was sell the truck and the Fairlane. I hated to let them go since my dad had taught me how to work on cars while he was maintaining them. But I couldn't keep paying for the storage and the insurance. I took the money and deposited it into my dwindling savings. I kept the jewelry though. At the time I was thinking I would give it to my future wife.

My professors mercifully gave me some time off to get it all straightened out and get my head together, but I had a terrible time catching up. I somehow managed to finish the semester, but just barely. My perfect 4.0 GPA was ruined, so in January I didn't start my final semester with any motivation. I had spent the Christmas holidays in a cheap hotel since the dormitories were closed, and I worked a temporary job at the local Post Office to make some money during the break.

I still went to class and did my homework, but my work wasn't the best. I did what I had to do to get by and nothing else. My professors saw the change and they would occasionally call me into their offices to check on me. The conversation would end with a suggestion to go see the school counselor, but I never did. I guess I should have.

I somehow managed to graduate, but I didn't bother with attending the graduation ceremony. I later picked up my diploma at the Registrar's Office. It didn't matter. College was over, and I had a good job lined up.

CHAPTER NINE

One of my friends helped me get the job. He was first in line for it, but he recommended me because he didn't want to move so far away. It was in a major city a few hundred miles to the north, and I decided the change would be good for me. My attorney friend offered to give me a job as a paralegal, but I was ready to leave. Nothing was keeping me near my hometown since it now had so many ugly memories.

I sold the Ford Falcon my parents had bought for me four years earlier since I now desperately needed some seed money. The city I was moving to had an extensive public transportation system, which meant I could survive without a car. I packed what few belongings I still had in a couple of suitcases, and I took a bus up there. I stayed at the local YMCA while I started my job and looked for a cheap apartment.

I was nervous when I started my first day. The night before I had considered calling my attorney friend and asking if it was too late to accept his paralegal job. But the next morning I went to work and found the routine and workload were going to be reasonable, and interesting.

As the weeks passed, I found the job to be therapeutic since it was a pleasant change of pace. My coworkers and my supervisor were all patient and supportive, especially when they heard about what I had just endured. As everyone around the office got to know me, they were excited to learn I knew how to hunt and fish. I also did light repair work on their cars now and then. That led to many Saturday-night home-cooked dinners with their families.

Most of my coworkers were left-brain types who had probably used pocket protectors and briefcases their entire lives. But now they had sons, and they wanted to learn how to do outdoor stuff. I was invited to several of their father-and-son weekend outings, which was fun because there were all kinds of new hunting and fishing opportunities in that part of the country.

I assumed I would get invited to a couple of their first trips, and then they would take it from there. But as my co-workers and their sons slowly (and I mean slowly) became somewhat competent outdoorsmen, they still wanted me to come along. All the kids started calling me "Uncle Buzz."

My immediate supervisor went on his first deer hunting trip with a couple of us, and then he was hooked. He didn't even shoot anything, but he was hooked, nonetheless. He told the owner of our company about the numerous employees who were becoming hunters, and a month later the owner announced he wanted to take everyone to a hunting resort in the mountains as an office retreat.

The owner of our company was tough by nature, but he was also extremely generous since we worked hard. We had just completed our best year in the history of the company, and he wanted to do something extra special for us besides the typical dinner at a nice restaurant.

The whole office cheered when the announcement was made, except me. I have never thought much of those guaranteed hunting resorts. In my opinion, they give the hunter too much of an advantage, but I was committed to going since it was heavily implied by my immediate supervisor that I should. The freezer portion of my modest fridge was already packed with frozen venison from recent trips, so I told the owner I would be glad to just stay back at the lodge in case someone needed me. He agreed that was a good idea.

If the trip had only consisted of the employees, it probably would have been a peaceful rest away from the office–like it was supposed to have been. But we encountered a snag. The trip was scheduled for the weekend after Christmas, and the wives didn't appreciate their husbands going off on a hunting trip and leaving them behind with the kids. Plus, none of the wives bought the story that it was supposed to be like a business trip. This led to several employees backing out because they were more scared of their wives than they were of the owner. So, for the good of the order, the owner graciously gave everyone the option of bringing their sons.

When the big day arrived, about fifty of us left on a Friday at noon in a caravan of station wagons and trucks. Everybody wanted me to ride in their car, but I politely declined and told them I needed to ride with my supervisor so we could discuss some important work stuff. I hated to disappoint them, but if I had ridden in one kid's car, the kids in the other cars would have felt slighted. This would have led to me changing cars at every stop, and there were several of those.

The plan was for us to arrive in the early evening. We would first get a quick orientation, and then we would have dinner. After dinner, we were scheduled to hear a scary ghost story by one of the hosts, and then we would all go to bed early so everyone would be rested for an early morning hunt beginning around five am. There would be another opportunity later in the day for an afternoon hunt, and then there would be one more hunt on Sunday morning. In between the morning and afternoon Saturday hunts, they were planning special outdoor learning activities for the kids and anyone else who wanted to participate. The learning activities were added to our itinerary since there were now children and teenagers involved.

I'm sure you have noticed by now I have not revealed the name of our company or the names of my supervisors and coworkers. I am going to keep that information to myself.

CHAPTER TEN

Under normal conditions, it would have been a four or five-hour drive to our destination, but the trip took about eight hours. Whoever planned our travel schedule didn't consider the needed bathroom stops when taking a large group of little boys on a long road trip. Each restroom break took no less than thirty to forty minutes since we had to explore every little town and truck stop.

But what put us behind was an emergency stop we made about twenty miles away from the resort. One of the station wagons started overheating because of a busted hose. Luckily, we were close to a huge truck stop that sold spare parts. I was able to find a hose, and it only took me a few minutes to put it on and fill his radiator with coolant. If I had not been there, they probably would have had to leave the car with a mechanic while the various passengers from that car froze in the back of someone's truck.

It was eight o'clock when we finally found the turn-off. Our little caravan slowly traveled down a gravel road for another ten miles. I am sure we would have been out there all night had there not been signs to guide us through the many turns. The owner, who was driving the lead car, could not read a map to save his life. We learned that the hard way after a couple of wrong turns earlier in the day.

We finally drove up to a giant wooden fence with a huge gate. It looked like something out of King Kong. Our instructions were to honk once we arrived, and someone would come let us in.

The owner honked his horn several times over the next twenty minutes while we all waited in anticipation. A very disgusted-looking man finally showed up to let us in. Everyone in our car smiled and waved as we drove by, but he just stood there looking mad at the world.

We drove another couple of miles on a winding gravel road, and even in the dark the countryside looked incredible. Several of the plots we passed were on small plateaus surrounded by hills and trees. For the first time I was getting excited about this trip, even though I wasn't planning to hunt. Then suddenly, a couple of nice-sized does ran in front of our car. My supervisor threw on the brakes, and they were quickly followed by a gigantic buck. We sat there in amazement for a few seconds, and then we proceeded on.

We arrived at a beautiful and massive hunting lodge that looked like it could have held an entire army. We were so in awe of the place we just sat there looking at it after we parked. After about a minute our hosts came out on the front porch smiling from ear to ear–but I could tell their smiles were forced. It never dawned on us that we should have called ahead and told them we were running late.

Everyone got out of their vehicles and started grabbing their suitcases, but we decided to leave our rifles for the time being. I counted twenty men on the porch and in the middle was a big guy who looked like John Wayne, only he was kind of fat. It was obvious that he was the one in charge.

"HELLO EVERYONE," he shouted. "EVERYONE CALLS ME BIG JIM AND THIS IS MY PLACE. I HOPE YOU ALL HAVE THE TIME OF YOUR LIVES DURING YOUR STAY WITH US. NORMALLY WE HAVE A LITTLE ORIENTATION WHEN YOU FIRST ARRIVE. BUT SINCE YA'LL ARE JUST NOW GETTING HERE, I AM GOING TO LET YOU PUT YOUR LUGGAGE IN THE FOYER AND THEN WE WILL HEAD TO THE DINING ROOM FOR SOME DINNER."

This sounded good to all of us. We were famished after our longer-than-expected trip. They led us inside and we dropped our suitcases in a large foyer. We proceeded into a meeting hall with about a hundred seats and a small stage up front. It resembled a little country church, except the walls were lined with numerous deer head trophies. We were led down the center aisle and around the stage to the left. One of the men slid open a large rolling door and we entered a huge dining room with several long dining tables with chairs on each side. Each table looked like it could have held about twenty people. There was a massive fireplace with a fire roaring on the right side of the room with some easy chairs and a couple of love seats in front of it.

Although our host had introduced himself as "Big Jim" there seemed to be an unspoken consensus among us we were not calling him that. The owner of our company, who now looked more exhausted than I had ever seen him, started this by saying, "Jim, I need to speak to you for a moment."

I could just barely overhear the conversation, but the owner said something about an unexpected breakdown, needing to find the right part, and then the time it took to make the repair. I heard my name come up a time or two as the owner motioned in my direction. I also heard a very emphatic apology for letting the time slip away from us. I didn't hear any mention of the time we wasted sight-seeing, but I did overhear the owner say that our untimely car repair had delayed the trip about three hours when it had only taken me about thirty minutes to get us back on the road.

Jim had been nice up to this point, maybe a little too nice—as if he was furious and doing his best to hide it in the name of good customer service. This would not have been a good way to begin the visit and it was important for the owner to explain our tardiness, even though he had just lied through his teeth.

This appeared to work because Jim eased off a good bit as he continued to nod in an understanding manner for the rest of the conversation. When the owner had finished his exaggerated explanation concerning our lack of punctuality, Jim gave him a wink and patted him on the shoulder. Jim then called his crew over and told them a condensed version of the story in about ten seconds. They all nodded, and all was well…for the moment.

While that was happening, the food was being brought out to a huge serving table in front of the room. The serving table had all the bowls and spoons on one end and the best-smelling stew I had ever smelled on the other. There were also huge plates of rolls and cornbread. But what really got my attention was the beautiful woman who was preparing it.

She had long black hair, green eyes, and a beautiful smile. The entire room sat in reverent silence as she gracefully and methodically performed her serving duties. When the table had been prepared to her liking, she looked up and smiled as she gracefully stepped back from the table.

Jim stood up and announced, "Everybody come and help yourself. I promise this is the best stew you have ever had in your entire life. Once you have your bowl, you can proceed to the drink table right over there." He looked toward the pretty lady and said, "Ms. Roisin will be happy to help pour your drink. We have plenty of food so don't be shy about getting seconds."

I would have expected the boys to charge up to the table in a mad rush of confusion with one serving mishap after another–especially since they had been bouncing off the walls with excitement all day. I lost count of the numerous displays they had accidentally knocked over in the various stores we had visited on the way up.

But with such a beautiful and graceful woman in the room, those boys were naturally on their best behavior–and scared out of their minds. None of them even wanted to move until their fathers started quietly encouraging them to go get their food. Everyone formed two lines on each side of the serving table, and they acted like perfect gentlemen as they carefully served themselves. It was hilarious watching them slowly walk up to the drink table. But Ms. Roisin was kind and gracious to all of them, and she never stopped smiling.

It was now my turn. I got my stew and casually walked over to the drink table. With a beautiful European accent, she asked, "Would you like coffee, tea, or water." I asked for coffee. As she was pouring, she looked at me and said, "I'm Roisin." I went ahead and told her my real name, but I also told her everyone just calls me "Buzz." She laughed and said, "I've never heard a name like yours before." Trying to play it cool, I said, "Well, I've never heard a name like yours before."

That was a misstep. Making light of a stupid-sounding nickname is one thing. But making light of someone's given name is something else. She stopped smiling and in a serious tone responded, "It's an old name. It means little rose." I recovered and said, "Well, in that case it appears to suit you." She smiled and I smiled back. I thanked her for the coffee and then I went back to my seat.

I decided to sit with my supervisor and the owner, and for the next hour, we mainly talked about hunting and guns. We also got seconds on the stew, and a few people got thirds. After everyone had finished eating, she went into the kitchen, and we didn't see her for the rest of the night. I guess she had a lot of work to do cleaning all those dishes.

It was after ten o'clock and we were ready to turn in, but Jim had other plans for us as he again stood up and announced, "I SURE HOPE EVERYONE ENJOYED THEIR DINNER. WE WILL NOW ADJORN TO THE MAIN HALL FOR AN ORIENTATION. AND BY THE WAY, ATTENDANCE IS MANDATORY IF YOU WANT TO BE ALLOWED TO HUNT ON THIS TRIP."

We all got up at a snail's pace and slowly walked back into the main hall. As we got settled in the uncomfortable wooden folding chairs, Jim informed us we were about to get the orientation we would have gotten at four o'clock. And over the next twenty minutes, we sat and heard a list of rules and procedures. We were informed that loaded guns were not allowed in the house, and we should not load our guns until we arrived at the plot. The guns then needed to be unloaded before leaving the plot. I had already taught everyone to be careful with their guns, so I wasn't worried about anyone doing something stupid.

Everyone started to nod off as Jim was completing his safety lecture, and just as he was about to lose the entire room, he said in his loud voice, "OKAY, I NOW NEED TO WARN YOU ABOUT THE GHOST."

That woke everyone up. No overnight trip to the woods is complete until you have heard a terrifying ghost story right before bedtime that makes everyone want to jump in bed and close their eyes. I will spare you most of the details, but basically, it was about a local lumberjack who went crazy one day and started offing anyone who had ever crossed him. Jim ended his extremely graphic story by telling us the very house we were in was a converted lumber camp and it was rumored the guy had once lived here. A coworker sitting in front of me leaned over and told his friend, "I remember when this place was built. It was never a lumber camp." I quietly told the guy to let it go.

There is a practical reason for telling a bunch of little boys there is a vindictive ghost seeking revenge in the area during an overnight trip in the woods. The camping ghost story is a scare tactic that has been used for years and is very effective when employed correctly. Otherwise, some crazy kid will swipe his dad's cigarettes and invite all his friends to come try one out in the woods while the dads are snoring away. We certainly didn't need someone sneaking off and starting a forest fire in the middle of the night since we were already on thin ice with these people.

Jim brought his story to a close by informing us the maniac was finally brought to justice, but his ghost was still occasionally seen roaming around the property and possibly in the house late at night. The bedrooms, however, were safe provided you stayed in bed until morning. The young boys were eating this up, but the teenagers and the adults were all beginning to look at each other and smile. We knew what Jim was doing. Especially when he ended by saying, "So remember, if you leave your room in the middle of the night, you might come face to face with the ghost in the hall. But if you do need something that can't wait until morning, just send your dad." We all laughed. The awkward evening was ending on a high note.

It was almost 11:00 and the first hunt was in six hours. Jim asked if we were up for it, and the entire room screamed, "YES." Jim asked again, "Is everyone here POSITIVE you are planning to get up at five in the am tomorrow morning?" Again, everyone screamed, "YES."

That wasn't a pep talk. It was obvious to me and no one else that Jim was hoping we would opt out of the morning hunt and then go out in the afternoon. He huffed a little and told everyone good night as he quickly left. I believe I was the only one who noticed he was silently simmering as he stormed out of the room. The meeting quickly adjourned, and we retrieved our luggage as we slowly went upstairs.

The second floor consisted of numerous small bedrooms. No one from the staff came up to help us get settled. We were left to find everything on our own. The rooms weren't very big, but they were clean. Some of the rooms had two single beds. Some had one double bed, and several rooms had bunk beds on each wall. Each room had a small bathroom and shower. The boys all wanted to sleep in the bunk beds, which led to several people sharing a room. And since this place could have accommodated well over fifty people anyway, there were plenty of rooms not being used. This thankfully led to me having a room to myself.

My small room consisted of a double bed, a nightstand, and a small chest of drawers that I didn't need. There was no alarm clock or radio, but fortunately I had thought to bring both. I planned to be ready at 5:00 am so I could offer support if needed, but now I wasn't so sure my help was going to be necessary. Jim and his crew appeared to have everything under control. I tossed that around in my mind until I fell asleep.

CHAPTER ELEVEN

The next morning came fast as my alarm started buzzing at 4:00 am. I took a shower and shaved before going downstairs. I normally wouldn't do those things before a hunt, but I wasn't hunting and there was a beautiful woman in the house. I began to regret not talking to her a little longer the evening before.

The smell of breakfast hit me as I walked downstairs. I proceeded through the dark meeting room and into the dining area. I followed the scent into the kitchen and Roisin was working frantically, looking very different. She wasn't wearing any makeup, her hair was pulled back in a little bun, and she was wearing a T-shirt and jeans. She was still pretty.

"Good morning," she said, sounding agitated. "If you will please wait outside, I promise I will have your breakfast prepared before you leave for your hunt."

I explained I wasn't planning to hunt, and I was only there to help the others. I asked if I could help her, and she politely said no. I persisted and promised I knew my way around the kitchen. She asked if I could flip pancakes and I told her I could. She smiled at me and we went to work. But I could tell she still wasn't in the mood for talking, so I kept quiet. That was something my mother taught me. It's never a good idea to try and make a woman talk when she doesn't feel like it. And frankly, at that time of day, I don't want to talk much either.

We had the first servings of bacon, sausage, eggs, and pancakes ready a few minutes before five am. I asked if she was planning to make grits, but she had no idea what I was talking about.

A few minutes later she asked me to go check and see how many hunters were waiting to be served. But as I walked into the dining room, I was shocked and embarrassed to only see Jim and his crew at the table. They all looked agitated.

"Good morning, Buzz," he said. "No one else from your group has come down yet."

That was disconcerting to hear since everyone had promised they were planning to go out first thing.

"Did everyone decide to sleep in and forget to tell us?" he asked, with not-so-subtle sarcasm.

I assured him almost everyone had expressed an interest in going out first thing that morning when we planned the trip. After an awkward minute of silence, Roisin came out with breakfast. She made a point of telling everyone I had helped her, and that broke the ice.

For the next two hours we swapped hunting stories, drank coffee, and ate a fine breakfast while the sun came up, but no one ever came down for an early morning hunt. We would later learn the long trip and the big meal late in the evening had taken the wind out of everyone, so they all stayed in bed thinking other people would take advantage of the early hunt. This meant Roisin, Big Jim, and the entire crew had gotten up at 4:00 am for absolutely no reason whatsoever. And to make matters worse, they had gone to bed later than they would have wanted because we arrived so late and delayed the evening itinerary. This trip was not starting well at all.

Around ten o'clock the first group of my coworkers started drifting downstairs. I checked with Roisin and asked if she needed any more help in the kitchen, but she assured me she had had more than enough time to prepare everyone's breakfast over the previous five hours. I was embarrassed and told her so. She just smiled and told me she appreciated my help. She then pointed at the door and told me to leave in a friendly, but direct manner. She still wasn't in the mood to talk, and I understood.

The early-morning breakfast became a late-morning brunch as the rest of the group finally joined us. Since everyone had gotten up late and completely blown the day's itinerary, it was decided we would just skip lunch and head out to the hunting plots in the early afternoon.

Once everyone had finished their late breakfast, the men all sat around smoking, drinking coffee, and swapping stories while the boys played tag or something outside. The outdoor activities planned for the kids were conveniently overlooked, and not giving the kids something constructive to do during that time nearly ruined everything.

A little after one o'clock the men called in their sons, handed them the car keys, and told them to go get their guns. This caused a stampede of elated kids running outside.

That made me nervous. I'm old-fashioned because of the way I was raised, but I believe anyone under the age of eighteen should always be supervised whenever guns are involved, and I am now sorry I didn't follow them out there.

Meanwhile, Jim announced to the room that everyone would be taken to the plots a few at a time in their small fleet of Jeeps, and the first group would be leaving in fifteen minutes. After his announcement, he was swiftly out the front door.

But once he was outside, our hearts sank as he started furiously screaming and cussing his head off. I don't want to repeat all of it, but I am positive I heard him say things like, "STOP THAT! STOP THAT NOW! YOU LITTLE FOOLS! YOU ARE ALL GOING TO KILL EACH OTHER! GUNS DOWN! GUNS DOWN! PUT THOSE GUNS DOWN ON THE GROUND YOU STUPID LITTLE.......!!!"

We all leaped out of our seats and bolted through the house to the front door. When we got outside the boys were all standing there in shock with their guns lying next to them on the ground. Most were beginning to cry. Everyone in Jim's crew was slowly walking through the group of kids, picking their guns up off the ground, and leaning them against the side of the house. Once all the guns had been confiscated, they began checking each one to see if any were loaded.

While his men were checking the rifles, Jim came over to the adults and explained what had happened. When he walked outside, the boys were having a pretend gun battle.........with their real firearms.

I don't believe little boys do this much anymore, but this was during a time when children grew up watching police, western, and war movies. Inspired by what they had seen on television, little boys would often take their toy guns and have pretend gun fights and battles in the neighborhoods and on the playgrounds. Playing this game with plastic cap pistols and plastic rifles is one thing, but playing with real rifles is something else. There was a lot of embarrassed yelling from the fathers as their sons insisted it was okay because they had checked, and none of the guns were loaded.

I couldn't help but feel responsible for this. I taught each of these kids how to hold a rifle, how to fire it, and how to clean it afterward. And through it all, I had done my best to impress upon each of them the importance of treating all guns as if they were loaded, even if they didn't think they were. But apparently, the lesson didn't stick.

While the kids were pleading a losing case to their mortified fathers, there were some furious rumblings among Jim and his crew as they continued checking the rifles. I walked over to see if I could help but was immediately told to back off. They wanted to inspect the guns themselves. As I rejoined my coworkers on the porch, a crew member walked up to Jim, handed him a rifle, and said, "This one has a chambered round, and the safety is off."

I almost lost my breakfast.

Jim walked over to the owner, and calmly informed him the hunting trip was over, and we needed to leave the property immediately. He also made it clear there would be no refund. The owner was incensed, but Jim reminded him they had violated the agreement by allowing the kids to blatantly ignore the gun safety rules. Jim's crew gathered behind him, and we all gathered around the owner. Even though we had them outnumbered, I don't think our crew against these guys would have been an even matchup. And even if a fight did break out, it wasn't going to change anything.

Then something happened.

"JIM, I WANT TO SEE YOU NOW!"

It was Roisin. She was standing there with her hands on her hips, looking furious.

Jim turned white as a sheet as Roisin directed him away from the house and out into the woods. We stood there shocked as she marched him out of earshot. She was about 5'8 and appeared to be in her mid-twenties. Jim must have been 6'5 and looked to be in his mid-fifties, but he was no match for her. She just kept pointing at him, pointing at the ground, and pointing at us as she yelled and yelled. After about five minutes, Jim slowly walked back with his head down and mumbled, "The first group of hunters will be leaving in fifteen minutes."

He walked over to the garage area to get one of the Jeeps as he shook his head the entire way. It was now clear who was in charge, and it wasn't him. We also learned something else; the young man who owned the loaded rifle was not part of the pretend battle. A few of the boys had the good sense to stay off to the side with the rifles resting on their shoulders. This young man didn't bother to check if his rifle was unloaded because he had wisely stayed out of the pretend war game. He was standing there patiently waiting for his father with the gun on his shoulder when Jim found them and started screaming.

I still felt responsible for what had happened, so I walked over to the owner and asked if I could say something to the boys before they left for the hunt. He agreed it was a good idea.

I gathered them all and said, "Okay, I believe almost everyone here has forgotten what I have been trying to teach you. The hunt is a sacred thing. You must approach it with respect, and you must always be ultra-careful with your guns. Remember, during every hunting season, especially at Christmas when someone has received a new rifle, people will often lose their heads in the excitement and foolishly throw caution to the wind. That is how they lose their lives or someone they love dearly. I want all of you to decide right now you are not going to be one of those people. I also want everyone to remain calm and approach what they are about to do with an adult mindset. And you must keep that mindset as you climb into the shooting house with your father. Then, if you are fortunate enough to get a deer today, I want you to wait patiently until someone comes to help you collect it. Remember, even though the deer has been shot and is lying still on the plot, it could still jump up and charge if you approach it too quickly. Then, once your hunt is over, remember the house rules and let your father unload your rifle before you leave the plot. In other words, do not get back in the vehicle and return to this house with a loaded rifle. If you follow the rules and stay in a mature mindset, you will have a memorable experience today. If not, then something horrible and tragic could happen and you will have to live with it for the rest of your lives."

The boys all promised to behave, and their fathers all thanked me. They all came up and shook my hand, and a few of the boys gave me a hug with tears in their eyes as they apologized for how they had acted. The mood of the group was now very serious, which was not a bad thing.

We were doing a lot apologizing on this trip, and once this round of apologies had finished, I happened to look over to my left. Roisin was standing right beside me. I hadn't noticed her walk up. She gave me a nod with a smile and then she went back in the lodge.

I stood on the porch and watched them leave for the various plots throughout the property. I said a quiet prayer of safety for each of them. I think I might have quoted Psalm 91. As I thought about the events of the morning, I really couldn't blame Jim for reacting the way he did, even though I wished he hadn't used profanity in front of the kids. It was his responsibility to make sure we were all safe. And if someone had gotten killed, he would have been held responsible since it was his place. Or was it? Roisin somehow had authority over him, and I began to wonder if this was really his place after all.

CHAPTER TWELVE

I noticed how cold it was getting once everyone left, and I went back inside. Someone had started a new fire in the dining hall, and I got some coffee as I made myself comfortable in front of it. I sat in peaceful silence for the next hour. It reminded me of my old home when I was a kid, and I started missing my parents.

As I sat there lost in my thoughts, Roisin quietly walked in. She was fixed up again and looking like she had the night before. She smelled nice too.

"May I sit with you?" she delicately asked.

"Of course," I responded. She sat down in an easy chair beside me. I asked if Jim and the crew were planning to stay at the house during the hunt, and she explained they were staying in small cabins strategically placed around the property so they could remain close to the guests who were hunting. I commented that was a good idea with this group. We laughed and for a while, we just sat in silence watching the fire burn. I was happy for us to have the place to ourselves.

She finally asked, "You're not from this part of the country, are you?"

I told her I was from the Deep South. She told me she liked my southern accent, and I told her I liked her accent as well. (Her accent maybe sounded Scotch, Irish, or English, but I couldn't tell which one.)

"Does your family live around here?" she asked.

I didn't mean to react so strongly, but the sudden look on my face told her she had touched a sore spot. I wish I could have played it cool, but I was in a weak moment because I had just been thinking about my parents.

"No," I answered, as my voice kind of shook. "My parents passed away a couple of years ago."

"I'm sorry," she said.

I had learned the hard way it was not a good idea to tell a girl your life problems when you first meet her. I ruined my dating life during my senior year of college because I was always so moody and depressed. I dated several girls up until my parents died, but the relationships were never serious. The first couple of years of college are like that for some people. There were opportunities to meet plenty of new people and we weren't thinking about the rest of our lives. Like most college students, I was getting used to my new surroundings and exploring new possibilities. But during the junior and senior years, many students start getting into their majors and realize their college days are numbered. As they start thinking about their lives after college, it's natural they should also begin to think about the person they might want to spend their lives with. Dating relationships become more serious as people mature into their early twenties, and plenty of engagements are announced during their senior year.

But it didn't happen that way for me. One of the first things young women will ask their potential boyfriends about will be their families. I was so bitter and angry about what my cousin had done, I couldn't help but get emotional whenever someone asked me about my family, and it quickly scared them off.

But Roisin was not like the girls I had known in college. She was a mature adult and didn't seem at all uncomfortable as I told her the whole story about losing everything and then starting over with this job. For the first time I told someone my story and I didn't get emotional or angry. It even felt therapeutic to tell Roisin about it as she patiently and empathetically listened.

When I finished my story, she was quiet for a while as she thought about what she had just heard. She finally said, "You truly must be an extraordinary person to undergo such a horrible ordeal. Even though you lost everything you held dear, you bravely pressed forward and created a new life for yourself. You are now well respected and admired. Those men are all much older than you, and yet for a few moments, you were their leader. You were the alpha male."

I had never been called an "alpha male", and no one had ever congratulated me for the way I had handled my life over the last couple of years. I began to feel that little quiver someone gets in their chest when they are about to get emotional. But I held it together and said, "I just did what had to be done. My parents taught me to never back down from adversity and to keep going."

After studying me for a few more seconds she quietly said, "I believe you are capable of greatness. You have potential you have not yet realized."

The conversation was getting heavy, and although I appreciated her compliments, my sense of modesty was making me uncomfortable. I decided to change the subject by offering to help with dinner. She told me the dinner was going to be catered, and the company handling the meal was due to arrive in an hour.

We went back to watching the fire. I decided it was my turn to ask a couple of questions.

"Does your family live around here?" I asked.

Looking straight ahead, and with no emotion, she casually answered, "My mother died when I was little, and my father is far away. I don't have anything else to say about my family."

I had just spent the last hour telling her all about me, and she had no interest in telling me about herself. I didn't know how to respond, so I didn't say anything. We went back to watching the fire.

The awkward silence was broken a few minutes later when we heard a shot ring out in the distance. We both jumped to our feet.

"Sounds like somebody got one," I said.

Roisin smiled and said, "It is almost dusk and time for the deer to visit the feeding plots. I expect we will hear a plethora of gunshots, and no doubt they will all need to pass by our abode on their way to the processor. Your young pupils will want you to see the fruits of their efforts."

I should now point out that Roisin had a unique way of putting things, and she used words I never would have expected someone of our age to use. Her way of expressing herself sounded more like one of my mother's elderly friends and not like a woman in her twenties. I guessed she was raised by older people like me and had not been around people of our generation much, if ever.

But she was right about my young "pupils". As the shots continued to ring out, every few minutes a Jeep would pull up with a happy kid and his proud father. I congratulated each of them and then I posed for a quick picture. Afterwards, they were taken off to the processor which was located about ten miles away from the entrance of the property. Almost everyone ended up with an impressive buck or a decent-sized doe. One kid shot a button buck because he and his father thought it was a large doe, but no one cared.

An hour later the caterers arrived with a fantastic meal of exotic meats and delicacies. I was thoroughly excited for everyone and was ready to sit down to a glorious celebration meal, but then I noticed one of my coworkers had not returned to the house with his son. I asked around, but no one had heard from them.

CHAPTER THIRTEEN

I took Jim and the owner aside and asked if either of them had heard from my coworker and his twelve-year-old son. I was beginning to think something was wrong since the sun had set and no one had seen them. I was especially worried because this was their first time to hunt without me and I wasn't sure they were ready to go out alone.

Jim got out his walkie-talkie and began asking if anyone had heard from them. He got a very faint response from one of his crew. He confirmed that he was with them, and they were heading back to the house. Jim asked why they were late, and although his man did try to explain, he was so far away that his voice turned to garbled static. We could tell by the inflection in his voice that something wasn't right.

It was becoming brutally cold outside, but I waited on the front porch anyway. Jim and the owner were out there with me. We stood there shivering for ten long minutes until we finally saw the headlights coming through the trees. We knew something was wrong when they pulled up. My coworker and the crew member looked tired and depressed. The little boy's face was red like he had been crying. Jim pulled his man aside and the owner and I talked with my coworker. Roisin put her arm around the little boy and took him inside.

My coworker explained, "Cecil (his little boy) and I were about to call it a day, and then right at sunset, the whole forest was suddenly quiet. It was almost eerie. We then heard some rustling in the leaves, and a gigantic buck bounced out of the brush and onto the plot. I know I must have counted at least ten points. I let Cecil take the shot, but I don't think he got him right in the heart. The buck jumped several feet in the air and then he ran off the edge of the plot. We waited for thirty minutes like you had advised, but by the time we went to look for him, the deer was nowhere to be found."

Jim and the crew member came over, looking very apologetic. The crewmember told his part of the story, "I found large hoof prints leading off the plot, but I couldn't find any trace of him. By then it was too dark."

We went back inside, and Cecil was waiting for us in the foyer. Jim patted him on the head and said, "I'm sorry little buddy. It happens that way sometimes. You must have missed, but better luck next time."

But my co-worker whispered to me, "He didn't miss. We were too close. I know he hit him. It just wasn't in the heart."

I spoke up and asked, "Why don't you take me out there? I'll be happy to go look." Jim and his crewmember both said "NO!" in unison. Jim quickly said, "It's not safe to crawl around in these woods after dark. And besides, if one of my men couldn't find it, I doubt anyone can. Now why don't we go get some of this tasty smelling dinner?"

Roisin walked up and gave him a dirty look. Jim turned, and said, "Okay, let's go see if we can find that deer." Jim, my coworker, the crewmember, and I headed out to the Jeep. We decided it was best for Cecil to stay behind. As we were about to leave, Roisin came running out of the house and plopped down next to me in the back. The five of us then set out in the darkness.

I saw parts of the property I had not seen coming in. Even in the dark, it looked impressive and dangerous. I could see why Jim didn't want to go back out. The roads to the various plots were hilly and steep. It would have been nerve-wracking enough to travel through here in a fast Jeep during the day, but it was terrifying at night when you weren't familiar with the terrain. Plus, although Jim was doing his best to hide his anger, it came out in the wild way he was taking turns and roaring down hills.

I jokingly whispered to Roisin, "This looks like real Bigfoot country." She sighed and whispered back, "Well, we certainly thought so at first, but alas no." I laughed because at the time I thought she was joking.

When we arrived, I noticed the plot had a steep drop on the outer edge. This was going to be a challenge, and I was regretting I had opened my mouth. We all piled out of the Jeep, and I asked my coworker to show me precisely where the deer had been shot.

He showed me and I easily found the fresh hoof prints, but I didn't see any blood. I still wanted to try and look for it anyway since they had taken the shot at such close range and my co-worker was so positive Cecil had hit the deer. I walked over to the edge of the plot and found a somewhat steep but climbable slope. I asked my coworker to show me where they had last seen the deer, and he pointed precisely where the prints left the plot. I asked the crewmember where he had gone to look for the deer and he pointed in the same direction. But interestingly, he also confirmed he never found a blood trail.

I asked for a flashlight, and I started climbing down. I asked everyone else to stay on the plot for the time being. One possibility was the deer did go in the direction they had thought, and either the crewmember had overlooked the deer as it was lying in the brush, or he didn't go far enough. The other possibility was the deer had changed direction at some point, and the crewmember had gone the wrong way. I was thinking this was the case since he never found the blood trail.

Even with a flashlight, it was hard to be certain, but I was reasonably sure I could not find any deer prints in the direction they thought the deer had gone. I double-backed and completed a slow semi-circle along the side of the hill. And about forty degrees in the other direction I found what might be part of a hoof print in the dirt. I went in that direction about ten yards through some leaves, and then I found part of another hoof print. I went another ten yards, and I found it–a small crimson drop of deer blood on a leaf. I screamed up to the plot in excitement, "HEY, I FOUND THE BLOOD TRAIL. COME ON DOWN IF YOU CAN."

Everyone else started climbing down and I proceeded a few more yards. I found another blood drop, and then another. I was getting close. I showed everyone each drop as we proceeded to the bottom and that's where we found the buck. Judging by the way he was lying on the ground I think he must have blacked out and fallen headfirst as he rolled over.

They all hollered in excitement, as Roisin ran up and kissed me right on the mouth. We then managed to carry the buck up the hill, but it wasn't easy. Each of the men took a leg as we carefully climbed.

We decided not to take the deer back to the house to show everyone. It was out of the way and this deer needed to be taken to the processor immediately. And even if the meat was no longer good, my coworker still wanted to mount the head. I didn't blame him. That deer had one of the most impressive racks I had ever seen. Jim radioed for a truck so Roisin and I could be taken back to the lodge in the Jeep while he and my coworker took the deer to the processor.

We all had to catch our breaths for a few seconds as we waited for the truck to arrive. Roisin was still excited and kissed me on the cheek. I would need a quick bathroom break before dinner to wash off her lipstick or I would have some explaining to do. Then, while we were admiring the deer, my coworker looked up and said, "Hey, who is that up there?"

There was a high hill on the right side of the plot, maybe about thirty yards high, and standing at the top was a large man staring down at us in the darkness. Had it not been a full moon, I don't think anyone would have known he was there. He was tall, broad shouldered, and slightly hunched over with his fists clenched. He looked furious about something. He was wearing a ski suit and a full-face toboggan—which made him look even scarier.

Roisin let out a shriek, and Jim just about jumped out of his skin. Jim and Roisin looked at each other in terror and then they looked at me. "I wonder how long he's been standing there," whispered Jim. Roisin told us to stop looking and to ignore him. "Do you know who he is?" I asked. Roisin answered, "He is no one important." I looked up again and he was gone.

A few seconds later we heard a truck driving up through the darkness. We loaded the deer into the bed, and Jim took my co-worker to the processer. Roisin and I climbed inside the Jeep, and we were taken back to the lodge. The ride back was not near as horrendous since we took it easy—but it was silent. Roisin insisted I sit in the front, while she sat in the back. Her mood was completely different.

Who was that guy?

CHAPTER FOURTEEN

I had the pleasure of telling Cecil we found his deer when we got back to the lodge. Dinner wasn't ready yet, so I poured a cup of coffee while Cecil and I sat by the fire, and I told him the whole story. After that, each father and son team came over to tell me their hunting story for the day. Roisin missed all of this since she was in the kitchen helping the caterers with the food. My coworker, Jim, and the crewmember arrived about an hour later. The processor confirmed that the buck was the biggest they had taken in all day.

We were now ready for the celebration feast of deer chili, turtle soup, roast duck, rabbit stew, and all kinds of other wild stuff I can't remember. It was the first time in years I felt so happy and at ease. I was hoping Roisin would come out and join us, but she never did. I guess she ate in the kitchen.

After dinner, Jim asked the room if anyone was planning to go out for a morning hunt. But this time everyone had the good sense to tell him they wanted to pass. The plan now was for a celebration breakfast at nine the next morning, and then we would go home. This was music to my ears.

Once this was decided, Jim and his crew happily turned in for the night. The owner, my supervisor, and all the rest of my coworkers slowly walked over. Something was on their minds.

The owner sat down and said, "Buzz, we have a favor to ask. Someone needs to come back in a week and pick up the deer meat from the processor. We were wondering if you would do this for us. I'll rent a nice pickup truck for you."

I agreed to retrieve the venison since saying no wasn't an option, but it was just as well. I didn't have anyone to spend the holidays with, and I didn't have any plans for the next weekend. Everyone thanked me as they headed off to bed.

It was ten o'clock and I was alone in front of the fire. It then dawned on me I had been up since 4:00 that morning, and the thought made me feel exhausted. I was about to go upstairs to bed, but I suddenly smelled a familiar perfume.

Roisin was standing next to me, looking more beautiful than I had ever seen her, and I should mention I was now sitting in the loveseat. Without saying a word, she sat down next to me, and I mean right next to me. I put my arm around her. For a while, we sat and watched the fire. Those quiet few minutes were my favorite of the entire trip.

She finally said, "That was wonderful what you did this evening. You are truly a gifted individual."

"Thank you, I couldn't let Cecil down."

We watched the fire for a few more minutes and then she said, "I'm sorry you didn't have an opportunity to hunt during your visit. You will need to come back before the end of the season, and maybe next time I could sit with you in the stand."

I didn't want to tell her this, but earlier I had heard the owner say we were never doing anything like this again. And in the future, it would be far less trouble to hand out cash bonuses. I also knew I couldn't afford to visit here by myself.

Roisin asked if I had any kind of special technique for the way I hunted deer, and I told her I did. It wasn't much of a secret, so I went ahead and told her about it. The first thing I pointed out was hunting on this property was not like hunting on public land. This area was densely populated with deer, and it was fenced off.

"Yes, that does make a difference," she agreed.

I then explained, "Most hunters are not successful because they don't know how to relax while they are in the stand. They sit there dwelling on all the money they spent to be there and how it will be lost if they don't get a deer. They get frustrated and their heartbeat goes up. They start fidgeting. And without realizing it, they are making just enough noise to scare away the deer. But my strategy is to clear my mind when I am in the stand. I typically have a two or three hour wait before a deer comes out on the plot, so there is plenty of time to relax. I then slowly control my breathing by taking slow deep breaths. This slows my heart rate down, which is important."

"I would fall asleep after doing that," she said.

"You probably would if you were lying down," I responded. "But in a shooting house, you are sitting straight up. Plus, watching nature unfold keeps me awake."

"What do you notice when there aren't any deer on the plot? Most people get bored waiting for the deer."

"Well, this part is difficult to explain. But nothing about the forest is ever boring to me. I watch the wind rustling through the trees and the birds that occasionally land and fly away. I watch the squirrels run through the tree limbs. And then, when the deer show up, they are just the closing act of my own personal nature show. I also love the plots where you can watch vehicles on a highway, several miles away in the distance. That's especially relaxing in the early morning before the sun comes up. Don't ask me why."

"So, is that it?" she asked.

"No, that's only the beginning. Once the deer arrives, you don't want to make a mistake and miss the opportunity. They will often show up right at dusk when the shadows have disappeared from the plot and the sun has gone down, but there is still a little bit of light left. During those precious few minutes before dark, the forest will get eerily quiet. That's when it is most important to remain perfectly still. Sometimes you will see the deer poke its head out from the brush and slowly come out, or sometimes a small herd gathers right there. But before I take the shot, I first let them get comfortable. Often, they will look towards the house and watch for movement. Those deer are smarter than you think.

They will start grazing once they're convinced the coast is clear. That's when I take the shot and I never miss."

Roisin was mesmerized by my story. When I was finished, she asked if I knew how to clean and maintain rifles. I told her I did. She asked if I knew how to maintain feeding plots. I told her I had grown up helping my dad and his friends maintain plots.

She then said, "Buzz, I believe you may have surmised that Jim is not really the owner of this property. My family owns and operates this camp, and I would like for you to come work for us. We have need of someone with your level of proficiency."

I asked if I would be living on this property throughout the year. She answered, "No, you will work here during hunting season, but during the offseason, we will have other projects for you where your skills would be beneficial to us."

I asked what those special projects might be.

"What difference would it make if you were with me?" she asked seductively.

I saw my opportunity. She had kissed me twice that evening and now it was my turn. But as I leaned in, I didn't get the response I was expecting. She pulled back and jumped to her feet. After a very long minute she said, "No, this is wrong. I can't do this." As she looked away, she said "Buzz, I'm sorry. I know I have misled you, but I must tell you something. I am engaged."

THE NIGHT PEOPLE

CHAPTER FIFTEEN

I know a lot about a lot of things, but I will never understand why some women do what they do sometimes. Nothing about Roisin's behavior over the previous twenty-four hours had given me any reason to believe she was engaged. She wasn't even wearing a ring. As you might expect, I was severely hurt, and furious. But I knew I needed to swallow it because if Roisin had known what I was thinking at that precise moment, I'm sure she would have made me, and the rest of the group, leave her property right then in the middle of the night. I also wanted to ask if the guy on the hill was her fiancé, but I resisted the temptation. Instead, I was somehow able to gather myself and play it cool as I apologized for coming on too strong.

She responded, "No, this was my fault. You see, my fiancé is not the man I became engaged to. He has changed so much over these past many years."

That statement didn't make much sense, but I still shouldn't have blurted out, "These many years? Good grief, how long have you been engaged?"

She slowly turned and gave me a look that could have cured head lice, as she curtly said, "Good night."

I got up and walked towards the door. I turned to say goodnight as I left, just to be polite, but she was gone. I didn't even hear her walk out of the room. The entire dining hall was empty. I went in the kitchen and turned on the light, but she was not in there. I looked throughout the entire first floor, and I couldn't find her. The scent of her perfume was so strong I could have sworn she was walking right next to me the entire time.

As I stood alone in the great foyer, the place began to have an eerie feel. People don't disappear like that. As I quickly climbed the stairs, in a strange way it felt like someone, or something, was following me. I immediately went to my room and got ready for bed. I was so shaken that if I had not been up for twenty straight hours, I don't think I could have fallen asleep at all.

As the alarm rang at eight o'clock the next morning, it was a great feeling to know we were soon leaving and going home. For obvious reasons, I wasn't as excited to see Roisin as I had been. I wasn't sure what I would say to her after our conversation the night before, but I still kind of wanted to see her.

When I got downstairs there was a big table with four large trays of biscuits. They were wrapped in wax paper, but they weren't hot and fresh, and there was no butter or anything to put on them. There was plenty of coffee, tea, and water, but the coffee tasted like it had been brewed the night before and reheated. No one was there to serve it, so we all helped ourselves. Jim and his crew said they had already eaten, but they visited with us as we consumed our cold biscuits and old coffee.

Roisin was nowhere to be seen. I went to look in the kitchen. But as I opened the door, Jim called out from his table, "Buzz, do you need something?"

"Well, you see, I was going to…"

"There's no one in there," Jim answered, and he went back to his conversation.

I sat down at a table with my supervisor and the owner, feeling humiliated as I tried to play it cool. The rest of the breakfast was uneventful, other than hearing the owner quietly complain that he had paid for a full breakfast on each day.

Precisely thirty minutes later Jim stood up and announced, "THANK YOU ALL FOR JOINING US THIS WEEKEND. I HOPE YOU HAD A BLAST. MY CREW AND I WILL NOW HELP YOU ALL LOAD UP YOUR GEAR, AND WE HOPE YOU HAVE A SAFE RIDE HOME."

Jim and his "crew" were ready for us to leave, and that was fine with me. I jumped up from my seat and ran upstairs to my bedroom to gather my stuff. Everyone else followed my lead as I hoped they would. Then it happened….

BOOM!!!

I had heard that sound many times, but never inside a house. I ran into the bedroom where I thought I had heard the shot. I found little boys looking at a hole in the floor and other little boys examining the hole in the ceiling. A split second later we heard all kinds of screaming coming up through the floor. I was down those stairs in a flash, and everyone else was right behind me.

This is what happened. There was a massive gun rack on the wall on the right side of the foyer for people to store their rifles. Someone was getting his rifle off the stand to put it in his gun case, and it had unintentionally gone off. He was so shocked he dropped it on the floor. It was a miracle no one was killed.

Jim came storming in and picked up the rifle. I believe he was madder than he had been the day before. Looking bright red with tears coming down his face and a little snot coming out of his right nostril he screamed, "WHAT FOOL? WHAT IDIOT FOOL BROUGHT A LOADED RIFLE INTO THIS HOUSE? I WANT TO KNOW WHOSE RIFLE THIS IS BECAUSE HE IS ABOUT TO GET IT WRAPPED AROUND HIS SORRY NECK!!!!"

This is where things got murky. The rifle in question was indeed the property of the man who had taken it off the stand when it had gone off, but he claimed to have loaned it out the evening before. The problem was he couldn't remember who used it since he had loaned out several other rifles as well, or at least that's what he told us. Yes, it would have been a good idea for him to check each of the rifles in his collection to make sure they weren't loaded before bringing them into the house. But the true culprit was the fool who forgot to unload it at the end of his hunt before leaving the plot, and no one was about to admit to it for obvious reasons.

After some quick finger-pointing, we were able to narrow it down to two possible suspects and their conversation went something like this:

"This was your rifle. I am positive this is the rifle you used. You must have forgotten to unload it in all the excitement."

"I beg to differ. I had the rifle with the synthetic stock. You wanted this rifle because it has a wooden stock. I remember because you thought a wooden stock would photograph better."

"No, I asked you if I could have the wooden stock rifle later for the picture if I got a deer. You then took this rifle with the wooden stock to the stand and left me with the rifle with the synthetic stock, which was fine with me."

"No, that doesn't make any sense. Since you wanted the rifle with the wooden stock for a picture, I went ahead and gave it to you. I took the rifle with the synthetic stock because I didn't care. And as you can see, the rifle with the synthetic stock is unloaded. Here, see? I remembered to unload it when I left the plot."

"No. The rifle with the synthetic stock is unloaded because it was mine and I unloaded it like I was supposed to."

"No, I don't think so……"

Jim interrupted. "GET OUT! GET OUT! GET OOOOOOUT!!!!! I WANT ALL OF YOU FOOLS OUT OF THIS HOUSE NOW! I NEVER WANT TO SEE ANY OF YOU EVER AGAIN! I DON'T NEED THIS! I HAVE A DOCTORATE FOR CRYING OUT LOUD! YOU'VE GOT FIVE MINUTES TO GET OUT OF THIS HOUSE AND TWO OF THEM ARE ALREADY GONE!"

No one said a word as we frantically grabbed our stuff and retreated to the vehicles. Jim's employees nervously helped us as they whispered things like, "Ya'll better get out of here now. I've never seen him like this." When we were outside and a safe distance away, I quietly asked one of them, "If he has a doctorate, then what's he doing here?" The guy shook his head and whispered, "He worked at several colleges, but no one would give him tenure. Now for crying out loud, will you please get in one of these cars and leave."

After the pictures were developed days later, we learned the rifle with the wooden stock had been passed around and used in several pictures because it was "so authentic and rustic looking." The two men who had argued about it in the foyer were each holding a different rifle in their picture and each of their rifles had synthetic stocks. Although the mystery was never officially solved, my theory is the man who owned the rifle, had indeed used it. It was a very rare and expensive gun, and even though he did lend out several less expensive rifles that night, I don't see him lending his prized rifle to anyone except for a quick photo.

Then, in all the excitement, he forgot to unload it as he proceeded to let everyone have their picture made with it. Meanwhile, those two idiots in the lodge were probably arguing over a different rifle with a wooden stock and didn't know enough about guns to recognize they were arguing over a gun that neither of them ever had in their possession. But who knows?

The owner paid the bill for the damage, but he never told us how much it was. He did confirm the bill was "outrageous." He also said he could have easily repaired the damage himself for a fraction of what they charged him.

The ride home was faster than the ride up and much quieter. We stopped a couple of times to gas up and use the restroom, but no one was in the mood for shopping or exploring. This gave me plenty of time to think.

It was my belief most of these men should never go hunting again. You need to have a practical and serious mindset to be a good hunter. And many of the problems we encountered on our little adventure were because most of them didn't take things as seriously as they should have. For instance, there were three opportunities to go hunting and they only went out once. They missed the other two because they all wanted to sleep in, even though they were visiting a spectacular hunting resort and the owner had paid for three hunting opportunities. The second misstep was when several men turned their young sons loose with their rifles without any adult supervision. And even though none of the boys were playing with loaded rifles, we still almost got kicked off the property. Then, once we barely got passed that, someone didn't adhere to protocol and unload his rifle at the right time. Plus, that same rifle was passed around to several people as a photo prop, and none of them had thought to make sure it wasn't loaded.

I would liked to have made each of these points to everyone for their own good, but I was no longer the "alpha male." Upon leaving the camp I had gone back to being an entry level employee who needed to watch what he said to his elder co-workers and supervisors.

When we arrived at the company parking lot, everyone got in their cars and drove home without saying a word. My supervisor gave me a ride back to my apartment. For some reason, I felt guilty, even though none of this was my fault.

Things were quiet around the office over the next week. On Monday morning I felt like I needed a vacation to recover from the vacation, and I believe everyone else felt the same way. The owner worked from home all week, and I didn't blame him. If I had been him, I wouldn't have wanted to be around us either. Rumor has it the poor man sipped wine and stayed in his pajamas the entire time. No one in his house was allowed to turn on a radio or television. He just wanted silence.

Late Tuesday afternoon he called me at work and told me the deer meat was going to be ready on Friday, as opposed to Saturday. So now he wanted me to go get it a day early. That was fine with me since it was a free day from work and I would not have to give up a Saturday, but there was a catch. In our haste to leave, one of the kids left his retainer in one of the bathrooms. That meant taking a quick side trip to the camp. I was glad we were on the phone, and he couldn't see the look on my face or the expletive I mouthed.

"I don't mind going to get the venison, but couldn't they just mail us the retainer? Because honestly sir, I think I am sensing a trap." At the time I was trying to be clever.

"You don't have to worry about going back there," he answered. "That sweet young girl was the one who called and told us she had found it. She also apologized for the way Jim acted when we left. Curiously, she specifically requested for you to come get it, and she was thrilled to know I was planning to send you anyway. All you need to do is honk when you arrive at the gate, just like we did last time, and she will bring it out to you."

(I should mention his short conversation with Roisin happened about three weeks before he got the bill for the hole in the floor and the ceiling.)

I left on Friday at 6:00 am in the pickup truck the owner had rented for me. It was fun to drive, and it only took a little over five hours to get there. It didn't take them long at the processor to fill up the bed with everyone's deer meat, neatly boxed with everyone's name on their order. It was a freezing cold day, so I didn't have to worry about the meat thawing on the way home. The ones who were having their deer heads mounted were planning to get them from the taxidermist sometime later.

With that chore out the way, it was time to return to the camp, or at least to the gate. I began to wish I had not come alone. When I arrived, I thought about just tapping on the horn slightly so I could truthfully say I had. Then when no one showed up, I could leave and tell the boss the attempt to retrieve the retainer was unsuccessful.

But then I realized I was being ridiculous. I gave the horn a good honk and about ten minutes later the gate finally opened, but it wasn't Roisin.

Jim came walking out and stood at my window looking disgusted. I slowly rolled it down and he handed me a bag with the retainer inside. He then said, "Roisin had to leave late last night on family business. She told me to give you this." Without saying anything else he turned around and started walking away. I called out, "Hey Jim, I'm sorry about everything." He stopped, turned, and said, "Buzz, I believe you should encourage all of those people to forget about hunting before somebody gets killed." As he turned to walk away again, I foolishly called out, "Hey, did you know that Roisin offered me a job working with you guys?"

Jim stopped in his tracks, turned, and stomped back to my window. Glaring at me he whispered, "You stay away from that girl. Don't go asking about her. Don't go looking for her. Don't even mention her to anybody. Just go on with your life and forget you ever knew her. And I don't care what she said, you should never come back here again. Do you understand?"

I was so shocked I didn't respond. I rolled up my window, backed away from the gate, and drove away with him standing there looking furious. I arrived back in town later that afternoon. Everyone was waiting for me in the company parking lot with a hero's welcome. They were all happy to get their venison, and as a token of their appreciation, they had all chipped in and bought me a hiker's full-sized backpack. It was just like one my dad had given me when I was in high school. I had mentioned to a couple of people I had lost my old one in the fire, and it felt good to have a new one.

Just as everyone was about to leave with their venison, I held up the bag and yelled out, "HEY, WHO LOST THEIR RETAINER? I HAVE IT RIGHT HERE."

But no one claimed it. There were only two men in the group with sons who used retainers, and neither one had left his retainer behind. I asked the owner what we should do with it. He shrugged and said he would send it back to them with a note saying it didn't belong to any of us. His thinking was someone would probably claim it at some point. My awkward side trip had been completely unnecessary.

About three months later my supervisor walked by my desk and asked, "Did you hear about the hunting camp we visited?"

"What about it?"

"The family who owned it has turned the property over to a timber company. They will probably clear-cut the whole thing."

I decided it was just as well.

CHAPTER SIXTEEN

A few days after I learned the fate of the hunting resort, my supervisor walked by my desk and said the owner wanted to see me in his office. I sighed and asked, "We're not going on another trip, are we?"

He informed me the owner had vowed never to take this group on any trip or business retreat. I was relieved, but he said something strange as I walked out the door.

"Buzz, make sure you tell him the complete truth. I promise there is no reason to lie to him. But you must tell the truth."

That was a weird thing to say. To my knowledge I had never misled anyone in this organization about anything, other than complementing someone's atrociously ugly tie. When I arrived at the owner's suite, his secretary sent me right into his office. The owner asked me to sit down on a couch next to his desk. I noticed the legs had been sawed off, which made it sit flat on the floor. When I had made myself as comfortable as I could, I found I was looking up at him. He had something on his mind.

"Buzz, you haven't been with us very long, but you have certainly made an impression during your short time. You're never late. You never call in sick. You don't mind taking on extra work or working extra hours, and you never complain about anything. When there is a tough job to do, you buckle down and do it. On top of that, your work is always perfect, and your co-workers love you. And I believe that nightmare hunting trip would have been an even bigger disaster without your help. For all we know someone might have gotten killed if you had not intervened."

"Thank you, sir," I said. But I could tell something bad was coming. He then looked me in the eye and said, "Buzz, something has come up and I am hoping you could shed some light on it."

My heart sank and I threw up a little in my mouth.

He continued, "As you know we sometimes have contracts in Hong Kong, and we have just been contacted by a company over there who wants to do business with us. It's a big contract, and we are happy with the offer. The peculiar thing is they have requested you, and only you, to be our in-country representative. Do you know anything about this?"

"No sir," I told him. I asked for the name of the company, and he told me. I had never heard of them, and I told him so. He wasn't convinced.

"Are you sure you don't know anything about this?" he asked.

"No sir. I don't know anyone in Hong Kong," I said.

"Do you think maybe a former classmate or instructor recommended you?" he asked.

"Well, maybe. But if they did, it was without my knowledge," I replied.

"Well, one thought that crossed our minds is maybe you knew someone connected with this company and you requested they specifically ask for you. Now be honest. Did you do that?"

"No sir," I quickly responded.

"Would you even want to do something like this," he asked.

"Well, no I wouldn't," I answered. "I don't know anything about conducting business in Hong Kong, and I don't think I'm ready to take on a project this big."

The owner nodded and replied, "Yes, although you have done an excellent job for us, I don't believe you are qualified for a project like this—not at this point in your career."

I asked him about a guy in our office who normally handles the contracts in the Far East. For this story, I am going to call him "Sam." Sam had declined the invitation for the hunting trip, and he wasn't at all surprised to hear what had happened. The man knew his coworkers and he knew them well.

The owner responded, "I told them Sam was normally the one who handles projects like this. And although they are familiar with Sam and have heard good things about him, they still insisted I send you. Now Buzz, I can forgive someone for being a bit too opportunistic. But I can't excuse someone lying to my face. I am going to ask one more time. Do you know anything about this?"

I again denied knowing anything about it.

He then said, "I pay huge bonuses to my men who take on big projects like this. Were you aware of that?"

"No, but regardless, I wouldn't want to be uprooted right now. I have been through so much over the past two years and I have enjoyed getting into a routine," I responded.

The owner sat back in his chair, chewing on his cigar. He finally said, "Well, I was hoping you'd be able to provide some sort of explanation. But if you truthfully have no idea what's going on here, then I am more confused than ever."

I understood his dilemma. No business owner in his right mind would want to pass on a deal like this, but the other company was making an illogical request without a good explanation. After about a minute he stood up and said, "I'm going to call and tell them Sam is the only man here who is willing to go. If they pass on him, then we will pass on the deal. Simple enough."

Sam had been working with the company for over twenty years and he was the best man for this project. He was of Chinese descent, and his family had always spoken Chinese at home. But his family had lived in the United States for three generations, so he also spoke perfect English. He had met his wife during one of the business trips to Hong Kong and she loved going on these long business trips with him since it allowed her to see her friends and family. They didn't have any children, and he had plenty of relatives here who were happy to take care of their home and personal affairs while they were away. This gave him the flexibility of being able to leave for months at a time on short notice.

The owner sent me back to work as I rethought every conversation I might have had about my job and business in general over the past several weeks—thinking maybe I had made a huge impression on someone without realizing it.

I took the elevator back down to my floor. My immediate supervisor called for me as I walked by his office. He asked how the meeting had gone.

"A company in Hong Kong wants me to come over and oversee a huge project for the company, but I have never heard of them, and I have no idea why they asked for me," I responded.

"Are you sure?"

"Yes, I am."

"Are you positive?"

"Positive."

"Well, you had better be right. Because if we find out you're not being honest with us, you're toast. You realize that don't you?"

I nodded. We stared at each other for a moment of awkward silence and then he motioned towards the door without saying a word. I turned and went back to my desk.

I tried to lose myself in the day's activities, but it was no use. They didn't believe me, and I was beginning to fear I was about to be fired. Three hours later my supervisor walked up to my desk and told me the owner wanted to see both of us in his office immediately. Neither of us said a word as we rode the elevator back up to his floor. His secretary directed us to the conference room. The owner was in there waiting for us and Sam was with him. The owner invited us to sit down as he told us about an update on the proposal.

"I have just been on the phone for an hour with a representative from the company," he began.

"Did you place a call to Hong Kong?" asked Sam.

"No, they have sent a representative who is staying at a local hotel. Anyway, they still want Buzz, and only Buzz, to head up this effort. I pressed him on this, and he did confirm that Buzz did not privately orchestrate this deal and knew nothing of it beforehand. All he would tell me is Buzz had recently made a strong impression on someone close to their organization, but the representative would not say who it was or when this meeting supposedly took place."

The owner sternly looked at me and said, "Buzz, I want you to think hard. Do you remember having a recent conversation with someone about our organization or what you do here? It could have been someone you met along the way in a restaurant, or at the gym, or maybe at church? You are not going to get in trouble. I just want to get to the bottom of this."

I told them I didn't eat out much since I knew how to cook. I didn't have a gym membership, and I had not yet found a church home, although I had visited a couple of places. During those church visits I had introduced myself to a few people, but I didn't remember having any extensive discussions about my job. Not to say it didn't happen, I just couldn't remember for sure.

"Maybe one of his professors from college put in a word for him," suggested my supervisor.

The owner replied, "I have already looked into that. I contacted the dean of the business school at his college. He told me that he and his professors are not in the habit of making formal recommendations when the student did not request it in the first place. He also informed me that Buzz had only requested one recommendation from him, and it was to us when he was hired here."

"Are you sure this is a real company?" asked my supervisor.

Sam responded, "I made a few phone calls, and they are a legitimate company that has been around for a while. They have conducted business throughout the Far East for many years."

The owner again sat back in his chair as he took it all in. After a very long minute, he looked at me and asked, "Buzz, have you had any kind of lengthy conversation with anyone lately, about anything? It didn't have to have been about business or your job."

I thought for a second and said, "The only person outside of this company I have visited with for any length of time was Roisin at the hunting camp. And we never talked about business or what I do here. We mainly just talked about hunting."

"Are you talking about that sweet young lady up at the camp?" asked the owner. "I doubt that she would have anything to do with this."

I agreed, but I did point out she was the only one I had visited with extensively who was from outside of our company.

The owner got a silly grin on his face and said, "You know Buzz, I think she was a little sweet on you. Several times I noticed her looking in your direction when you didn't realize it."

By then all three of them were giving me that silly grin which immediately turned to disappointed astonishment when I told them she had admitted to being engaged on Saturday night after everyone had gone to bed.

The owner then thoughtfully said, "You know, I don't remember seeing her at all on Sunday morning. I think Jim and his band of miscreants were the ones responsible for serving us those stale biscuits and coffee. My suspicion is they were left over from another meal from days before."

My supervisor changed the subject and asked, "So where do we go from here?"

The owner toked on his cigar and said, "I told them we are pleased with their offer, and we appreciated them for thinking of us, but Buzz simply wasn't available….and then they doubled the offer."

I was shocked and not in a good way. But the owner reassuringly said, "Now Buzz, don't worry. I am not going to pressure you to do this if you don't feel up to it. This deal is not going to make or break us. And regardless of the offer, I'm starting to get a bad feeling about this. It isn't logical for someone to make such an odd request and not offer a good reason why."

The owner of our company could be demanding. But he cared about his employees like we were his own family. I was thankful to be working for a man like that. I believe my parents would have liked him.

Sam and my supervisor agreed we were most likely doing the right thing by saying no, but none of us were completely sure because of the money involved. The meeting adjourned, and we went back to work.

CHAPTER SEVENTEEN

I later received a call from the owner to come up to his office, and he told me to come alone. That made me nervous, but I went up anyway. What choice did I have?

I could tell he was agitated when I walked into his office. He asked me again if I was sure I had no idea what was going on. I told him I was as confused as he was. He then pulled out a shotgun and blew my head off as I heard him scream, "LIAR!!!"

I screamed out in terror as I sat up in bed. I looked at my alarm clock and it was three a.m. I have always been prone to having horrifyingly vivid nightmares during times of stress. It was almost an hour before I went back to sleep, and for a while, I considered getting up and starting the day.

The next morning, I dragged myself out of bed and went to work. I was behind because of the interruptions from the day before, so it wasn't hard to lose myself in my assignments. A couple of hours later my supervisor stopped by my desk and stared at me without saying a word.

"Another meeting?" I asked, already knowing the answer.

He sighed heavily and said, "Yeah, let's go back up there."

We walked back into the conference room, fresh coffee was brewing. The owner had also brought some of his wife's pastries. I assumed they were for someone else, but the owner invited us to have some. I had already eaten breakfast, but I had been warned to accept when the owner offered his wife's cooking. The three of us sat at the table eating the treats as the owner told us Sam would join us in a few minutes. My supervisor and the owner discussed something else happening in the company while I sat there drinking my coffee and slowly eating my Danish since I was still full after eating my first breakfast. Sam finally showed up and the meeting began. The owner took the lead:

"I have called you here to give an update on our business proposal from Hong Kong. Last night I called the representative, and I declined the new offer. I also recommended another company that might be interested. Two hours later he showed up at my house unannounced as my wife and I were getting ready for bed. I was furious, but he had yet another proposal. They are now willing to pay ten times their original offer, and they are adamant that Buzz is the only one they want."

I began to feel flushed, so the owner called for this secretary to bring me some water. Once I had collected myself, he looked at me and said, "Buzz, here is what you will be paid if you agree to do this."

He handed me a slip of paper with a number on it. It was the equivalent of three years' salary. As I stared at the paper, the owner said, "Now remember, you still don't have to do this. I will understand if you decide this is not right for you, but I didn't want to turn this new offer down until I let you know what kind of money you could make."

I didn't know what to say. I wished I could call my dad and ask for his advice. He would know what I needed to do.

The owner continued, "You won't be going alone if you decide to do this. Even though they said I could only send you, this contract is so lucrative I can justify secretly sending Sam to help you behind the scenes. You will secretly report to him, and you will both report to me."

I thanked him for the offer, and I told him I needed time to think about it. The owner told me to take the rest of the day off. It was a Friday so I could take a long weekend. I excused myself and then the owner, my supervisor, and Sam met privately.

I rode the elevator down to the first floor, without even going to my desk to get my briefcase. The door opened, and I walked through the lobby and into the sunlight. It was spring, but there was still a cold nip in the air, and it felt exhilarating to be away from the job on a beautiful workday. My high-rise apartment was only about a mile away, so I took the bus home and changed out of my formal work clothes before doing anything else.

I walked around my neighborhood for a while and thought about how the trip would change my life. I would be gone for about six months and living in a foreign land where I didn't know anyone. That was scary to think about. But on the other hand, the money was good. It would be enough for me to buy a new car without going into debt, and

I really wanted a new Mustang. I could now pick one up and still have plenty of money for savings.

I continued walking for several blocks over the next couple of hours, oblivious to everything happening around me. Around noon, I started getting tired, so I sat down on a bus stop bench. That was when I noticed something odd. I looked to my right and saw a man walking towards me about a block away. When he saw me sit down, he got an awkward look on his face. He quickly sat down on a bench in his corner. At first, he just sat there looking straight ahead, but then he slowly glanced in my direction. When he saw I was watching him, he turned and looked right in front of him. He was tall and robust like he could have been a football player. His hair was dark and cut short. I began to feel uneasy, so I got up to leave as I headed in the other direction. When I got to the street corner, I decided to turn right. Out of the corner of my right eye, I saw he had also gotten up and was now walking behind me. I crossed to the other side and started heading back up the opposite side of the street. And sure enough, he crossed the street where I had, and he was walking behind me again. I thought I was about to get mugged, so I hailed a taxi.

I felt uneasy and stayed close to my building for the rest of the afternoon. Around five o'clock, I walked to the local diner across the street and got a cheeseburger and fries. I sat facing the door and watched it the entire time. After I finished eating, I went next door and hung out at a local coffee shop with a huge magazine rack. I picked up the latest issue of Outdoor Life and sat down with some coffee. Eventually, the sun went down, and I went back to my apartment.

I ventured out a little on Saturday and Sunday, but this time I stayed close to home as I continued to think about the offer. The only consolation I had when my parents died was I could either live in my old home or sell it to have seed money. Ever since I lost it all, I had been living with a nagging sense of urgency that I was one wrong move from being destitute. That was why I felt driven to do well in this job and get along with my coworkers. But taking this offer would remedy all of that. I would have savings, and the ability to do almost anything I wanted.

As I sat by my window watching the traffic, I convinced myself the owner would always resent me for not taking this offer and it would cost me my job. Looking back on it, I know that wasn't true. But I couldn't shake the fear at the time. So even though I didn't want to, on Sunday evening I called the owner and told him I had decided to accept the offer. He firmly told me to be in his office at 7:00 am the following morning. Man, I wished I had waited until the next morning to tell him.

I needed to go to bed since I now had an early meeting, but it was no use trying to fall asleep. About eleven o'clock I got up and attempted to watch television, but there was nothing on worth watching. I turned on my small radio and pulled a kitchen chair up to my window. Sometimes watching late-night traffic and listening to a local jazz station relaxed me enough to fall asleep–but not this night.

I looked out the window and nearly had a heart attack. The man who followed me on Friday afternoon was outside my building on the other side of the street. He was looking up at my window and smiling. He knew I could see him and was glad I was startled. He pointed directly at me for a second, and then he brought his index finger across his throat–giving me the cutthroat sign.

I backed away from the window and called the police. They said there was a car in the neighborhood, and that they would check it out. In the meantime, they advised me to stay in my apartment and not open the door until they arrived.

I turned off all the lights and went to the window, but I stayed back about two feet so he would probably not see me looking out. He was no longer there. A police car came by a minute later and they drove around the block a couple of times. They were at my door a few minutes later, and I told them what happened on Friday afternoon and what had just happened a few minutes before. They asked if I was sure it was the same guy, and I told them he was. He was even dressed the same. They asked if I knew who he was or what he might want. I told them no. They said they did not find anyone matching that description anywhere in the vicinity, but I should call them again if the guy doesn't leave me alone. They also told me to lock my door and be vigilant anytime I left my apartment.

Leaving the country for a while was starting to sound like a good idea.

CHAPTER EIGHTEEN

I met with the owner, my supervisor, and Sam in the conference room the next morning at 6:59 am. They each looked exhausted, and with good reason. The owner had asked them to come in at midnight and they had spent the previous seven hours setting all of this up. That may sound crazy, but there was a ridiculous amount of money involved with this contract, and time was of the essence.

I was informed that Sam would be preparing me for the trip and these preparations would now be my full-time job. I was also reminded I could still back out at any time, but I knew I would never respect myself if I did that. I had committed, and I was going to follow through with it. I also wanted a new Mustang. The company in Hong Kong was covering my travel and living arrangements. I was also informed I would fly first class and stay in a very nice place.

Over the next couple of months, I spent a lot of time with Sam and his wife as they helped me prepare, and we became good friends. They would often invite me to their home for dinner and we would have long discussions about contemporary Chinese culture and their customs. We also had long discussions about my job responsibilities and how I should handle various situations while keeping with the cultural norms in the workplace.

He advised me we would have to be careful about being seen together in public since the company was still adamant that I come alone, and the owner was reminded repeatedly. That should have tipped us off, but it didn't.

The next challenge was deciding what to do with my apartment while I was away. Sam suggested that since I was planning to find a new place after I returned, I should put my things in storage during the trip. Then I wouldn't have to worry about rent and utilities for an empty place. When the owner learned about this, he offered to let me keep my things in a small storage facility in the basement of a building he owned. He also promised to pay for a hotel while I looked for a new place after I returned.

I moved out of my apartment the day before I left. The owner paid for the move, and an overnight stay in a five-star hotel so I wouldn't have to sleep on the bare floor of my empty apartment. It was all coming together.

The owner and my supervisor took me to the airport and waited until it was time to leave. (Sam and his wife had already left a few days before.) The owner took me aside five minutes before I was about to board and whispered, "Buzz, I'm glad to give you this opportunity, but I'm still uneasy about all this. Although these people have been extremely cordial, and there is an enormous amount of money involved, they have also been mysterious about a lot of things. Honestly, I am on the verge of calling this whole thing off right now. But I am going to ask one last time. Are you still sure you want to do this? You don't have to. I promise I will understand."

Without hesitation, I assured him I still wanted to go.

He then whispered, "Okay, I have one final instruction. If something should go wrong and you are in danger, if you can contact us, but you are not able to say outright you're in trouble, I want you to say the following words: please remember to feed my goldfish. I promise we will use every resource at our disposal to come find you."

I thanked him and promised I would remember to do that, but privately I thought he was just being paranoid. We said our goodbyes, and I boarded the plane.

This wasn't my first time flying. My parents and I had flown to California a couple of times to visit relatives, so I wasn't nervous about the flight even though it was a long one. This was my first opportunity to sleep on a plane and it wasn't bad. I woke up when we hit some rough turbulence along the way. But then we all calmed down, and I fell back asleep.

We landed at the Hong Kong International Airport, and I was ready to see my temporary new home. The plan was for me to pick up my luggage, and then I would look for someone holding a sign with my name on it. This person would give me a ride to my new place. I was also told I should not ask any questions since the person picking me up did not speak English. Once I arrived at my new home, I was to wait for a phone call, and someone would give me further instructions. Sam was planning to call later that evening, and we would discuss those instructions.

After I picked up my luggage, I looked through the crowd and found a smiling young lady holding a sign with my name on it. I was hoping they would send someone who could help me with my luggage since my bags were extremely heavy, but the only thing she could carry was the small bag I had with me on the plane. I struggled with my luggage as she led me outside to a delivery truck. She motioned for me to put my luggage in the back and then she motioned for me to climb in. The floor of the van was dirty with grease and oil. I should have known something was off. A reputable company never would have transported someone this way, but I went ahead and sat down on the spare tire.

Once I was settled, the young lady handed me a bottle of something and motioned for me to drink it as she closed the door. I had worked up a good thirst carrying all the luggage and was happy to have it. She stood and watched through the back window as I drank it down. It had a weird medicine-like taste. I figured that it was some kind of foreign soft drink. That was the last thing I remembered.

CHAPTER NINETEEN

I woke up sometime later in total darkness. I was sitting upright in a chair with my hands and feet in chains. I was on a ship–down in the cargo hold. I could see I was surrounded by several wooden crates when my eyes finally adjusted. I could hear the squeak of some rats in a corner.

I had heard of people traveling to other countries and being shanghaied into permanent servitude, but in my wildest dreams, I never thought it could ever happen to me. I was more terrified than I had ever been in my entire life. Why would someone lure me across the world to chain me up and take me away?

My anxiety overtook me as I started screaming, "HEYYYYYYYYYYYYYYYYY!!! WHO ARE YOU? WHY AM I HERE? WHAT DO YOU WANT? WHERE ARE YOU TAKING ME? WHY DID YOU TAKE ME? I WANT TO SEE SOMEBODY NOW!!!!"

No one answered.

Then in desperate exasperation, I just started screaming at the top of my lungs, "HEYYYYYYYYYYYYYYY", over and over. I did this for several minutes until I was out of breath. The screaming released some of my anxiety, which gave me the presence of mind to contemplate my situation. I wasn't dead, so obviously my captors had plans for me. That wasn't much consolation, but it was something.

After I had been quiet for several minutes, I heard a door slowly open overhead. The light of the sun came in. I was chained down so tightly I couldn't turn around to see who was coming. My anxiety nearly reached its breaking point as I heard someone slowly walk up behind me. That was when I heard a familiar voice say, "Buzz, my friend, be calm. There is nothing to fear. I promise."

It was Roisin. Jim's warning about her was not an idle threat. I didn't know what to say, so I didn't say anything. She finally said, "Buzz, I am so sorry for taking you away. But when Jim told us you didn't want to join us, we had no choice but to lure you here. We need you. And although you do not yet realize it, you need us as well."

"I never told Jim I did not want to work for you," I said. "I just told him you had offered me a job, and then he told me to leave."

Roisin gasped, and then she was silent. After a few seconds, she slowly asked, "Am I to understand......he did not tell you about the specifics of our offer that day when you came to pick up the retainer?"

"NO," I loudly responded.

Roisin took a deep breath and asked, "Buzz, would you have been interested in helping us track down a rare animal for a fee of a hundred thousand dollars?"

This was the late 60s and I would have been lucky to make that over ten or twelve years. I immediately said, "Yes, of course, I would have gladly quit my job for that kind of money."

It was quiet for a few seconds, and then Roisin let out a prolonged shriek. When she was done, she quietly muttered, "That buffoon lied to me, and he will pay dearly. No one lies to me, ever."

After she collected herself, she softly said, "Buzz, my dear friend, there has been a horrible misunderstanding. I believe the best thing for us to do now is unchain you. But know that you are on a ship in the middle of the South Pacific and we are not near land. Can I trust you not to do anything foolish?"

I assured her she would have my full cooperation, so she went back upstairs for the keys. When she came back, I could hear several heavy footsteps walking with her. I figured she was bringing some muscle, and I was right. When she unchained me, I slowly stood up and saw she now had ten large men with her. Sure, I was furious, but I wasn't stupid. I played it cool.

With a forced smile, I said, "Roisin, it is wonderful to see you again. But I'm sure you can understand why I'm confused."

I didn't think she was buying my nice act, but she nevertheless said, "Come. We have your suitcases upstairs. I will show you to your cabin."

I followed Roisin up the stairs and her bodyguards were close behind. I let her stay six or seven stairs ahead of me the whole way up, just so her friends wouldn't think I was about to try something. We walked out on the deck and the intense sun was blinding after being held in that dark hold. For a few seconds, I painfully couldn't see a thing. When my eyes adjusted, I saw we were in the middle of the ocean with no land in sight. But if I had seen any kind of land or maybe a ship, I would have jumped overboard and taken my chances.

As we walked down the deck, I started thinking about Sam and the owner. They were going to be sick with worry, wondering where I was, but there was nothing I could do. Roisin led me into my cabin where my suitcases were neatly lined up next to a bed. She dismissed her bodyguards, and we were alone. She invited me to sit down on the bed with her. I could tell she wanted the first word, and I let her have it.

"Buzz, let me apologize for them chaining you to the floor. They were supposed to bring you in here, and let you wake up on this bed. My comrades do not always follow directions as well as they should."

I didn't believe that for a minute. I knew they put me in chains so I wouldn't be able to strangle someone when I woke up, but I just kept quiet and listened.

She then explained, "My family and I are conservationists. We use our vast resources to save lost animals that are on the verge of extinction. To accomplish this endeavor, we endow a foundation that researches ways to help them survive. One of the ways we do this is to bring them to our private animal sanctuary. My apologies for deceiving you and your employer, but we so need your help and expertise. And I knew that if you could see for yourself what we are doing, then you would surely want to assist us."

"I will be happy to help in any way I can, but my supervisors are going to be frantic if I don't check in with them soon," I said.

She responded, "For the time being we'll inform them you are performing your duties admirably and we are abundantly satisfied with your efforts. Then, when you see what we have for you, you can inform them personally that you have decided to become a permanent member of our organization. Truthfully, we need you much more than they do."

That was the most pretentious thing I had ever heard in my life. But I continued to play along since I didn't want to go back in the hold, or worse, over the side. Besides, I knew the owner was smarter than that. He wouldn't be satisfied if he couldn't hear directly from me. Plus, when he learned from Sam that I never checked in to the place where I was supposed to be staying, I had no doubt he would start asking questions.

I wanted to know how long it would be before I could contact the owner, but I didn't want to ask directly, so I asked, "Will this job take six months like we originally planned?"

"Oh no. It will take another three days to arrive at our island where you will be our special guest, and I promise they will be the most memorable days of your life. During that time, you will see some of the rare species we have collected. You will then be trained on how you will complete your mission to find the rare animal we have been searching for. After that, you will be taken to the area for your hunt. You will be given up to seven days to accomplish this, but I doubt it will take you that long. Once we have collected the animal, you will be paid handsomely for your services. You can then return to that miserable job…if that is what you want."

"So, I guess you're saying this trip will take about three to four weeks?" I asked.

"Yes, surely your owner can go that long without hearing from you directly and not become suspicious. By the way, you did travel to Hong Kong alone, didn't you?"

I knew telling her about Sam would probably put his life in danger, but I still managed to screw up. I should have just said no, but I foolishly blurted out, "Not to my knowledge."

That was what Dad would have called a "political answer" and saying it that way aroused her suspicion. She studied me for a few seconds and asked, "Buzz, do you think it might be possible that your superiors would send someone to secretly look after you? Someone who might try to look for you?"

"No, they have complete trust in me, and are confident I can handle all of this on my own."

"Really? Because as I recall he repeatedly demanded to send someone else. I believe his name was…Sam?"

For the past several minutes I had been wondering what repercussions Jim was going to face because of my big mouth. Jim was trying to warn me, and in return I might have just put him in grave danger. I was not doing that to Sam if I could help it.

I responded, "Yes, Sam helped train me for this assignment."

I didn't say anything else.

She then asked, "And to the best of your knowledge, neither Sam nor anyone else from your organization, is in Hong Kong right now?"

"If our owner didn't have the confidence in me to do the job by myself, then he wouldn't have sent me for any amount of money."

That answer seemed to satisfy her. I could now only hope that Sam would not blurt out to someone in their organization I knew he was there. The plan had been for Sam to never have any direct contact with their company. But since I was now missing, there was no telling what he or the owner might do or say.

Roisin continued, "Although we can't allow you to speak directly to your employer just yet, do you have a personal message you would like us to tell them? It should preferably be something that could only come from you so they will know you are okay."

"Yes, please tell them to remember to feed my goldfish," I said.

Roisin got a big smile on her face and asked, "Oh, you have goldfish? What are their names?"

I had to think fast, so I told her they were named John, Paul, George, and Ringo.

"Oh, they are named after the famous guitar group?" she asked.

I had never heard of those guys referred to as "the famous guitar group." Roisin was aware of the outside world, but she was not part of it.

But back to the goldfish, I did confirm they were named after The Beatles. And I also added, "The problem is I can't tell them apart."

We both laughed and that lightened the mood. She asked if I kept them in an aquarium or a regular fishbowl.

"I keep them in an aquarium. I like to sit and watch them in the evenings. It helps me to relax," I said.

I wasn't sure how long I could keep this charade going because I had never kept fish in my entire life. My parents had a twenty-gallon tank before I was born. They went away for a weekend, and it leaked all over the den while they were gone. Their expensive fish were all dead and the carpet had to be replaced. My mother then refused to have a fish tank in the house, and a fishbowl was too much trouble.

I wanted to stop talking about nonexistent pets, so I changed the subject by telling her I was looking forward to seeing her home and I was now thankful she had pulled me away from that horrible and mundane job. I also told her the owner of our company was a complete ass, and I was happy to be rid of him.

None of that was true. But I believed it was smart to tell her something she would want to hear.

"Well, if you relish looking at little goldfish, you will be amazed at the various animals I have to show you," she replied.

She then stood up and left the room. I tried to follow her, but she was already gone by the time I walked out of my cabin and into the hall. I figured she had gone into another cabin or something, and it was just as well. I had a terrible headache, which was probably from whatever they had drugged me with. I went back to my cabin to sleep it off. A few hours later a crewmember woke me and said I was "expected" for dinner. I told him I was feeling seasick and didn't feel like eating. He stared at me for a second and then he walked away.

CHAPTER TWENTY

So, there I was the next morning. I was standing in front of the entire crew, along with Roisin. Someone had tied my hands behind me as Roisin said, "Buzz, we have decided you are not what we are looking for after all. We are going to release you." They all laughed as I was forced to walk a plank. Someone pushed me along with an extremely sharp sword. Then, just as I hit the water, I woke up.

I was still in my cabin, and it was the middle of the night. I had broken out in a cold sweat. My clothes and sheets were soaking wet. I got up and walked around my cabin because I was too nervous to go outside. I eventually went back to sleep.

The next morning a rolling cart with a decent breakfast was brought to my room. I still wasn't hungry, but I decided I needed to eat something. About four hours later they brought me a bowl of soup and I downed that too. By midafternoon my boredom was overtaking my anxiety and I decided to venture out to the deck to look around. The crew noticed I was there, but no one said anything to me as they went about their business. I tried to nod hello to a couple of them, but they ignored me. As I turned a corner, I heard one of them whisper, "We should have kept him in the hold until we dock. I tell you it is too risky to let him walk around like this." I wanted to ask the guy what he was afraid of, but I resisted the urge to do that.

That evening Roisin invited me to eat with her in a private dining room, but I told her I wanted to eat alone in my cabin. I also asked for a small table and chair because I was tired of pulling the cart up to my bed. She was disappointed. But she did comply by having a small desk and chair brought in. I pulled the desk and chair up to the porthole and ate my dinner while I looked out at the ocean. I was accustomed to eating alone anyway.

Over the next two days, when I wasn't eating, I just sat at the porthole and looked out at the ocean. I was hoping I would see another ship I could swim to. But I never saw anything but water.

As I sat watching nothing but water hour after hour, the gravity of my situation began to overwhelm me. I was on a ship heading to an unknown destination, and no one knew where I was or how to help me. The owner would probably get the cryptic message I was in trouble, and at least he would know I didn't run out on him. But other than that, I didn't see how alerting him I was in danger was going to do much good. Thinking about that made my blood boil so bad, I thought my head was about to explode. And having to hold all that anger in made me sick.

As I resigned myself to the fact that I was now a prisoner, my contained rage slowly began to turn into depression—the kind where you feel emotionally and physically numb, and you no longer care what happens to you. At the end of the third day, Roisin came into my cabin when it was time for dinner but without my food. She invited me to sit on the bed with her again as she had done on the first day, but I told her I preferred to remain at the desk. She made a face, but she went ahead and proceeded with what she had to say.

"Buzz, I have been thinking and now realize it was inappropriate for us to uproot you like this. Please hear me when I say it was never my intent to hurt you in any way. All I wanted was for you to see my beautiful and glorious home and maybe reconsider working for us," she said.

"How does your fiancée feel about me staying on your glorious island?" I asked sarcastically.

She looked down and quietly muttered, "He is no longer my fiancée."

It never ceases to amaze me how some people make things much harder than they should be. If Roisin had split with her fiancée and wanted to see me again, all she needed to have done was call me at work and I would have met her for coffee or something. She then could have made the job offer herself. With the kind of money she was offering, I would have gladly accepted. And sometime after that, who knows? I guess maybe something might have happened between us. But at that moment, I didn't feel anything towards her. She had just thoughtlessly taken my life away. I turned away from her and put my head down on the desk. I was so emotionally drained I no longer cared if I made her mad or even if it meant I was about to be killed.

She started pleading, "Buzz, don't do this. Please don't turn your back on me. Don't turn your back on this opportunity. I promise. I am taking you to a wonderful place. But you must snap out of this before you meet my father."

"Why is meeting your father such a big deal?" I asked.

"Buzz, he has the power to make your life more fantastic than you ever dreamed possible. But if he sees weakness in you, it's over," she responded.

"Over? Could you explain what you mean by that?" I asked.

She nervously paused for a second and said, "It means you will go home with absolutely nothing. But if you help us, you will be rich beyond your wildest dreams."

I let that sink in for a moment.

"So, I will see some rare animals on this island?" I asked.

"You will see amazing things you never dreamed could exist," she answered.

"And what exactly am I going to see? Giants and unicorns?" I asked flippantly.

She just smiled and said, "You'll see."

A feeling of intrigue began to overtake my depression. I told her I was getting hungry and asked if we could continue this conversation over dinner. She smiled and led the way without saying a word.

The sun had gone down and there was a full moon shining over the water. We slowly walked down the deck and she led me into a small room near the bridge. There was a dining table with a white tablecloth and two candles that were already lit. As we sat down a couple of stewards in white coats came in and set the table with knives and forks. Thereafter we were treated to a spectacular five-course meal. To this day it makes my mouth water thinking about it. I would love to tell you what we ate, but I honestly had no idea what most of it was and I was too embarrassed to ask.

The stewards silently stood off to the side for the entire meal. Although they made me uneasy, they provided excellent service the entire time. Whenever one of us reached the bottom of a glass it was quickly refilled. When we ate all the rolls, they immediately returned with another plate. Roisin and I never said a word to each other. We just ate our food silently as we occasionally smiled at each other.

After we finished our desserts, the stewards took our plates and utensils away. We were alone again, and I felt more at ease. I believe she did too.

"Did you enjoy your meal?" she asked. I told her I did, and I thanked her. She asked if I would like to sit on the deck and look at the stars. I said I would.

She led me outside and up some stairs to the top deck where there were two Adirondack chairs. We made ourselves comfortable as we looked out on the ocean. It was beginning to feel like the evening at the hunting camp, other than having to deal with the fact she had just kidnapped me and chained me up. I still had trouble getting past that—even after the nice dinner.

For about thirty minutes we sat quietly as we watched the water and the night sky. She finally broke the silence and said, "Buzz, I hope this evening was to your liking. I can promise the next few days will be even better."

"I guess I am starting to look forward to it," I said. I was about to say something else, but then the magic of the moment fell apart as I looked down to my right. The entire crew was standing silently below with their arms crossed. They did not look happy. And for the first time, I also noticed that although they were of various nationalities, they all seemed to resemble each other a little in the face. I believe it was seeing them stand side by side with the same expression that caused me to realize that. I leaned over and quietly asked, "What are they doing?"

"Oh, them. They are just keeping watch over me. I believe you should know if you were to hurt me any more than you already have, they will most certainly end you," she said.

Why did she have to say something like that? A frightening thought then crossed my mind. Roisin was promising a huge payday for my cooperation. But under the circumstances, could I trust these people to pay me for my services and send me on my way once this was done? Having realized that, I decided I needed to get away from these people if I could.

Leaving their island on my own was probably not going to happen. But if this big deal hunt was supposed to take place on the mainland, there might be an opportunity to get away and contact someone for help. It wasn't much of a plan, but it was all I had.

As I thought about that, Roisin broke my concentration.

"What are you thinking about, Buzz?" she asked with clear suspicion.

She had been studying me and I hadn't realized it. She could tell I was doing some heavy thinking. I had to think fast, so I brought up something she had said earlier that seemed like a safe subject.

"Am I going to see giants and unicorns?" I asked.

I began to hear snickering and laughing from the men below. I didn't realize my voice had carried, but I guess my anxiety had caused me to speak louder than I needed to. Roisin gave me a thoughtful look for a second, and said, "I believe it's time to retire for the evening."

She walked me back to my cabin. We exchanged goodbyes and she kissed me. I was so surprised I turned around and walked into my cabin. Realizing I was being rude, I turned around to say good night and thank her for the evening. But in just barely a second, she had already disappeared. I looked around the deck, but she was gone. I went to my cabin to prepare for bed but couldn't sleep for hours. I think I finally dozed off around 3:00 am.

One of Roisin's men woke me up around 10:00 am the next morning. He informed me it was time for brunch and Roisin was waiting in her private dining room. He also advised me not to keep her waiting. I showered, shaved, and was ready in about ten minutes. It was like one of those mornings where you oversleep and must get ready in a hurry. I went to the private dining room, and she was there with another spectacular meal that included a choice of every breakfast food you could imagine.

"I am going to gain weight on this trip if you keep feeding me like this," I said. She just smiled and we proceeded with our meal. This time the stewards left us alone and we talked more freely. But after what she had said the night before, I knew I needed to be careful. I decided to take more of an interest in my upcoming hunt.

"You had mentioned I was going to be trained during my time on your island, can you tell me a little more about that?" I asked.

"We are going to show you how to load and use a tranquilizer gun. It is not difficult, but you will need to know how to fill the syringe. You will also be told everything we know about the animal you will be hunting. I am sure your prior knowledge of tracking and the information we will share should make it simple for you to accomplish this objective." she replied.

I asked her if anyone else had ever tried to find this creature and she replied, "Oh yes, we have sent people to look for this animal for many years."

"Do you have any idea why the other attempts failed?" I asked.

"Honestly, we are not sure," she replied. "We have sent many experienced hunters, and they have all returned with nothing. We paid them for their efforts, of course. But they always left disappointed since they couldn't find the creature and collect the big bonus."

"Why do you think I will be successful? What is it about me?" I asked.

"Well Buzz, we have never seen anyone with your tracking skills. You are almost superhuman in your abilities. We are convinced that if we put you in the proximity of the animal, you will surely find one for us," she replied.

I knew what she was doing. Roisin was attempting to win me over by feeding my ego. Good grief, she had only seen me track down one lousy deer that had fallen to the bottom of a hill. That idiot at the camp would have found it on his own if he had just looked a little more thoroughly. Now that I think about it, maybe he did find it and didn't want to fool with hauling it back up there.

Then she said, "If you can track a deer's hoof print, I know you can track the hoof print of the creature we want you to find."

"You are still not ready to tell me what I am supposed to be looking for?" I asked.

"We will discuss it soon enough. There are some animals I want to show you first," she said.

One of the stewards walked in and whispered something in her ear. She looked horrified and nodded as he quickly left the room.

"Buzz, I have just learned our arrival will be delayed. A terrible storm is passing over the island. We are slowing our speed to avoid sailing right into it. I am disappointed because I had planned for you to see my glorious home for the first time during the day, but that will no longer be possible."

She got up and left.

I don't know if this is a widely accepted superstition. But I had an Aunt Nora who believed it was a bad omen on a trip for a thunderstorm to pass over your destination prior to your arrival. Whenever this happened, she would refuse to go any further. She was married to my mother's brother. She believed weird things like that, and we often had to drastically change our family plans at the last minute whenever she spotted one of her stupid omens. She nearly drove my poor uncle crazy, but he somehow managed to put up with it. Her defense was her strange beliefs had kept her alive up to that point, and it is impossible to argue with someone who follows that kind of logic—even though my parents tried many times. Mom was convinced she was out of her mind, but Aunt Nora was always good to me, and I miss her sometimes. She later left my uncle so she could live off the grid, claiming the evil empire was coming for her. I remember he took her departure very well.

CHAPTER
TWENTY-ONE

I waited in my cabin for the rest of the afternoon. Roisin and the other crew members stayed in a closed-door meeting for hours. I could hear them furiously talking to someone over a two-way radio. They all sounded upset about something, but I couldn't hear what they were saying. I tried to casually make my way over to the vicinity of the door, but one of the crew stopped me before I could get within a few feet. He shook his head and pointed towards my room without saying a word. I shrugged and walked off.

When their meeting was finally over, Roisin went up to the steering room to meet with the captain, and she stayed there for the rest of the trip. She and the rest of the crew looked stressed, which made me begin to wonder what was going on.

Was the storm heading our way? Or were they upset about something else? I went out on the deck and this time no one tried to stop me. I walked down to the bow and casually looked off in the direction we were heading. I pretended to just wander up there aimlessly, but my intention was to look out on the horizon for any sign of a storm in the distance. I didn't know how close we were supposed to be to the island, but I saw nothing but clear skies in front of me.

A few hours later the sun went down, and the night was pitch black as we slowly arrived at our destination. I was getting uneasy again. I couldn't explain it, but as we got closer to the island, I began to feel a terrible sense of danger.

At that moment I would have given anything to be in my crummy little apartment with my boring and mundane desk job the next morning.

We gradually sailed into a natural port with a small dock. It was so dark I couldn't get a sense of how big the island was. I could hear the voices of several men outside waiting for us, and I would later hear these periodic excursions to the mainland were necessary for supplies.

Roisin and a couple of the men arrived at my stateroom to help me with my stuff, but she could immediately see something was wrong with me again as she looked into my eyes. She told the men to leave us alone for a minute. They reluctantly walked out of the room and closed the door.

She turned to me and angrily said, "You are disheartened again, aren't you? Well, snap out of it. You can't show fear here. Your very life will depend on it."

I know I should have been alarmed to hear that, but I wasn't. I was again starting to not care about anything, and I felt so depressed I could barely stand up. Honestly, I had never felt so bad in my entire life. But after a couple of minutes, I pulled myself together enough to get up and walk out of there. There wasn't anything else to do.

"Here, I can carry these bags, but I will need help with the rest," I said as I looked down at the floor.

She called for the men to come back, and the door immediately swung open. They were probably listening on the other side. They took the other bags and Roisin led us off the ship. Everyone else continued to unload the cargo and didn't seem to notice us.

The dock was nothing like I would have expected. The boat had all the modern conveniences you would expect a small cargo ship in the late 1960s to have. But as I disembarked, it appeared the conditions here were going to be primitive.

The men who had come to greet us were all carrying torches, and no one had a flashlight. I also noticed there were no gas-powered vehicles. They were all driving horse-drawn wagons, which they began to load with giant crates from the ship. One of the men was watching for rats as they climbed down the ropes. Whenever one of them made it down to the dock he would immediately slash it with a sword. I am not a fan of small rodents, especially rats, but this was still an unsettling thing to see. Roisin commented, "Rats are not indigenous to this island, and we aim to keep it that way."

I decided to go for broke and ask Roisin if I could just remain on the boat during my stay here. But before I could say anything, I heard the captain announce they would be leaving port as soon as the cargo was unloaded.

Roisin led me to a wagon and my luggage was in the back. She told me to climb on as she took the reins of the horses. As we slowly traveled down a small gravel road in the pitch dark, I noticed something odd. I had expected to see evidence of a recent storm, but everything was perfectly dry. It didn't look like there had been any rain in quite some time.

If there wasn't a storm, then there was another reason why our arrival had been delayed. I wanted to ask Roisin about it, but I stayed quiet. I was their hostage, and that fact was not lost on me.

Our caravan of wagons slowly continued through the darkness for another thirty minutes or so. It was astounding to think an inhabited island this size had been kept secret from the rest of the world. I asked Roisin about that, but she just shrugged. She had something on her mind and didn't want to talk much.

We came out of the forest into a clearing, and in the moonlight was a colossal medieval-looking castle made of stone sitting majestically on a hill. It was surrounded by mountains in the moonlight. It looked like something worthy of King Arthur. There were giant turrets in each corner, and I could see men with high-powered rifles moving slowly along a walkway on the roof. They were also shining spotlights off into the darkness.

These men were guarding the place from something, but what? I now had mixed emotions. I felt nervous about going into the castle because it looked like something that would have a dungeon—but I also didn't want to be outside anymore.

"Isn't it glorious?" whispered Roisin.

"Yes, it is," I responded, too nervous to say anything else.

"I wish you could have seen it for the first time during the day, but it is still wondrous at night," she said.

We pulled up to a giant metal door that was slowly lowered. Roisin stopped the wagon and got out. I remained sitting, waiting for instructions. After a few seconds, she laughingly said, "We're here. You can get out of the wagon now you silly dolt."

I jumped out and unloaded my suitcases from the back. One of Roisin's men walked up and helped me carry everything inside. I noticed the rest of the wagons were continuing around to the right side of the castle. I asked Roisin where they were going and she replied, "There is a loading dock over there, but the main entrance is for our special guests. Come, you have had a long trip, and it is high time for you to enjoy some luxurious accommodations."

We proceeded into a gigantic main hall. The man who had been helping me with my bags dropped them next to me without saying a word and he went back outside. The big metal door slowly closed.

Roisin and I stood there alone. Against the wall to my right was a colossal stone staircase that went up into the darkness. I was expecting the conditions here to be primitive but fortunately, a few electric lights were giving some illumination.

I looked at Roisin and asked, "So, what now?" She smiled and clapped her hands. The overhead lights came on and about fifty people came running out and lined up in a single row in front of us. They were all smiling and looked happy to see us. This was a welcome change after dealing with those cretins on the ship, and more light made the place seem more hospitable.

Roisin gestured towards them and said, "Buzz, this is the entire waitstaff of my home. They are here to serve you and provide anything you might need during your stay."

I was feeling very conspicuous so I just kind of smiled and waved at everyone. A short man who appeared to be in his sixties stepped away from the line and offered his hand. He smiled as he said, "I'm Otto. It is a pleasure to meet you, Buzz. I will be your valet during your stay here."

"It's a pleasure to meet you Otto," I replied. The little guy put me at ease.

"You must be hungry. Let me show you to the main dining room where we have a five-course meal waiting for you and Ms. Roisin. I will have someone take your luggage to your room," he said.

As he said that, I realized there was a heavenly smell of food coming from somewhere. As Otto began to lead me and Roisin in the direction of the smell, someone suddenly started pounding on the outside door. A deep booming voice screamed, "ROISIN. ROISIN, MY LOVE. I KNOW

YOU ARE NOW HERE. LET ME IN. LET ME IN NOW.
IT'S YOUR ONE TRUE LOVE."

CHAPTER
TWENTY-TWO

Everyone looked terrified. Otto grabbed his heart and Roisin began to cry. She looked at Otto with a "What do we do?" look on her face. Otto turned to me and said, "Buzz, I am sure you must be tired after your long trip. Before you have your dinner, why don't I give you a chance to see your room and let you freshen up?"

He didn't give me a chance to answer. Several men from the wait staff grabbed my bags and a couple of them helped Otto usher me up the stairs. The men and women who stayed behind quickly gathered around Roisin.

More lights were turned on as we quickly ran up to the second floor. I almost fell a couple of times because the stairs were not exactly even. When we reached the top, I was quickly led down a long hallway with lantern-type electric lights mounted to the walls. At the end of the hallway was a large door. Otto threw it open and led me into a large and luxurious bedroom. There was a king-sized bed with a canopy, several Persian rugs, a small sitting area with some easy chairs, and a hi-fi stereo with several records. I walked around the room, taking it all in. I asked if there was a television and he said, "No, we are too far away from the mainland for television or radio. We do have a well-stocked library with thousands of books downstairs. You will see it and the rest of the house tomorrow. You will also notice we have several records for your listening pleasure. I do hope we have something you might like, but please do not play them or make any kind of loud noise right now. Here, let me show you the lavatory."

He took me into a gigantic bathroom. He asked if I might be interested in taking a shower before dinner, but I told him no and that I had already showered before we arrived. I was ready to eat, and I told him so. Otto sighed and led me out of the bathroom.

The men had left my bags in a row at the foot of the bed. As Otto walked out the door he turned and said, "I will return shortly. Buzz, please do not attempt to leave this room until I return. Do you understand? Do not attempt to leave this room until I return."

Before I could answer or ask what was going on, he rushed out the door and locked it. I was incarcerated again, but at least this time I had better accommodations.

I paced around the room as I wondered what was happening downstairs. No doubt the idiot at the door was Roisin's ex-fiancé, and as far as he was concerned their break-up was not yet finalized. That was when I started hearing voices coming out of the wall.

I looked in the direction of the voices and noticed there was a dumbwaiter in the room. I opened the doors, and the waiter part was not anywhere to be seen, but I could clearly hear Roisin's furious voice in the room below me. I pulled up a chair and looked down the shaft as I listened, but I didn't have to try very hard.

"WHAT ARE YOU DOING HERE YOU FOOL? YOU WEREN'T GIVEN PERMISSION TO COME HERE. HOW DID YOU GET HERE? DID YOU

SECRETLY STOW AWAY ON THE SHIP?" she screamed.

"I sailed here on my yacht. The yacht you gave me as an engagement gift. Why do I need to be given permission to see the woman who is to be my wife?" he asked.

"YOU ARE SUPPOSED TO BE IN MONGOLIA. WHY ARE YOU NOT CARRYING OUT YOUR ASSIGNMENT?" she yelled.

"I think you sent me on an impossible mission to die. I already risked my life to find the other creature for you. That is enough. You said we would live here together forever and that is what we will do. I stay now. I stay here forever. Send that other man away."

"YOU ARE NOT STAYING HERE, IVAN. YOU ARE TO LEAVE NOW! WE HAVE RADIOED THE BOAT. THEY ARE COMING BACK AND YOU WILL BE ON IT."

It got quiet for a few seconds. I leaned way into the shaft as I strained to hear. Ivan then screamed at the top of his lungs, "YOU BRING THAT OTHER MAN HERE. WHY? YOU NEVER BRING HUNTERS HERE BEFORE THEIR HUNT. HE WAS TO GO TO TRAINING FACILITY. HE WAS NEVER SUPPOSED TO COME HERE. YOU NOT EVEN BRING ME HERE BEFORE MY HUNT. WHY HE HERE? HE WILL NOT TAKE

WHAT IS RIGHTFULLY MINE. WHERE IS HE? I WILL TEAR HIM APART WITH MY BARE HANDS AND EAT HIM ALIVE IN FRONT OF YOU."

It was beginning to dawn on me that this Ivan dude was probably the nut who was following me when I was in town, and most likely the furious guy on the hill at the hunting camp. I wanted to yell down the dumbwaiter shaft and let him know that coming here was not my idea. But I didn't have my gun with me, so I didn't. I then heard a third voice. It was much older, but no less powerful.

"IVAN, YOU WILL STEP AWAY FROM MY DAUGHTER. YOU WILL NOW GO TO THE DOCK WITH THESE MEN AND YOU WILL GET ON THE SHIP. YOU AND I WILL DISCUSS YOUR BEHAVIOR AT A LATER TIME."

There was a long period of silence, and then I heard Ivan ask, "What about my boat?"

I heard the older voice calmly say, "The boat can remain where you left it on the north shore of the island until you return."

There was a long period of silence, and then I heard Ivan say, "Okay, I go, for now. But this is not over. You take that other man out of here or I will take him out of here in pieces."

I could hear several footsteps walking out of the castle and then the giant door closed. Roisin and the man that I assumed was her father, started to warmly greet each other. That was when I heard Roisin say "Hey, doesn't this dumbwaiter shaft lead up to the room where we put Buzz? I could hear her opening the doors at the bottom, so I closed my doors. I slowly walked over to the bed and sat down shaking.

Otto came back about thirty minutes later. I was still sitting on the side of the bed scared out of my mind. He cracked the door and said, "Buzz, we were thinking that after your long voyage, you might want to enjoy your dinner in the privacy of your room this evening. Would you like for me, and some wait staff, to remain in here and visit while you eat?"

I told him I wanted to be alone. He nervously nodded and brought in a covered dish on a cart. I guess someone had helped him carry it up the stairs, or maybe there was a dumbwaiter on this floor that worked. He left the room and again locked the door behind him.

I opened the cover and inside was a bowl of soup and a plate with a large roast beef sandwich. This was far from the five-course meal I had been promised earlier this evening, but it didn't matter. I was beginning to feel nauseated, and I didn't feel much like eating anyway. Instead, I walked over to the small sitting area near the window and thought about what I had just heard.

An hour later I heard a knock at the door. It was Roisin. She came in and joined me in the little sitting area. I let her start the conversation.

"Buzz, I know you heard all that. I saw you close those doors when I looked up the shaft."

"I am sure I would have heard even if I had not opened the doors," I said.

She shrugged and said, "Yes, I should have been more careful about where I chose to have that discussion, but I was not thinking about dumbwaiter shafts at the time. Look, I believe I should clarify a few things. Yes, Ivan has been my betrothed for a long time, but we will not be wed after all. My father is traveling to the mainland soon and he will inform Ivan of that himself. He will also be told he is never to come back to this island ever again, but probably not at that time."

"He wants to be here," I said.

"Yes, he does. But nevertheless, he is never coming back. Everyone is terrified of him, and he has repeatedly abused his status as my fiancé." She began to cry a little as she said that.

"What about his boat?" I asked.

"Well, it was an engagement gift, but if we are not getting married then............on second thought. That is none of your concern. Forget about the boat. It doesn't concern you."

"Was he serious when he said he wanted to eat me alive?"

I didn't want to ask about that, but I had to.

Through her tears, Roisin took both of my hands, looked me in the eyes, and said, "Buzz, if you ever encounter him again, and you don't have access to some kind of weapon you know how to use, I want you to run. Just run as fast as you possibly can and don't stop."

"Why would I ever have a reason to see that man again?" I asked.

"Well, as I'm sure you have observed, Ivan can be almost anywhere at any time. And yes, he is capable of doing precisely what he says he wants to do. He doesn't make idle threats."

"When you were bringing us here earlier, I didn't see any evidence of a bad storm outside. The ground was perfectly dry. He was the reason our trip was delayed, wasn't he? You were watching out for him while we were traveling to this castle, weren't you?"

She sighed and said, "Buzz, you are correct. There was never a storm here. Our arrival was delayed for another reason. And yes, I was watching for something very dangerous on our way here. But it wasn't Ivan. I had no idea he was even on this island until he started banging on the front door like an imbecile. One of our special creatures is missing, and for all we know he might already be dead."

"I'm not safe here, am I?"

"Buzz, other than when you are in this room, you will never be alone on this island. And when you are in this room, there will always be someone right outside your door. I could even arrange for armed guards to stay in this room with you at all times if that's what you want. As for the creatures we keep, they are all wonderful in their way. But yes, some of them are horribly dangerous as well. However, if you always do what we say, and never, ever go out alone, you will always be perfectly safe."

I was hearing all kinds of warnings about being in a place I had not asked to be brought to, and it made me mad. I also knew there was nothing I could do about it, and that made me feel worse.

I slowly walked over to the wall, leaned my back up against it, and slowly slid down to the floor. The enormity of what I had just heard was weighing on me, and I couldn't hold back. I started crying. I couldn't help it. I missed my parents, but I also couldn't help but think they would be ashamed of me for getting myself into this giant mess because of greed. I guess I was on the verge of a complete nervous breakdown.

Roisin didn't say a word. She walked over to me, helped me to my feet, led me over to the bed, and we sat down on the side as she put her arms around me. She held and rocked me as I cried my eyes out like a baby. This went on for a while, maybe an hour or so.

Although Roisin looked like she was still in her early twenties, it didn't seem like she was my age. It's hard to explain, but it felt like I was being consoled by someone much older. She just had a patience and maturity I wouldn't have expected someone of her age to have.

Once I had just about cried myself out, she looked at me and said, "Buzz, I am sorry you were introduced to my home this way. You were supposed to be led through this island peacefully in the bright sunshine and then you were going to see this beautiful home in all its glory in the afternoon sun. That is what I had planned. But instead, you have been threatened with your very life for reasons that are no fault of yours, and I don't blame you at all for being disheartened."

She then stood up, took my hand, and said, "Come with me. I am to blame for all of this, but I am now going to correct my egregious aberration. I have something that will give you the heart of a lion."

She pretty much had to drag me off the bed and pull me to my feet. I was surprised to learn how strong she was, but at the time I attributed it to sheer determination. She led me out of the room and down the hall. The guard outside my room remained at attention and never acknowledged we were there. But I am sure he must have been wondering what was going on.

We walked down the hall to a door that was near the top of the staircase. She looked at me and said, "You are about to see my bedroom. Don't tell anyone I brought you here, or what you are about to see. And you should never ever come here unless I bring you here. Do you understand?"

I nodded and we proceeded into her room. She locked the door behind us. Her bedroom was more like a small apartment with a sitting room in the front. She pointed to a room on the left and said, "That is where I sleep, but we are going to go this way."

She took me into the room on the right which was some kind of small library with hundreds of books. The room also had a chaise lounge and a hi-fi stereo that looked identical to the one in my room.

Roisin walked over to the back wall and touched something near the floor. She did it so fast that I'm not exactly sure what she tripped. A secret door opened behind one of the bookcases. She picked up a big flashlight and said, "Follow me, but be careful. The stairs can be slippery."

"Are we going back downstairs? Why don't we just take the main staircase outside your room?" I asked.

"This secret staircase will take us to another place that cannot be accessed from anywhere else in this castle," she said.

As we made our way down into the darkness Roisin explained, "This entire castle was built hundreds of years ago for the sole purpose of hiding and protecting an extremely valuable resource. My father and I are the only ones alive who know of its location. You will be the third. And again, you must tell no one you have seen it. If you do reveal you know where it is, you could very well be tortured in the most horrible way imaginable until you disclose the location."

We continued our slow descent for another several minutes. Someone in the past must have spent years creating this stairway to whatever was down here because we were descending deep into the earth. When we finally reached the bottom, Roisin turned and somberly said, "We have reached the entrance."

She turned her flashlight up, and I saw we were standing in front of a stone wall. She touched a small place to the side, and the wall in front of us slowly moved out of the way. We proceeded down a path through a small cave that led to an old well made of stone. The cave did not go any further. If she had not brought a flashlight, we would not have been able to see a thing.

Roisin asked, "You don't know Latin, do you?" I told her no, but that wasn't true. I had taken a year in high school, but my curiosity was at its peak, and I didn't want to sabotage this. She led me over to the well, and then she lit a small lantern sitting on a large rock. The lantern lit up the entire room, and over the well was a stone marker that said, "FONS JUVENTAE." It was all I could do to hide my astonishment. In Latin those words mean, "The Fountain of Youth."

CHAPTER
TWENTY-THREE

Whenever we went camping, my dad used to tell stories around the campfire about myths, legends, and mythical creatures. His stories would always keep you on the edge of your seat the entire time. But he would always finish by reminding us it was all just folklore, and not to be taken seriously. He did acknowledge that sometimes legends do have a basis in fact. But he also warned us to always keep a healthy perspective. Although my dad loved telling stories, he was also a realist. He had raised me to think the same way, and I never would have believed it if Roisin had claimed her family was guarding the mythical fountain of youth. But after this creepy descent halfway to hell, I was ready to entertain the thought there was something special down here.

Roisin dropped a bucket into the well that was attached to an old-looking rope. It fell for several seconds before we heard a splash. She slowly began to pull it back up. I offered to help but she snapped at me to stand back. When she had brought the bucket back up, she picked up an old metal ladle that was sitting off to the side. She scooped out a small sip, and then she offered it to me. I carefully took it from her and drank it without asking any questions.

Yeah, I know. I should have known better than to do something stupid like that. When I was in college there was a girl who liked dating straight-laced guys from conservative households. Her goal in each of her twisted relationships was to convince, or better yet trick, her young suitors into trying something they had never done before. And sometimes, it was something they had never planned to do under any circumstances. One of her favorite tricks was to offer them a glass of soda which was secretly spiked with LSD. The crazy bitch would then watch a hapless dude go out on his first trip unexpectedly and love every minute of it.

But one night her cruel little acid joke backfired. The poor guy got away from her and attempted to fly out of a six-story window. He was dead the second he hit the ground. The girl was arrested and expelled from school. I have no idea what happened to her, but hopefully, she went to prison for a long time.

I was now taking my own sip of something, and it was not like anything I had ever had before. It had a strong sparkling taste to it, but not like soda pop. The water almost felt like it was alive as it went down my throat and into my stomach. From there I felt a tingling all through my torso and then throughout my arms and legs. A couple of seconds later the tingling feeling went up my spine and into my head. My entire field of vision suddenly turned completely white. Normally it would terrify me to suddenly go blind, but it didn't. I was revitalized in a way I had never felt before or since, and my fear, depression, and anxiety were gone. As my vision quickly came back, I felt like I could take on the entire world. I looked over at Roisin and she had a huge and almost evil grin on her face.

I didn't say a word as I walked over, picked her up, and gave her a big kiss right on the mouth as I stuck my tongue right down her throat.

She gagged and immediately pushed me away.

I was still me, but at the same time, I had turned into someone, or something, else. It was an elation at the very edge of sanity.

"Am I going to feel like this forever?" I asked.

With intense disgust, she said, "No. You will continue to feel this dangerous ecstasy for a short time and then you will come back down to a more healthy level of consciousness, which is why I am going to keep you down here for the moment. We can't have you running through the castle tongue-kissing all the women."

She was right about that. The way I felt, I wanted to walk up to every woman in that place, kiss her, and possibly something extra—and damn the consequences. Since 1 had completely lost my sense of fear, I saw nothing wrong with blurting out, "Is this really the fountain of youth?"

"YOU TOLD ME YOU DID NOT KNOW LATIN!!!" she screamed.

She looked mad enough to kill.

My common sense hadn't left me completely. So rather than admitting I had lied, I pointed out that someone would not necessarily need to know Latin if they were familiar with the words: "juvenile" and "fountain." From there they could just figure it out since the activity had involved drinking a small sip of water from a secret well in the bowels of an ancient and fortified stone fortress on a secret island in the middle of the ocean.

Roisin rolled her eyes, folded her arms in haste, and huffed.

"So, am I now going to live forever?" I happily asked.

Roisin was having none of it.

"No, you are not going to live forever. And if you ever again fondle me like that against my wishes, you will not live another second," she barked.

I was not about to let her get away with saying that, and I responded, "Oh come on Roisin. Let's stop playing these silly little mind games. I know what's going on here. Ever since that night at the camp we've been carefully and foolishly stepping around the fact that you have fallen madly in love with me. It's obvious. You threw your fiancé over the side when you met me, even after giving him a boat. You then kidnapped me, drugged me, and brought me to this freaky place. And now you have dragged me down here so I could drink your special water the rest of the world is not supposed to know about. I've resented you up until now because of the way you tricked me, but now I realize you did all this because you are in love with me. And you know what? I am now thinking, I want to see, if maybe, I can somehow love you too, at some point, someday.......maybe."

I'm not sure what made her more enraged, my abrupt accusation she was in love with me or the foolish way I had just told her I did not love her back. But regardless, she smiled, walked over to me, and grabbed my throat with both hands. Come to find out, she was way stronger than I would have guessed. She nearly squeezed the life out of me as she pulled me down to my knees and looked into my eyes with deadly infuriation.

I could barely breathe, but with the only hint of air that I could muster, I strained to ask, "Are you as turned on as I am right now?"

She responded by slapping me on the side of my head so hard that I flew across the little cave room and into the wall headfirst. Under normal circumstances, I guess that kind of impact would have given me a concussion or even killed me. But fortunately, the water had given me a level of strength and invincibility I normally wouldn't have had. She started coming for me again, as I managed to get on my feet.

I felt like she and I needed some space, and I ran towards the stairwell for dear life. She tried to stop me by tripping the mechanism that closes the door, but I managed to dive through as it slammed shut behind me. I heard her scream a nasty expletive as I took off up those creepy stairs. I knew the door would slowly reopen in a few seconds, and she would be right on my heels, but I had a plan.

I now wanted to find Ivan's boat and see if I could get away from this crazy place. If they had taken him away on the big boat, I figured his boat still had to be docked somewhere on the north shore of this island as they said. I just had to figure out where it was.

I hadn't driven a boat in years, and I didn't exactly know where we were in the world, but I was still willing to give it a shot. I was bursting with energy and not really in a mindset for thinking something through. But I was ready to run across that island all night looking for that stupid boat if I had to.

I got to the top of the stairs and into Roisin's room. But when I tried her bedroom door, I remembered she had locked it. I attempted to tear the door off its hinges (and probably could have) as some kind of sharp needle hit me right in the upper thigh. I reached behind and pulled out a tranquilizer dart. The last thing I remembered was examining it before I blacked out on the floor. I felt Roisin kick me in the butt real hard as I blacked out, but fortunately, she didn't kick the cheek that had been hit.

The next morning, I woke up right where I had dropped on the cold stone floor of her room. Normally sleeping on the cold ground makes me feel stiff and grouchy, and this floor wasn't much different–but I felt neither. I felt rejuvenated and chirpy. I was no longer elated out of my mind, but I did feel more confident and at ease–like I had just walked out of a final exam of a tough class, and I knew I passed with an A. I sat up and looked around, and Roisin was relaxing in an easy chair watching me come to life. She had no expression on her face as she said, "Good morning. We are now going back to your room."

We walked down the hall in complete silence. I knew I was probably in big trouble, but I felt so good I didn't care. A new guard was standing in front of my room. He opened the door like nothing was wrong. Roisin closed the door behind us, and she invited me over to the sitting area. I casually sat down and got comfortable.

"I know Otto promised to show you around the castle today, but you are going to spend the rest of the day in here. I believe most of the adverse side effects from our special water have worn off by now, but I would still rather you stay away from everyone for the next few hours. It was my fault. I shouldn't have given you a pure dose, but no matter. You are welcome to get more sleep if you need it. Tonight, you will be meeting my father and the three of us will dine in his private dining room. In the meantime, I will arrange for your breakfast and lunch to be brought up here. I dare say this will be the most important dinner meeting of your life, so I suggest you clean up and wear the suit that we have for you in the closet. I also recommend you spend some time thoughtfully preparing yourself. Now that you have tasted from our private well and your body has had some time to adjust, you will find controlling your emotions and acting more like a man will not be nearly as difficult for you."

She got up to leave. As she was walking out the door I said, "Roisin, from the bottom of my heart I want to apologize for what I said and did last night. It was wrong for me to….."

She interrupted and softly said, "Let us never speak of it ever again. You should be ready for dinner at seven this evening. I will come for you. And remember, you are not to speak of last night to anyone." She smiled at me as she closed and locked the door.

CHAPTER
TWENTY-FOUR

After she left, I began to feel exhausted again, like my body had just undergone some kind of intense workout. I collapsed on the bed, and I guess I slept for another couple of hours. Around nine o'clock I heard a knock at the door. The guard rolled in a food cart with a covered dish, and he told me to knock when I was finished. I opened the cover and found a stack of pancakes, which is normally my favorite. But strangely I was in no mood for carbohydrates. I was craving protein and plenty of it. I knocked on the door and asked the guard if I could have something like steak and eggs instead. He nodded and said, "Yes, my lord. Right away."

He had just called me "my lord." At the time I had no idea why, but I would eventually find out why he was already starting to treat me like I was his superior, even though I still felt like a kidnapped prisoner.

About thirty minutes later he came back with the best steak and egg breakfast I had ever eaten. I'm not sure it was beef, and I'm not sure the eggs were from chickens, but it was good, and I ate all of it. My appetite had changed, along with some other things.

I have always had normal hearing, vision, and smell. But those senses were far more enhanced. I could hear flies buzzing around in the room. I could see deeper textures in the mortar and stones in the wall, and my sense of smell had picked up the steak and eggs long before it had arrived.

I also felt much stronger, right down to my toes and fingertips. The ceiling was about fifteen feet high, and I suddenly had the compulsion to climb the stone wall of my room. I dug my fingertips into the tops of a couple of stones just over my head, and I pulled myself up easily. This would have been way too painful before, but I found I could now scale up the wall with ease. I climbed to the ceiling and let go as I landed back down on the floor. My knees, ankles, feet, and back absorbed the shock with no problem. I felt like a sudden superhero who was discovering his new powers.

I walked over to the window, opened the shutters, and before me was the most beautiful view I had ever seen in my life. I was sick I didn't have my camera. If I were an artist, I would have later painted this wonderful scene from memory. It's hard to put it all in words, but I could see mountains and jungles, with the ocean off in the distance. There were all kinds of exotic birds. The air smelled of sweet tropical winds and the colors were all vibrant in the island sun. Before today I would have been too wrapped up in my fear to notice any of this. But with my enhanced senses, the immense beauty before me was almost overwhelming.

For the next couple of hours, I was so enamored with what I was experiencing that for the first time I began to feel happy about being there. It no longer mattered I had been kidnapped and stolen away to a place where someone I didn't know wanted to rip me apart. I was just glad to experience such a beautiful scene most people will never have an opportunity to see.

Otto brought my lunch around noon and left me alone to eat. Whoever prepared it must have been aware of my earlier request for protein. I was served several grilled swordfish steaks, and they were amazing. Although it had only been three hours since I finished breakfast, I was still famished.

I knocked on the door when I had finished. The guard came in and took my food away. Otto came back in and asked if we could talk. We sat down in the sitting area. I put my feet up and casually asked what was on his mind.

"Buzz, Roisin asked me to speak with you about last night."

"I have no idea what you are talking about," I quickly answered.

"No Buzz, it's okay. I know she told you not to tell anyone about it, but you can trust me. I have been looking after her ever since her mother died when she was just a little girl."

My suspicion was Roisin and Otto were testing me to see if I would slip and discuss what had happened with a third party, even though I had been told not to, so I continued to play it cool.

"Seriously Otto, I have no idea what you are talking about. I was alone all night."

I said that with a blank expression and with no hint of anxiety in my voice. Roisin was right, it was now easier to control my emotions, and I found I could believe my lies.

Otto sighed and walked out of the room. Five minutes later Roisin barged in dripping wet with a soaked bathrobe clinging tightly to her shapely body. Her hair was rolled up in a towel. She blurted out in one breath, "I know I said not to disclose the events of last night to anyone, but you now have my permission to discuss it with Otto."

She turned and stomped out of the room. Otto came back with a mop and bucket for the water she had dripped all over the place. Once he was done mopping, we sat down again.

"Okay Buzz, let me start by saying I know you received a pure dose of the water last night, so we now need to discuss a few things."

I didn't say anything. I just nodded.

"I am also aware she showed you the source of the water."

He rolled his eyes as he said that.

"You should know she did that because she thinks you are truly something special, and she was anxious to share this important part of her life with you—even though she was never supposed to show it to anyone, ever. But what's done is done. The important thing now is you never, under any circumstances, betray her trust to anyone and reveal the location of the well or even confirm you know where it is. Truth be known, I don't even know exactly where it is, and I have lived in this castle for many many years."

I stayed quiet and nodded.

"She has taken a big chance with you. So again, if you ever encounter someone who demands to know where it is, you must never tell them. And above all, if they say I want you to tell them, you should know this person is intending to do us great harm."

I continued to nod without saying anything.

"I know our original plan was for me to show you around the castle today. But truthfully, we were going to walk around and discuss your dinner meeting tonight and what you should expect for the remainder of your visit. So why don't we just stay in here and talk? I think that will be much better under the circumstances."

I nodded and said, "Yes, I would appreciate it. I now see the wonder of this place and I want to learn as much as I can."

Otto smiled and said, "That is good to hear. Because before today Roisin and I were concerned the shock of seeing what was on this island was going to be too much for you. That's another reason she decided to share the wonderful gift of the water. And as a result, it sounds like you are now wisely embracing your unexpected and wonderful blessing. This is good. Alright then, before we discuss how the water has blessed you, I think you should know Roisin's father is under the impression you came here of your own free will. In other words, he doesn't know Roisin had you kidnapped."

That was shocking to hear, but without any emotion, I casually said, "Do tell."

"Roisin and the others at the camp knew you were special from the very beginning. You have abilities at a level they had never seen before, but you are now even better. You have heightened senses that have strengthened your already amazing abilities."

I asked him if the changes were going to be permanent and if I now had eternal youth.

"Buzz, the sign you saw is very old and it was created long before anyone understood what those amazing waters are precisely capable of doing. But as to whether the changes you are experiencing will be permanent, well, that will eventually be up to you. Roisin will explain that to you when she is ready, but do not under any circumstances ask her about it in the meantime. The only thing you should be thinking about right now is impressing Roisin's father with your knowledge of hunting and your insatiable appetite for adventure. And later, everything will take care of itself."

"Otto, did Roisin have Jim killed for not telling me about the offer?" I asked, suspecting I already knew the answer.

Otto didn't say anything. He just looked down at the floor.

After an awkward silence, I quietly asked, "Why did she ask Jim to make the offer? Roisin could have contacted me herself and made the offer directly. I would have gladly accepted."

"Roisin was planning to make the offer the day you arrived to pick up the retainer that didn't belong to anyone in your group. As I am sure you have surmised by now, the retainer was just a ruse," he answered.

As I thought about it, I wish the owner had asked around to see if anyone was missing a retainer. It should have tipped him off no one reported losing one after the trip. Plus, if someone had left a retainer behind, they could have gone back up there to get it themselves or had someone from the camp mail it to them.

As I rolled that around in my mind, Otto continued, "She had to leave the camp and come back here unexpectedly. It was time for her to accept the position of watching over the well since her older sister had just perished in a horrible accident. She left Jim with instructions to make the offer. Thereafter we fully expected you to accept and return to the camp once you had delivered the frozen venison to your friends and resigned from your job. We were then going to help you move your things to a nice house on the property you didn't have a chance to see during your earlier visit. Once you were settled in your temporary home, you would have been trained right there at the camp as to how you would collect the animal we need and then we would have sent you to the secret area for the hunt. If Jim had just done what he was told, by now you would have your fortune, and we would have our special animal on this island safe and sound with the others."

That was infuriating to hear, but I continued to calmly listen without emotion.

"Poor Roisin was devastated when Jim sent word you had rejected her offer......and I will tell you something about Roisin, she will fiercely take whatever she wants. In her mind, it was completely justifiable to bring you here because then you could see what we have on this island and understand what we are trying to do. Thereafter she believed you would jump at the chance to help us find what we are so desperately looking for."

We sat in silence for a few minutes as he let me take that in.

He finally said, "Buzz, please understand she is the most kind and generous woman you could ever meet...providing she gets what she wants. But if not, she can become absolutely savage, more so than any female I have ever known. So that said, whenever she offers you something, no matter what it is, I highly recommend you graciously accept. The consequences could otherwise be extremely dire."

It was disconcerting to learn just how ruthless my captors were, but not surprising. I was getting set up for some kind of big offer, something other than hunting a lost animal. I wanted to know what it was, but I saw no point in asking at that time. Instead, I asked, "Doesn't her father have a problem with her behavior?"

"Oh heavens no. He admires her for having that kind of drive and determination. That is how he raised her, and she is his favorite, mainly because they are so much alike. That is why she was chosen to watch over the well and preside over our wonderful island when he eventually passes."

If her father was planning to pass away at some point, then the well in that glorified watering hole did not bring eternal life after all. But the water was something special. Before tasting it, I had wanted to give up and throw myself from the top of this place, but now I was thirsty for the challenge of regaining my freedom—even if it meant risking my life.

Otto continued, "Buzz, although her father admires determination, he also demands honesty and loyalty. So please, do not disclose to him that Roisin had you kidnapped. He is capable of unimaginable things when he finds someone has deceived him—even his own daughter."

I nodded, and we sat in silence for a while.

He then said, "Look, I know Roisin has her quirks, but I promise she did all this out of admiration for you. So much so that I think her judgment was clouded last night. Rather than take you to the well and give you a drink of the water, I would have suggested she come back with a diluted sample for you to drink here in your room. That easily would have been enough to help you without driving you to near insanity."

I agreed that would have been a better plan. I wouldn't have thought twice about accepting a simple glass of water.

"But it pained her so to see you falling apart, and she felt completely responsible. Plus, she knew you would be far better equipped to face Ivan if you happened to encounter him soon. Otherwise, the deck would not have been stacked in your favor. That was the other reason she wanted to give you some of the water."

"Wasn't Ivan removed from the island?" I casually asked.

"Yes, but Ivan can appear anywhere unexpectedly. And he hates you with a passion since you are now getting Roisin's full attention."

"I believe it would have been better if she hadn't kissed me in front of him when we were on the plot," I commented.

"She had no idea he was up there. No one did. At the time he was supposed to be on an assignment on the other side of the world. But that is a perfect example of what he is capable of. After you and your little hunting party left that morning, Jim and his men climbed up that hill to see if they could figure out how he was able to enter the property and then leave without anyone knowing. But they couldn't find any sign he had ever been up there. They searched the entire property and found nothing."

"Well, it's a big place," I said.

"Yes, it is. But although it's a big place, the walls around the perimeter are high, and the security is tight, more than you realize. There is a special staff of security guards who are always patrolling the outside walls. The guests at the camp never know they are out there. No one should have been able to come and go without our staff knowing about it."

"Were they sure Ivan did leave the property?" I asked.

"Later the next evening it was confirmed Ivan was already hundreds of miles away. When he saw you with Roisin, he must have left and kept right on going."

"I heard the property was later sold to a timber company," I said.

"Not exactly. It was turned over to a timber company, but that company is also owned by Roisin's family. It is still going to be maintained as a hunting property, but it will no longer be open to the public."

"What's the point of that?"

"We decided it would be beneficial to have a private hunting resort for some select clients of our various companies and corporations in that part of the country. As a matter of fact, Roisin's family owns many successful businesses around the world, and they have numerous similar retreats for select guests."

"I am guessing this island is not normally one of those places."

"That is correct. The wonders on this island are typically only experienced by select members within our organization and not outsiders. You should feel extremely privileged to be here, and I am hoping you are now beginning to realize what a wonderful place this is."

"I get the impression I have stumbled into something quite extraordinary."

"Oh yes, I am so glad you are starting to realize that." "I do have a question though."

"I will answer if I can."

"I've noticed Roisin can slip away in the blink of an eye. And you've mentioned Ivan can turn up unexpectedly without warning. Do they have some kind of special invisible ability that comes from drinking the water?"

"Oh heavens no. Ivan can seemingly turn up anywhere because he is crafty, resourceful, and devious. Roisin, on the other hand, does have a special ability to make herself scarce, but it has nothing to do with the water. She will share the secret with you when she is ready, but please wait for her to mention it."

I went ahead and told Otto about my experience with the stalker in my neighborhood. Otto asked for a description of the stalker, and he confirmed it did sound like I had an encounter with Ivan.

"They didn't send him to check me out while they were making the offer to my company?" I asked.

"No, at the time Ivan was supposed to be somewhere else. But you were right to be cautious; it is good you contacted the authorities. Ivan could have disposed of you instantly."

After about a minute Otto said, "Look, you shouldn't worry about Ivan. I understand he will be closely watched from now on, especially since Roisin has decided to break her engagement with him."

"Yeah, back to Roisin. Now that I am aware of her physical strength, you can bet I will be watching my step around her from now on," I said.

"Well, again, she is not that hard to handle if you remember to always give her what she wants and allow her to think she is in control. And when you think about it, aren't all women that way? As for her father, the best way to handle him is to always appear confident and fearless, and never be intimidated or frightened in any way. You want him to believe you are fully capable of accomplishing what he and Roisin have for you. In the meantime, you will be truly amazed as you experience our private animal sanctuary."

"I've been to plenty of zoos. What's so special about these animals?" I asked.

"Buzz, you are about to see some creatures that will take your breath away. I believe you will want to watch each of our animals for at least an hour, maybe longer."

"When will I see them?"

"I understand you might be seeing one of our fabled animals tonight after dinner."

"Fabled animals?" I asked.

Otto put his hand over his mouth as he whispered, "Oh, I shouldn't have said that. Please don't tell Roisin I said that. I slipped."

Otto looked genuinely scared for his life, so I put his mind at ease.

"Relax Otto, we will keep that between us. And besides, Roisin had already dropped a weird hint about giants and unicorns."

Otto let out a deep breath and asked, "Look, I hope Roisin and I can count on your full discretion tonight while you are visiting with her father. It's very simple. You cannot mention anything about being kidnapped, knowing about the well, or knowing we have fabled creatures. Do you understand?"

I assured him he and Roisin would have my full discretion. He didn't say another word. He just smiled, patted me on the shoulder, and left the room. I went back to the window to look out on the tropical scene for the next few hours as I contemplated the strange conversation I had just had.

CHAPTER
TWENTY-FIVE

Around five o'clock I decided it was time to start getting ready for dinner. I shaved and took a long shower, and I continued to keep my cool. I was ready to get some more information about this weird trip, and I wanted to see a "fabled animal" as Otto had put it.

I found an Italian-made suit in the closet that fit like it had been tailor-made to my exact measurements. I began to wonder what had happened to me during the time I was drugged and passed out at the beginning of my incarceration. To this day I still have no idea how long I was out.

I sat at the window waiting in my new suit, cool as a cucumber. Then, at about five minutes to seven, a thought came to me. With my new body strength and the dexterity in my fingers and toes, I was willing to bet I could scale down this wall in the middle of the night and look for that idiot's boat. But first I would need someone to disclose our location or at least point me in the direction of the shipping lanes. Maybe then I could get picked up by a merchant ship or something. With my anxiety cured, I was feeling more and more confident I could somehow figure out how to save myself.

I heard a knock at the door. It was Roisin. I greeted her and I was still not the least bit nervous. Roisin, however, looked terrified. I asked if she was okay, and she took me to the sitting area. (I was getting very used to that part of my room.) She took the chair Otto had used, but I told her I wanted to mix it up and use her chair for our talk because I now wanted to sit facing the other side of the room. She looked at me for a second. She then told me to sit down and shut it.

"Buzz, I know Otto told you about our little secret."

"What secret?"

"My father thinks that you were brought here willingly. Can I count on you not to divulge otherwise?"

"Sure, no problem. I just can't believe you engineered that entire con with my company all by yourself," I said.

"Oh, I had a substantial amount of assistance. Buzz, I will one day be the matriarch of this family. And the most powerful members of our organization know it is best to get in my good graces now. But my father is still the leader, and he will be very cross if he learns we spent all that time and money to bring you here when you didn't agree to come in the first place."

"Isn't he going to find out eventually when he looks over the expenses?"

"Father isn't involved with the day-to-day expenditures of his many companies and organizations. He's more of an overseer. He meets with kings, presidents, dictators, and prime ministers regularly all over the world to ensure his business interests can continue to operate efficiently in their respective countries."

"So, what's the deal with this private zoo? I've seen plenty of zoos. What's the big deal about this one." I asked.

Roisin sat quietly for a few seconds as she thought about how to answer. She finally leaned over and said in almost a whisper, "Buzz, first and foremost my father is a conservationist. He loves this earth and all its creatures. We can care for the rare species we have brought here in a way no one else can. Each of the creatures you are about to see would have been lost if they had not been brought here. In addition to being his secret place for his special animals, father considers this island to be his true home."

"Roisin, you said you will be the head of the family when he passes, does that mean you will one day travel all over the world meeting with various heads of state?"

Instead of answering, she quickly snapped, "Look, try not to ask so many probing questions tonight. Just sit, listen, and be cooperative. Do you think you can handle that?"

I needed to say something she would want to hear.

"Roisin, I have been thinking and I am now honored you have chosen me to experience this place. And I am ready to accept whatever challenges lie ahead, providing you are always by my side."

That nearly brought her to tears as she responded, "Buzz, that is so wonderful for you to say."

Even with all the sweet talk I still had not forgotten I was still a prisoner, only now I could deal with it. I stood up, took Roisin by the hand, and said, "Take me to see your father. I want to know the man who has brought such a wonderful person into this world."

She gave me one of those smiles where the bottom lip poked out a little as we walked hand in hand out of the room and down the hallway. The guard nodded and smiled as we walked by. She led me down the stairs and through the main hall. The entire staff stood on either side as we proceeded to the back of the castle. I know they were trying to impress me, but the whole experience was still pretty weird, and the weird experiences in this place were just beginning.

I had not realized how big this place was when I first saw it. Most of the castle was built down the back of a hill, making it look deceptively smaller from the front. It looked as if the back part was added later in an expansion. Various stairwells appeared to lead under the main floor and down into the hill itself. Roisin explained the castle was built over a series of caverns, as she led me into the most impressive trophy room I had ever seen before or since. It looked like some kind of natural history museum with all kinds of animal trophies from all over the world.

On one side of the room were full-sized panthers, leopards, lions, and tigers—all in attack mode. On the other side were several full-sized polar bears, black bears, brown bears, and Kodiak bears. Some were on all fours looking docile and some were standing on their back legs looking fierce. There were numerous deer, elk, and ram heads all over the walls. There was an elephant head with giant tusks hanging over the fireplace.

But the most impressive trophy of all was a gigantic gorilla-like skeleton which stood about twenty-five feet tall. I took a close look to make sure it was real, and the bones appeared to be authentic. It was in full attack mode with bent knees, fists that were ready to strike, and its mouth hanging wide open.

King Kong is my all-time favorite movie. Dad and I used to watch it whenever it was on, which was usually late on Saturday nights. I still remember the first time I saw it when I was about eight years old. When Kong picked up Fay Wray, I was so scared I started crying. He calmed me down by saying, "It's just a movie. It can't hurt you. If you don't stop acting silly, I'm going to make you go to bed."

He always knew just what to say.

I stood there for several minutes, fascinated by the giant ape skeleton, wishing I could have seen it when it was alive. Roisin walked up beside me and said, "This is my father's favorite piece."

"I never knew gorillas could get this big," I said.

"Normally they don't."

I was so enthralled with everything I was seeing I lost my head and blurted out, "Is this the fabled creature I am supposed to see tonight?"

Roisin immediately shot me a look and snapped, "Why did you call it a fabled creature? What made you say, fabled creature? Who said you were going to see a fabled creature?"

In addition to losing a healthy sense of fear, Roisin's secret water also caused me to lose a keen sense of discretion. That is never a good thing, and for Otto's sake I started trying to cover.

"You were the one who said I was going to see giants and unicorns on this island. Those are fabled animals, aren't they? Sure, they are. I've been looking forward to seeing those *fabled* animals ever since you mentioned them."

Roisin furiously responded, "I never once said you were going to see those things. You asked me if you were going to see those things, but I never confirmed you would."

"Sure, you did. You told me I would be seeing giants and unicorns, and then everyone laughed their heads off."

"No, that is not at all what happened. Now shut it!"

I was about to respond, but we were interrupted by a deep booming voice that called out, "Oh for Pete's sake. No Buzz, this is not the fabled creature you are going to see tonight."

Roisin and I slowly turned around, and there, with a big grin on his face, was the father I had heard so much about. It was fortunate Roisin had given me the water because without its influence, I probably would have fainted. (And I would like to say before being Shanghaied on that crazy trip,

I was never a fainter.) He walked over to me and extended his hand.

"I'm Lorcan. Welcome to my home."

He was a little over six feet tall and had a grip like an iron vice. He had dark red hair, with a red mustache and beard. What you could see of his face looked weather-beaten. He was of medium build, but I was guessing he was pretty strong. He was wearing a sports coat and white shirt with no tie.

"Thank you, sir. I would have to say this has already been the most memorable trip of my life," I said.

Lorcan threw his head back and laughed out loud.

"Yes, I'll bet it has," he said.

Roisin stood there looking like a frightened deer as she watched us get acquainted, but I was feeling pretty good. Lorcan seemed like a decent guy, and he was putting me at ease. Roisin and Otto had me believing I was about to meet Genghis Khan or Attila the Hun, but this guy seemed more like Ben Cartwright. I could see why supposedly so many world leaders liked him.

As I glanced around the walls, I couldn't believe one person could bring in this many trophies over his lifetime, and I commented, "Sir, this is the most impressive trophy room I have ever seen. Are you and your family responsible for all of these trophies?"

I was thinking this trophy room was the result of numerous hunts over a couple of generations, but Lorcan quickly clarified that.

"This is my trophy room. I hunted all of these animals. My various offspring have their trophy rooms at their respective homes."

He had just referred to his kids as "offspring." Although that is what they are, I still thought it was odd to refer to them that way. I nearly blurted that out, but fortunately, I caught myself.

"I'll bet you have some incredible hunting stories to tell. I would love to hear them," I said.

"And I would love to tell them, my boy. I believe they are ready for us. Let us now adjourn to the dining room."

Lorcan led us out and we walked through the main hall of the castle. At the end was a huge dining hall that looked like it could seat a hundred people. But Roisin quickly whispered in my ear we would not be eating here.

We followed Lorcan into a smaller dining room at the end of the main dining hall. This dining room was much smaller with a table that could seat six people, and I liked it much better. Lorcan took the head chair. Roisin and I sat on either side. We were treated to a five-course meal. And yes, it was all excellent.

Throughout the evening Lorcan told several hunting stories and I was completely enthralled. He had hunted all over the world and each story was more fascinating than the last. Roisin watched us talk and she looked pleased. Whatever she was hoping I would accomplish with her father, I guess I was doing it. I found him to be a very patient and kind man. He was not someone I would have initially feared.

After we were done with dessert, Lorcan let out a loud belch. About a minute later he asked one of the servers to bring him a cigar. As he sat and puffed, he asked if I wanted one. I said no, but the servers did bring some excellent coffee. The three of us then sat back and let our food settle without saying a word. After a few minutes of silence, Lorcan looked at Roisin and said, "I believe I am going to retire my dear. Why don't you take our new friend downstairs to see tonight's fabled creature? I believe it is about time for him to surface."

Roisin got a big grin on her face and said, "Yes Father." Lorcan turned to me and said, "Buzz, I want you to stay with Roisin. This animal is unlike the others in that he is not in an enclosure. We just happen to be living over his natural habitat. I don't want you to go anywhere near it. Just remain on the observation deck."

"Does he have a name?" I asked.

"No, we have never thought to give him a name. He's really not much of a pet."

CHAPTER
TWENTY-SIX

Lorcan said goodnight as he firmly shook my hand and kissed Roisin. Out of the corner of my eye, I saw him leave through what appeared to be a hidden door in the back of the room. Roisin took my hand and said, "Come, let's go. It's almost feeding time." She led me out of the dining room and into the main foyer. We walked over to a large metal door, and I helped her open it. We then proceeded down an old spiral stairwell made of iron.

"Will anyone else be joining us?" I asked.

"I don't believe so. Everyone else on this island has already seen this creature numerous times," she answered. She picked up a couple of flashlights and handed one to me. We had just enough light to walk, but that was it. I believe we must have walked down about sixty or seventy stairs.

At the bottom was a wooden observation deck with a couple of wooden chairs. It wasn't very big, maybe ten feet by ten feet. But to the side was a wooden staircase that led down into the darkness. I asked Roisin if we were going to take those stairs and I was relieved to hear we wouldn't be going any further.

"Remember what my father said. We are going to remain on the deck," she said.

"I am happy to remain right here, but I can't see anything," I said.

About a second later some overhead stadium lights came on and I could see the entire cavern. The giant cave room was about fifty yards high and maybe two hundred yards long. At the bottom was a sandy beach and a large underground lake that extended from one end of the cavern to the other. The lake extended into the dark, and I couldn't see how far it went. Near the edge of the water were some goats feeding from a trough. There was a large door on the far side wall of the cavern. I assumed that was where they had brought in the goats.

"It looks like you have your own indoor beach down there. Have you ever thought about having an indoor beach party or something?" I ignorantly asked.

"We tried to, once. But the only indoor party we held down there nearly ended in carnage. That was how we learned about the special creature living in the depths of this cave. Anyone who goes down there now is extremely careful and doesn't stay for more than a few seconds. The creature has been trained to know that when the lights are on, the goats have been brought in. But again, please don't be tempted to run down there for a closer look. Just pull up your chair and watch the water," she said.

We sat silently for several minutes, waiting for something to happen. And then…I saw a small disturbance on the surface. It started with a small splash or two, followed by something coming slowly out of the water. At first, it looked like some kind of giant snake, but it got bigger and fatter. It was a tentacle, a giant tentacle, moving and undulating, up above the surface. Another tentacle surfaced and then another, until finally I saw eight giant tentacles rising out of the water. It was a giant octopus, about fifty yards long.

Dad used to tell me the story of the Kraken and how big it was rumored to be. We would have a good laugh over it because we never believed an octopus that big could really exist. But here it was, in the depths of this castle. Neither of us said a word as we watched the creature slowly proceed out of the water and partially out onto the small beach. The goats continued to obliviously eat from their trough, not realizing what kind of trouble they were in.

One of the tentacles began to slowly make its way along the beach until it stealthily reached one of the goats. It then proceeded to wrap around the animal like a snake squeezing the life out of a rat. Once the octopus had a good grip, it pulled the animal towards its beak. I watched in amazement as that poor goat was devoured in his mouth right before my eyes. The rest of the goats kept on eating their dinner, completely oblivious. Another tentacle slowly did the same, and then another, until finally all eight tentacles had a goat with each of them calling out in terror. The thing's appetite was atrocious.

Roisin and I continued to watch without saying a word. If I had been watching a regular-sized octopus eat its dinner in a giant fish tank, I am sure I would have been bored long before now. But Otto was right, there is something about seeing a fabled creature that makes you want to sit and watch, even when the animal is doing something completely revolting. It's as if your mind can't fully accept what it's seeing. Roisin finally broke the silence, but we never took our eyes off the creature.

"Buzz, while I have you alone. Please remember I permitted you to tell Otto about seeing the fountain, but no one else," she said.

"In other words, I shouldn't mention it to your father. Right?"

"I believe I just said you were not to discuss it with anyone but Otto. But yes, that is correct. Father would be mad enough to kill if he knew I showed it to you." she said bluntly.

"It's hard for me to imagine your father killing anyone. He seems like such a nice man."

"He is a nice man. But don't try him….ever," she warned.

We sat in silence for the next few minutes while we watched the thing pull one poor goat after another into its beak. I finally asked without looking away, "Do you think Otto will say something to him?"

That was when I heard Otto say, "I assure you I would never betray Roisin's trust."

Roisin and I turned around, and Otto was standing behind us. We were so transfixed by what we had been watching that neither of us had heard him walk up. For all I know he could have been standing there the entire time.

Roisin got up and hugged his neck. I turned again to take one last look at the creature as it slid back into the water. The goats were all gone. I assumed our entertainment for the evening was finished.

I stood up and said, "Thank you. I can't believe I had an opportunity to see that."

They both smiled and we started back up the stairs. When we reached the main hall, the overhead lights had been turned off and only the lantern lights on the walls were still on. The castle appeared to be deserted, and I assumed everyone had gone to bed.

I had no idea where the time had gone. We continued down the main hall and up the stairs to our bedrooms. When we reached the top, Roisin turned and said good night to both of us as she went into her room. Otto walked with me down to my room. I figured we were about to have a debriefing, and he was about to tell me I had done well, but I was way off. He again ushered me over to the sitting area and I could tell he looked nervous about something. I decided that on my last day, I was going to throw these chairs out the window.

When we got settled, he said, "Buzz, I hope you had a wonderful evening. I trust you did."

I nodded, waiting for the other shoe to drop.

"Buzz, Lorcan is a very gracious and agreeable man, but I should inform you he wasn't completely impressed with you this evening. I'm sure you felt right at home with him at dinner because he can make virtually anyone feel that way. But please remember, you should never cross him or Roisin in any way."

"I guess he was a little put off by my discussion with Roisin when he first showed up," I said.

"Yes, you hit the nail on the head. He demands complete loyalty from his subordinates and that expectation extends to his favorite daughter as well. So please do not confront her that way again, especially in front of him. He can be particularly ruthless when he sees someone is not taking him or his favorite daughter completely seriously. The way you were speaking to her, it sounded very disrespectful to him. He nearly had you removed right there."

It had not been my intent to be disrespectful when I brought up the discussion about giants and unicorns on the boat. To me, a little light-hearted sarcasm was just another way of flirting. No big deal. But on this island, it was obvious anything could be as big a deal as Lorcan wanted to make it. Otto looked at his watch and continued with what he wanted to say.

"Now let me prepare you for something else. He and Roisin are going to tell you about the animal they want you to find very soon. But no matter how utterly ridiculous the request might sound, I want you to take it seriously, or at the very least, act like you do. I do hope you realize you are now skating on thin ice."

That made me mad, and I said, "Otto, I didn't ask for any of this. Do I need to remind you I am not here of my own free will? It would not have bothered me in the least if Lorcan had sent me home tonight."

Otto looked aghast and another thought hit me as I sarcastically said, "You know, I hope he doesn't find out about what I said to her at the well. I would probably be drawn and quartered."

Otto sighed and said, "Well, he hasn't done that in a while. Lately, he's been doing something else."

I watched him for a second and looked for any sign he might be joking, but he just sat there looking deadly serious. After several long seconds, he got up and walked out the door without saying anything else. The door was again locked the second it was closed. I took off the suit and hung it in the closet. I went to sleep listening to the sounds of the tropical jungle.

CHAPTER

TWENTY-SEVEN

So, there I was, on the little beach in the cavern with my hands and feet tied. I was lying in the sand against the edge of the water. Roisin, Lorcan, Otto, Ivan the Terrible, the entire house staff, and the entire crew from the boat were all back against the wall watching. Even the girl who had drugged me at the airport was there. It was silent for a few seconds and then a tentacle came out of the water and pulled me in while everyone laughed and applauded. Right before I was about to be pulled into the thing's beak, I was awakened by a loud knock at the door.

"Buzz, are you ready to see some more fabled creatures?"

It was Roisin. It was still dark out, so I called back, "I didn't know we were getting up so early. Is it okay if I shower first?"

"Yes, please do, but try to be ready in about ten minutes. We have a long day ahead of us."

Nine and a half minutes later I was running down the stairs of the main hall with a little soap in my ear. Fortunately, someone had unlocked my door. Roisin was waiting for me, and she led me into the main dining hall for breakfast. Lorcan and Otto weren't around, but some of the kitchen staff were in there. I was served another breakfast of steak and eggs, still not knowing what kind of animals they were from.

When we finished, Roisin led me outside to another horse-drawn wagon, but this one was bigger and nicer than the one we had used on the first night. We climbed aboard and she drove us into the night, or early morning, depending on how you look at it. I tried to start a conversation, but Roisin didn't feel like talking, so I left it alone. I remembered from the camp she doesn't like talking in the morning, and that was fine with me. After several minutes we arrived at a giant enclosure made of stone and concrete with a wooden door.

"We're here," she said.

She led me inside and down a small path to an observation tower that looked like a huge shooting house for hunting deer. We walked up a spiral staircase and into the small viewing house on top. There were two chairs inside which looked out onto a small pasture. The observation window was completely open with no glass. We sat quietly in the darkness until the sun slowly came up. She rested her head on my shoulder while we waited. She smelled nice, but that would soon change.

On each corner of the plot were medieval-looking banners flying in the air. It was eerily quiet, and then I heard some kind of rustling in the trees. I knew that sound. Something was about to make an appearance, but what?

A small white head pushed its way through the brush, as it slowly walked out into the pasture. It was a pony, just a simple little white pony. I was confused. Because although it was a fine-looking animal, I would have hardly called it a fabled creature. We watched it graze while a few other ponies joined him.

Watching this small herd of white ponies graze in the morning sun was pleasant enough, but I didn't see why it was a big deal. I whispered, "How are these fabled creatures?" Roisin whispered back, "Look to your right."

And there was the most noble and majestic animal I had ever seen in my life. It was a beautiful white pony, with a single horn about a foot long sticking out of his head. It was standing proudly in the morning sunlight at the end of the pasture. It was, indeed, a unicorn.

I sat up and Roisin took her head off my shoulder. I could see her grinning at me in the corner of my eye. She was enjoying my reaction, as I sat there mystified. It slowly walked out to the plot, but it didn't join the others. It just stood apart by itself, as well as it should. A few minutes later two smaller unicorns came out of the trees. They went to eat with the big one, and apparently, they were going to be the only ones allowed to do so. Roisin whispered the two little unicorns were eating with their father.

We watched them graze for most of the morning. Just like the Kraken from the night before, there is something indescribable about watching a mythical creature in the flesh. I would have been ready to leave after a minute if they had just been regular horses, but I couldn't take my eyes off real live unicorns. At some point, Roisin put her head back on my shoulder, but I was so transfixed I didn't notice precisely when she did. I felt like a time traveler visiting Old England in a lost chapter of their long history. Then, something incredible happened.

Roisin told me to stay where I was, as she got up and left me alone in the observation house. She proceeded out to the pasture and sat down in the grass, not far from where the big unicorn was gazing. When he noticed she was there, he walked over and knelt next to her as he put his head in her lap. Roisin began slowly stroking the animal's mane.

I can't say how long I watched Roisin and the Unicorn, but it was a long time. Eventually, she rubbed his belly, and that seemed to be his signal the visit was over, and it was time for him to stand up and walk away. She quickly came back up to where I was, smelling like a horse. She poked her head in the door and said, "Come, it's time to see the other animals." We left the enclosure and climbed into the carriage. We discussed the experience as we drove away.

I began by asking where the animals had come from and she explained, "Those ponies are from England. We found a genetic strain among a few of them that causes a growth in the center of their foreheads, and yes, I believe it is safe to assume this is where the unicorn legends come from in that part of the world. Although only three of our ponies have horns, each of the ponies you saw carries the recessive trait. They are kept together with the hope more unicorns will be forthcoming. I'm sorry I couldn't invite you to visit the plot with me. The big unicorn is extremely territorial and will attack any man who happens to be with me when I come near him. I believe he regards me as his girlfriend. As you can imagine, he is capable of great harm when he is agitated."

I asked why only three of the ponies had horns, and she responded, "A mare that is carrying a foal with a horn never survives the pregnancy, since the horn does profound internal damage during the gestation period. Whenever we see a pregnant mare starting to hemorrhage, it's usually safe to assume she is carrying a little unicorn. Since we know we are about to lose the mother, we go ahead and try to save the foal. But the foal rarely survives the birthing process, which is why we only have three right now. Most likely this is why they were thought to only exist in legend. I can't imagine how a foal was ever able to survive through birth in the wild. But it must have happened a time or two in the past. Hence the legends."

We slowly rode in peaceful silence for another thirty minutes or so. We eventually went over a small hill, and on the other side was a small parking lot with three four-wheel drive Jeeps. "I thought this place only had horse-drawn carriages," I said.

Roisin giggled and responded, "No, you assumed we only have horse-drawn carriages on this island. My father regards that side of the island as his private retreat, and he likes to keep things traditional over there. It took a great deal of convincing for him to allow us to install an electrical system for better lighting and cooking."

Roisin unhitched the horses from the wagon and led them into a small stable. We climbed into one of the jeeps, and I noticed the keys were already in the ignition and the doors were unlocked. I foolishly asked Roisin about this. She laughed and said, "Well, if an outsider were to seize one of our Jeeps, he wouldn't go too far from the island."

The road on this side of the island was paved and she drove very fast. We sped directly towards a mountain, and I asked Roisin if we were going over it. She responded, "Yes we are, and we are going to go fast so hang on."

The road to the top was windy and steep, and Roisin drove it like a racecar driver. I felt like I was riding something at an amusement park and loved every bit of it. The ride increased my adrenaline and I was more excited than ever when we got up there.

The top of the mountain was a plateau with some small cottages and each one looked out onto a spectacular view of the island and the ocean. I blurted to Roisin, "If I could live here, I think this is where I would want to build my home."

She didn't say anything at first. She just stood there with almost a tear in her eye and appeared to be very moved by what I had just said. She quietly responded, "I believe this is where I would like to live as well."

After a few seconds, she collected herself and took me by the hand to a high observation tower. We slowly took each step up to the top deck. At the top, it felt like I had been higher than I had ever been in my life without being on a plane. We could see for miles and miles out into the ocean, and that's when I saw it–a cargo ship, off in the distance.

It was the first time I had seen some sign of the outside world since the beginning of my incarceration. I did my best to contain my excitement as I asked Roisin if the ship was one of theirs.

"No, that ship doesn't belong to us. Unfortunately, we're not far from the shipping lanes. We would rather our secret island be more remote. But no one ever interferes with our lives here, so don't give it a second thought."

My plan to steal Ivan's boat and escape this place had just gotten some traction. As I contemplated that, I suddenly got a disconcerting thought as to what might happen to anyone who accidentally stumbled on this place.

"Do you ever worry one of those ships will be blown off course and end up here? The world would then know about what happens here."

"It is common knowledge there is an inhabited island here and it's private property. We used to keep our island a secret, but there is no way we could ever conceal it in these modern times, especially since the advent of air travel. Ships have even requested to dock here in an emergency, and we have always accommodated them. It is also known we have a sanctuary for rare and exotic animals. Only they don't know the animals are fabled creatures," she said.

"Don't they see the animals from the air?" I asked.

"The unicorns are almost the only animals here that live outside. From the air, they look like a normal herd of white horses. The rest of the animals are kept in large, enclosed habitats designed to be nearly identical to their natural environments, and one is kept in an enclosure so densely wooded he can hardly be seen from the air—but never mind about him. Let's continue our journey. I have more animals to show you today, and then we will return to the castle."

We jumped in the Jeep and quickly sped down the other side of the mountain. The road down was also winding and steep, which made it even more scary because we were going very fast. Several times it felt like we were about to go right off the edge as we took a curve at the very last second, but we never came close to going into a skid. Roisin knew this road and she knew it well. Meanwhile, I never flinched, even though a couple of times I thought she was going to kill us. I guess I was still reaping the courage benefits of the water.

As I caught sight of what was on this side, I noticed it was completely different from the medieval side. It looked like a modern industrial complex with several windowless buildings lining a wide paved road. The buildings were all made of steel and concrete and looked like they could withstand a hurricane. Right past the last enclosure on the right was a modern harbor able to accommodate a decent-sized ship. There were numerous trucks which I assumed were for hauling supplies away from the dock.

Roisin stopped in front of the first enclosure and climbed out of the Jeep. Several people were walking around, but they didn't stop and talk to us. They just smiled and went on about their business.

The buildings were bland and gave no hint as to what was inside. Near the dock was a large apartment-looking building that was also made of concrete and steel. I asked Roisin if the crew on this side of the island lived in there and she confirmed they did.

"But you will not have a reason to go in there. You will continue to stay with me in the castle for the remainder of your visit," she said. I asked who the people were, and she explained they were there to take care of the animals and maintain the facilities.

She invited me into the first building. We walked into a small foyer with a metal circular stairway going upward. We went up the stairs and into an observation room that looked out into a gigantic aquarium from just under the surface. There were several comfortable chairs, and she invited me to sit down.

At the top of the aquarium were metal walkways with a few people standing at strategic points. They each had a large barrel of something. Someone gave a signal, and the barrels were dumped into the water as several fish were released. They looked like sea bass to me. I was too busy watching the fish swim through the water to notice what was happening at the bottom. Roisin directed my attention to several cave-like structures down there and coming out of them were the strangest-looking aquatic animals I had ever seen.

They appeared to be some kind of green aquatic amphibians about five and six feet long. Their skin was light green. The lower parts of their bodies consisted of a giant amphibian-like tail which propelled them through the water at amazing speeds. The upper part of the body looked similar to a human's torso. They each had two arms which allowed them to grab the fish. I watched them for a few seconds and realized what I was seeing.

"These are mermaids, aren't they?" I asked.

"They are a rare species of amphibians that live in remote parts of the ocean. They rarely come to the surface, and they almost never come near land. And yes, we do believe they are one explanation for the mermaid legends."

They moved through the water gracefully and were fascinating to watch. Their fingers were webbed, and their faces were flat. They did almost look like they could be considered half human and half fish, but there was one more distinct difference. They had incredibly sharp teeth and no problem devouring their dinners. It was both wondrous and terrifying to watch as it dawned on me what might happen to a hapless human being that got too close to them in the ocean.

I believe we watched them for another hour or so, and I could have sat there all day. Roisin finally grabbed my arm and said, "Come, we still have more to see."

CHAPTER TWENTY-EIGHT

She took me to another building right across from the mermaids, or merpeople, or whatever those things were. We again walked up a metal stairway to an underwater observation area that looked out into another giant aquarium. This aquarium looked like the other one, but there was a huge layer of silt at the bottom with some huge snake-like creatures slithering around in it. To me, they kind of looked like giant snakes.

"What are these?" I asked.

Roisin directed my attention to the top of the tank high above us. And just like before people were standing along the walkways, ready to pour in barrels of live fish.

As they poured in the fish, giant snake-like creatures slowly started coming up out of the silt. They each had four little protuberances coming out of their bodies that looked like small limbs. They were all about eight to twelve feet long. I again asked Roisin what we were looking at, and she said, "They are a subspecies of eels that are only found in a certain part of the world."

To me they almost looked like some kind of aquatic dinosaur, but Roisin assured me they were in the eel family, and not reptiles. I asked her where they were from and she quietly said, "Loch Ness."

"Are you saying we are looking at a family of Loch Ness monsters?" She looked at me and smiled. I had just answered my question.

I asked why the rest of the world didn't know about them.

"We believe they are all but extinct in Loch Ness. But if there are any left, they live deep in the bottom of the loch and seldom come to the surface. When they do, it is rare for someone to be watching at the right time, in the right place, when they surface."

We stood and watched them feed for a few minutes and then she pulled my arm and said, "Come, we have more yet to see."

As we left the building, I couldn't help but feel a little disappointed to learn that the fabled Loch Ness Monster was nothing more than a group of over-sized eels. Roisin noticed the look on my face and asked what was wrong.

I responded, "I had always hoped the Loch Ness Monster was some kind of lost dinosaur that had somehow survived to the present day. And now I find out they are just giant eels. Don't get me wrong. They were impressive, but I have always hoped that maybe in some remote part of the world a few dinosaurs might still be around waiting to be discovered. And about those first animals, I've never believed mermaids could exist, but I still can't help feeling let down to learn the animals behind those legends are just a strange amphibian and fish combination."

Roisin got a sly grin on her face and pointed towards the building next to the first one, and diagonally across from us. "Follow me," she said.

The third building held a giant aquarium just like the first two. But this one had a spiral staircase that went straight to the top where we stood on an observation deck about fifteen feet over the water. It was completely open, without any walkways. This time several people were standing on a deck on the opposite side with more barrels of live fish.

As the fish were dumped in the water, two large reptile-like creatures began to slowly swim to the surface. They had long necks and flippers. As they reached the surface, one of the feeders threw a couple of fish into the air. The creatures poked their long necks out of the water and caught them in their mouths as I stood there dumbfounded.

I couldn't say a word for the longest time. I finally muttered, "These are plesiosaurs, aren't they?"

"They most certainly are," answered Roisin with a big grin.

I asked if they were also found in Loch Ness and Roisin explained they were found in the North Sea of Scotland, but it was certainly plausible some of these animals might have made their way down to Loch Ness and been sighted on rare occasions. I stood and watched as I again lost all track of time.

Roisin finally pulled on my arm, and I told her I didn't want to leave.

"Would you like to have lunch here and watch them while we eat?" she asked.

I told her I would, and she led me down the side of the observation deck to another set of stairs. We walked down into an observation area under the surface. From there we could look out into the aquarium. As impressive as these creatures were on the surface, they were even more spectacular underwater. There was a table and chairs where our meal was waiting for us on a rolling cart.

"You planned for us to eat here all along, didn't you?"

She giggled and we sat down to another delicious meal. We didn't talk much. We just sat and watched the plesiosaurs swim peacefully in their tank while we ate.

I asked Roisin if she knew why the creatures had never been discovered. She explained they had mostly died out and the few that are left mainly stay up in the North Sea area where they are rarely seen. These days they rarely swim down to the Loch.

As we finished our lunch, Roisin looked at her watch and said, "I have two more creatures for you to see this afternoon, and then we will return home." She led me back out into the street, and I commented, "It is going to be hard to top seeing a dinosaur." And again, she gave me that sly smile and led me into a building across from the plesiosaurs.

We went up another spiral flight of stairs and at the top was an observation area like the others, but this one looked out into a jungle-looking habitat. We were about twenty feet up, which I assumed was a safe height, but for some reason, I felt uneasy since there was no glass separating us from whatever was down there. I was about to say something, but then Roisin put a finger to her lips and directed me to two chairs sitting close to the railing. I quietly took one and she took the other.

I felt like I was sitting on a branch in the middle of the jungle. There was vegetation everywhere, and all of it was growing from up from the ground. There was a clearing in the middle with a small pool. I couldn't be sure if the building had a real floor with a thick layer of dirt or if a real floor was even there at all. It was very hot in there, and I was about to ask Roisin if I could have something to drink.

That's when we saw it.

As she smiled and pointed towards the clearing, out of the dense vegetation walked a small dinosaur. It appeared to be a small brontosaurus, maybe a little bigger than a cow. The animal drank from the pool and then he proceeded in for a swim.

I remained completely mesmerized, just like before. So much so I never noticed Roisin had gotten up and left. Before I knew what was happening, she was in the middle of the habitat holding some giant leaves. The little dinosaur came over to the edge of the pool and ate the leaves right out of her hand. When he was done, she gently rubbed his head and he seemed to like that. She then walked back up to where I was, and we watched him wade around in the pool for at least another hour.

The little creature then crawled out of the pool and back into the trees. Roisin quietly took my hand and led me back outside.

When we were back in the street, I asked, "Where did you find him?" Roisin explained, "He was found deep in the Congo of Africa. His species is believed to be behind the Mokele Mbembe legends. But sadly, we believe they have died out, except for him. He was found when he was just a calf. He was looking sullen and standing next to a larger brontosaurus that had just died. We assumed that was his mother, and for all we know they were the last ones. We did find some other ones, but they were deceased as well. We're thinking it was some kind of virus or parasite. This one did not appear to be affected and he has been happy here ever since. He is so tame, that when he first arrived, we let him roam around the island on his own until we had this habitat built."

"How long has he been here?" I asked.

Roisin didn't answer. She instead pointed to a building that was diagonally across from us and said, "I am about to show you the last animal you will be seeing today. He is very docile just like our sauropod, but we must keep it extremely frigid in this building. You will see why."

When we walked in, she led me to a coat room filled with several fur-lined coats. She helped me find one that fit, and she recommended I put a scarf over my mouth. Fortunately, I was already wearing pants. When we were properly bundled up, she led me back into the hall and opened the door to the habitat.

The cold hit me right in the face. It was well below freezing in there. We went up a spiral staircase and at the top was another open observation deck. The room itself was bland and the smell was ungodly. But standing in the middle of that room, eating peacefully at a trough, was a wooly mammoth.

There wasn't any place to sit, and I was okay with that. As happy as I was to see a real live mammoth, I didn't want to stay in this room very long. And after everything else I had seen that day, seeing a mammoth wasn't nearly as captivating as seeing the other animals. Just as the cold was about to give me a headache, I looked towards Roisin to ask if we could go back outside. That was when I noticed she looked like she was about to cry. I asked her what was wrong, and she just shook her head. I asked her if she wanted to leave, and she nodded. We went back downstairs and straight to the coat room. Once we had taken off our coats, I asked if I had said something wrong.

She shook her head and said, "Ivan located the mammoth for us in Russia many years ago. It was his first assignment. He used to be so different." There was a bench in the coat room. She sat down and put her face in her hands as she started to cry.

I didn't know what to say. I sat down and put my arm around her. She finally took a deep breath and said, "Come, it's time to go."

There were two more buildings we had not seen at the end of the row. When we walked back outside, I asked if we were going to see the animals in those buildings and she responded, "No, you will not be seeing those creatures today." I expected we would walk back up to the Jeep and head back to the castle, but Roisin went the other direction. The road extended past the two buildings with the animals I wasn't supposed to see and into a densely wooded area. I quietly followed several steps behind. The road led to a natural port where we found a yacht docked in the water. Painted on the back were the words "Ivan the Terrible", which had to be the worst name for a boat I had ever seen in my entire life. But in this case, I guess it was accurate. Roisin walked up to it and screamed, "OH IVAN, WHY?"

I felt awkward. I didn't know whether to walk up and console her or to just leave her alone. As I stood there wondering what to do, a thought suddenly hit me. I now knew the location of Ivan's boat. Day before yesterday when I had gotten the bright idea to maybe find his boat and escape, I suppose I would have found it if I had made it to the road outside the castle and followed it straight here. Yeah, the road over the mountain would have been tough on foot, but that night I probably would have had the energy to conquer it. But on the other hand, after seeing these animals, I was starting to take a different attitude about being brought to that place. Within twenty-four hours I had seen unicorns, a sauropod, a wooly mammoth, a possible explanation for mermaids, two viable explanations for the Loch Ness Monster, and an extremely solid explanation for the Kraken. As I thought about that, I began to think maybe Roisin dragging me here wasn't such a rotten thing to do after all. Then it happened.

CHAPTER
TWENTY-NINE

A small helicopter buzzed right above us heading in the direction of the castle. Roisin looked terrified. I asked what was wrong and she explained the helicopter is called when someone needs to make an emergency trip to the mainland. I asked if the helicopter could fly all that way and she said, "No, the helicopter takes someone to one of our nearby islands that has a small airstrip. Whoever needs to visit the mainland is then taken to Hong Kong in a Lear jet, but we only do that in an emergency. Something must be wrong. We need to return to the castle now. Run fast."

We sprinted back up to the buildings. The helicopter had gotten everyone else's attention, and several people were in the street asking if anyone knew why the helicopter had been called. When they noticed Roisin was there, and she had been crying, they all swarmed around her wanting to know what was wrong. But she was adamant she did not want to talk about it. Some were looking at me suspiciously, like maybe I had done something to her.

But the awkward situation was interrupted by something else. In one of the two buildings I was not supposed to see, we suddenly heard loud, thunderous banging on the wall from the inside.

Everyone turned towards the building looking horrified. And one of the keepers nervously said, "The helicopter must have woken him up. This is usually his nap time." A loud roar came from the building as whatever was in there kept banging on the wall. I could tell it was very tall since the point of impact was about thirty feet off the ground. The walls must have been steel reinforced because otherwise I believe they would have crumbled. Roisin immediately took control of the situation.

"I don't think he will be able to get out since he is in the new enclosure, but I want you, you, and you to be ready with your tranquilizer guns just in case. The rest of you go back to your assigned areas and stay there until he calms down. Buzz, you are coming with me."

As we ran back to the Jeep I asked, "Roisin, is there a giant gorilla in there like the one in your trophy room?"

One of the trainers overheard my question and said, "Well, not exactly."

Roisin gave him a look and told him to shut up.

As I said earlier, King Kong is one of my all-time favorite movies, and my mind was racing with the possibility that there might be a giant ape in there. But I knew it was pointless and potentially dangerous to ask any more questions. At this point, I was well aware Roisin didn't appreciate being asked about things she was not ready to discuss.

We jumped in the Jeep and Roisin drove like a maniac towards the mountain as I braced myself for an even wilder ride than earlier in the day. But as we approached the base, she suddenly took a right turn down a road hidden by trees.

This road led us around the base of the mountain, and we avoided going over the mountain.

Roisin giggled a little as she saw me looking around confused. She explained, "The road we took over the mountain was originally unpaved, and it only went up one side. It was built to provide access to the top so we could build the cottages and the observation tower. When we got the Jeeps, I told my father I wanted a paved road that went up one side and down the other. He had the road paved just for me. Wasn't it fun?"

"Yes, it was. Your father is a wonderful man who is to be respected and admired," I responded.

Yeah, I know. I knew it was wrong as soon as I said it. The weird look I got from Roisin confirmed I had just poured it on a little too thick.

"Buzz?"

"Yeah?"

"What did Otto say to you last night after we parted company?"

"He told me your father was ticked off at me for getting smart with you about the giants and unicorns when we were looking at the giant ape skeleton. And by the way, I didn't mean any offense. I was just flirting a little."

"Yes, and you were also trying to cover for Otto because he had let it slip you were going to see creatures that only exist in fables."

I didn't know how to respond. There was no point in denying Otto had spilled the beans since I had already let it slip that he had let it slip. I was getting tired of having to be careful of what I said and to whom, especially since I didn't ask to be brought here in the first place. I was about to tell her so, but there was that comment about having to endure something besides being drawn and quartered, so I let it go. For the next few minutes, we rode back in silence. I assumed we were going to take the wagon back, but she sped right on past the stables without slowing down.

"Doesn't your father forbid gas-powered vehicles on this side of the island?" I asked.

"Normally yes, but he tolerates them in an emergency and the presence of the helicopter means something is wrong," she answered.

The helicopter then zoomed back over our heads going the other direction. Roisin screamed and started driving even faster. We pulled up to the castle and Otto was outside waiting for us. Roisin jumped out of the Jeep and ran over to him.

"Otto, what's wrong? Did father leave?" she asked frantically.

"My dear, your father was called away to the mainland. I don't know why. He said he would be back soon, but in the meantime, he wanted you and Buzz to continue with your visit."

Otto invited us back inside and led us up to our rooms. That was where Roisin and I parted company.

"I had an amazing time today," I said.

She turned around and said, "Oh, I will see you again this evening. We will be having dinner later in a special place, so be ready."

Otto escorted me down to my room, where a guard nodded at us as we walked in. I figured I was about to get a briefing about tonight or a debriefing about the events of the day. I was ready for either.

"Buzz, I didn't want to alarm Roisin, but her father told me there was a problem with one of his companies in Hong Kong, and it happened to be the one Roisin used to abduct you. Lorcan didn't say what the problem was, but I am thinking it might have something to do with the fact that your employers are raising a stir because they haven't heard from you. We might need to place a call and let them hear your voice. Don't worry. We will tell you what to say."

I knew it was best to cooperate, so I told him I would be fine with that.

"Oh, that is wonderful to hear. But I am not sure it will even be necessary. For all we know, the problem Lorcan needs to address might not have anything to do with you. In the meantime, I suggest you clean up and put on the suit we left for you in the closet. Roisin will come for you at seven this evening. Make sure you are ready."

And at precisely seven that evening there was a knock on the door. Roisin was standing there looking beautiful in a form-fitting black dress covered in sequins. She took my hand and led me down the hall into a room next to hers. In that room was a staircase that led up to the roof.

And out on the roof was a beautiful dining area lit by tiki torches. There was a line of waiters standing ready to serve our food and fulfill any request. Otto joined us, and we were treated to another fantastic meal. I don't think I have ever eaten so well and so much in such a short period.

I was now on an emotional high like I had never had before. Over the previous two days, I had seen and drank from the mythical fountain of youth. I had seen animals believed to be extinct, and other animals thought to only exist in legend. And I had done it all in the company of the most beautiful woman I had ever seen. I don't think any writer could have imagined it all.

As we enjoyed our meal under a spectacular night sky filled with bright beautiful stars, I was now beginning to feel like a true guest rather than a prisoner.

After we finished the main course, Roisin looked at me and asked, "Should I assume you are now enjoying your visit?"

"I am. And I must ask, are we going to see any more animals before it is time for me to leave?"

Roisin thought for a moment and said, "Yes, tomorrow I will take you to our second island and you will see other animals in our collection. But I will not tell you anything else right now. I want you to be surprised."

Otto looked panicked and immediately said, "Roisin, if you are going to take him to the second island, then it would be best if you prepared Buzz a little for what he is going to see. I know you love those animals, and you like to surprise people, but the creatures on the second island are just, well….."

Roisin gave Otto a fiercely demonic look, and I am not exaggerating. He immediately shut up and sat there looking terrified. After a few seconds of awkward silence, she rolled her eyes and said, "Okay, maybe I should prepare you a little. Buzz, I believe all animals are wonderful in their way. But many people in this world tend to have unfair prejudices about what is beautiful and what isn't. And if a creature doesn't happen to have the aesthetics that others do, we tend to judge that animal as being evil and overlook its true beauty."

"I believe that also happens with human beings," I responded.

"Yes, you are correct", she said.

Otto was still not convinced as he shook his head and said, "Roisin, he is already sold on what we are doing here. He doesn't need to see the second island right now. Let's just send him off to the training first thing tomorrow so he can begin his hunt for the animal you want so badly."

Roisin again glared at Otto and told him to leave the table. He hung his head and left quickly. The mood had become awkward, and I didn't know what to say. I hated that because up to this point, this had been my favorite meal of the trip.

When we finished eating, we just sat there in silence looking at our plates. Someone on the wait staff asked if we wanted dessert. I said no thank you and Roisin told them to leave. They quickly left us alone, at least I think we were alone. You never knew for sure in this place.

Roisin had gotten so mad at Otto, I was scared to say anything. But then she finally huffed and said, "Otto tends to be overprotective. But I promise there is nothing to be concerned about. Tomorrow will be every bit as glorious as today, but in a different way. You will be amazed, and perfectly safe. I promise."

She seemed kind of embarrassed with herself for losing her cool. I didn't know what else to say other than, "I'm looking forward to it." She smiled and stood up. The evening was over.

We walked back downstairs, and we went our separate ways for the night with a light kiss. As I walked back to my room, I turned and watched her walk back to her room. In that dress, I could see she was the most perfectly shaped woman I had ever seen. And as stupid as this might sound, I began to feel privileged that I would be seeing something the next day that only Roisin had wanted me to see.

CHAPTER THIRTY

So, there we were. Roisin and I were standing over a lake of molten lava in a deep underground cave. It was so hot that I was sweating profusely and could barely breathe. Then, out of the lava came four horrible-looking winged animals that looked like demons with sharp teeth and horns on their heads. I couldn't understand how anything could live in molten lava, but obviously these horrible looking creatures were tough to the point of invincibility. As they flew closer, I could see they had gargoyle-like faces and leathery skin. They made a beeline for Roisin as they swarmed around her. She laughed to the point of ecstasy as each one proceeded to kiss her right on the mouth. Normally it was beautiful to see Roisin interact with her animals, but this was disgusting.

Once they were finished greeting Roisin, they flew back out over the surface of the lava in circles. As I stood in horror, Roisin looked at me and said, "Clearly these creatures are the explanation for all of those silly legends about demons and hell."

"You don't believe in heaven or hell?" I asked.

"Oh no, we don't have those beliefs here," she responded with a laugh.

The creatures then flew over to me and each one grabbed a limb. I screamed in terror as they flew me out to the center of the lava and dropped me in the fire as Roisin stood there laughing.

I woke up screaming in terror. I turned on the nightstand lamp and looked at my watch. It was three a.m. Of all the nightmares I have had in my life before or since, that one made me feel the absolute worst. And even though it had just been a nightmare, I still had an overwhelming sense of betrayal.

The guard outside my room knocked on the door and asked what was wrong. I told him I had just had a nightmare. He asked if I needed anything, and I said no. It was an hour before I could go back to sleep. I began to wonder if the water was already beginning to wear off.

Roisin woke me up herself the next morning. Thankfully she had allowed me to sleep in a little. She had a pitcher of water with her and an empty glass. I knew what that meant.

"Do you think I need a refresher already? What if I start running around like a maniac again?" I asked.

"Oh, don't worry about that. This is a diluted dose, but I do think you will need some liquid courage today. I heard about your little outburst last night."

I had always understood the phrase "liquid courage" to mean something else entirely, but I complied. It did give me kind of a jolt, but not like before. This time the effects were more manageable. I leaped out of bed and told her I would be ready in a few minutes.

She asked if I wanted to talk about the dream. I told her no.

About ten minutes later I was showered, dressed, and running down the stairs ready to face the day. Roisin was waiting for me in a Jeep. I asked her about breakfast, and she informed me we would be eating on the way. We raced to the boat dock on the other side of the island near the enclosures, and it was a much quicker trip since we were taking a gas-powered vehicle the entire way and we didn't go over the mountain. When we arrived at the dock, there was a large yacht waiting for us that had not been there the day before. I believe it must have been over a hundred feet long. We quickly boarded and were led to a small dining area where we were treated to a fantastic breakfast.

After breakfast, she told me to go take a seat outside and she would join me in a few minutes. I found a couple of Adirondack chairs and I sat down, thinking maybe she just needed to powder her nose, or something. I was looking out across the water when I heard her walk up behind me. I turned and was completely shocked. Roisin was now wearing a small black bikini and sunglasses. I became very nervous, and she seemed to enjoy my reaction.

"Oh Buzz, relax. I just wanted to get a little sun."

She sat down in the other chair, and we didn't say much of anything as I stole an occasional glance at her when I didn't think she was looking. Since we were facing the stern, and there was a nearly naked woman sitting right next to me,

I wasn't paying any attention to where we were going. About an hour later Roisin told me we were almost there, and I turned around to check out our destination. My first impression was jarring.

This island was nothing like the other one. It was a giant mountain with no vegetation. I looked to see if there were any kind of animals roaming around, but there was nothing but giant rocks on the beach. I asked if we had arrived at the right place and she said, "Yes, the animals on this island are kept underground in an elaborate cave system since they can be extremely dangerous to humans. I told you this place was different."

I was glad Roisin had given me another drink of special water because it would have otherwise been too unnerving to learn I was about to explore a cave system with deadly creatures after the dream I had just had. We sailed into a huge cave and docked inside an underground complex. There were people everywhere waving at us, but they immediately went back to what they were doing once the pleasantries were over. I watched them and the overall mood among these workers was different as compared to those on the other island. These people were on edge. Roisin told me to wait for her while she changed. I had hoped that she would wear the bikini all day, or maybe the top with a pair of cut-offs, but I didn't tell her that.

When we got off the boat, Roisin led me into a cave with a lighted path, just like you would see in a public attraction. In all directions, you could see colored lights illuminating giant stalactites and stalagmites. It was mind-blowing to think this was not open to the public and could only be seen by a select few. We walked through this amazing cave system for about five minutes, and then we arrived at a large metal door. Roisin turned and said, "Buzz, I promise you will be perfectly safe in here, but I do want to stress you are not to go near these creatures, and you must stay with me the entire time. Do you understand?"

I promised to stay out of the way. She threw a lever on the wall and the giant door slowly opened. We proceeded into a cave system consisting of several enclosures. The rooms were gigantic with cinderblock walls about fifty feet high. We walked across a metal walkway about twenty feet off the ground.

The first room had a dirt floor with some giant boulders. I stood there quietly looking for some kind of animal, and then a small door opened on the far end. A small goat was quickly shoved inside. It seemed curious, but otherwise content. I know what happens to goats around here, and I was scared for him.

Nothing happened for several minutes as the goat just walked around checking out his new surroundings. Roisin then silently pointed to an opening in the side wall, and the biggest wolf I had ever seen in my life slowly came out of his den. It was all black with big glowing red eyes. It was terrifying to think something like this was roaming around out in the wild somewhere. He stealthily crept behind some giant rocks as he quietly stalked his prey. I believe he was about ten or twelve feet long.

The wolf began to rear up like it was about to strike. And then to my horror, it stood up on its hind legs like a human and slowly walked a few feet. My mind began to race as I considered the many legends that could be explained by the existence of this amazing and ferocious creature.

The wolf slowly crept up behind its prey while still walking on its hind legs. It paused for a second, and then it pounced on the defenseless animal as it furiously devoured its prey in a matter of seconds. Blood and animal parts were flying in every direction. We stood and watched the carnage in stunned silence.

When the giant creature was finished, it lay down on its side to let its food digest. Roisin explained, "This animal was found in the Moors of England and is believed to be behind the black dog and hellhound legends."

"What about the wolfman legends?" I asked.

"The lycanthrope legends go back centuries, but I believe the modern legends of a man shape-shifting into a wolf mainly come from the cinema. But yes, I guess you could say this animal could very well explain any legends in that area about a werewolf. Personally, I think the lycanthrope legends originated back when people were ostracized because they suffered from a severe mental disorder such as schizophrenia. Those poor souls were often banished from society and forced to live in the wilderness and fend for themselves. Over time their hair grew long, their facial hair grew, and their fingernails became long and sharp. They probably developed a penchant for eating raw meat and might have attacked humans if they felt scared or hungry."

I let that sink in while we stood there looking at what was left of that poor goat. Roisin had an interesting theory about the werewolf legend, and it made sense.

She went on to say, "We have reason to believe there are similar animals living in the Bayou of Louisiana. They call them the Rougarou. But anyone we have sent to the area has never returned."

"Do you have any idea what happened to them?" I asked.

"We are not certain. We once found a human jawbone that did not appear to be very old, but that was all."

I decided not to ask her anything else about it.

CHAPTER
THIRTY-ONE

The next room was a giant terrarium with all kinds of vegetation. The walkway was now enclosed in glass. Roisin directed my attention to another goat roaming around in the dirt below us. It seemed content, with no idea it was about to become dinner for something. As we waited silently for this poor animal to meet its demise, I foolishly asked, "Do you ever feel bad for these little goats?"

She answered my question with a question: "You consume meat, don't you?" I nodded and she said, "Then stop being a hypocrite and shut it."

We continued to watch for something to happen for several more tense minutes. Roisin finally let out a huff and said, "Well, I guess he's not hungry. I can't even see where he is in all the foliage. Maybe we need to refurbish this habitat."

I was getting bored and ready to leave, but then I thought I saw one of the logs move–only it wasn't a log. It was a snake, a giant snake. It must have been about forty feet long and maybe about three feet wide. I had never had a problem with snakes. My dad and I used to pick up water snakes and rat snakes all the time. I had always wanted to keep them as pets, but mom always refused. It then dawned on me that if I could get out of this alive, I could now have my own snake. I was planning to name him "Kenny" after Kenny Stabler, the famous quarterback.

Roisin asked, "Am I correct to assume you have witnessed a snake feeding on a rodent?"

I told her I had, and she said, "Good, then you shouldn't be surprised by what you are about to see."

The gigantic snake then proceeded to wrap itself around the helpless goat as he slowly squeezed the life out of it while I almost lost my breakfast. Once the goat was dead, the snake turned loose of its lifeless prey as he prepared to swallow it whole. I thought we were going to stay and watch that part of it, but Roisin said, "It could take some time for Titan to finish his meal. Why don't we proceed to the next enclosure?

"Why do you call him Titan?"

Roisin explained this snake was called a Titanoboa, hence the name. They were believed to have died out millions of years ago, but unknown to the rest of the world, a few have survived deep in the Amazon.

We slowly walked into the next enclosure. It was dark with very low neon lights. The walkway was covered in a steel mesh, making it hard to see much. I first started looking up at the ceiling, but Roisin pointed to the floor, which appeared to be moving. Something or some things were moving around down there.

My eyes adjusted and I could see tarantulas, gigantic tarantulas, all over the place. They must have been about six feet across, and they were crawling everywhere. I was only feeling slightly unnerved, but if I had not been under the influence of the water, I probably would have croaked. I have never had a serious issue with spiders either. This, however, was something else entirely.

The day before had been exhilarating, but this was all turning downright weird. I was silently hoping we were nearing the end of this, but no such luck. Roisin nudged me into the next room as she said, "Come, we still haven't viewed the very most fantastic creatures."

I didn't like the sound of that, but I kept walking. I had no choice.

In the next room, we went down a flight of stairs which took us to floor level, which I did not like at all. The walkway was enclosed in thick glass on all sides. This enclosure was a giant swamp, like you would see in Florida or Louisiana. When we were in the middle of the room, Roisin stopped and whispered, "Slowly look over to your left, but try not to move too much."

To my left was a pool of water with some kind of alligator or lizard poking its giant head slightly above the surface. I had seen alligators before and at first, I was feeling unimpressed. The creature then slowly walked out of the water upright like a man. To my horror, I was standing face to face with an actual lizard man with a long tail. He was about six feet tall.

His body looked muscular like a human, but his head looked like that of a crocodile. He had long sharp teeth and was covered in green scales. We locked eyes and stared at each other for about a second. I was in awe of him, but he was only sizing me up.

Then, in a split second, he pounced at the glass so hard I immediately jumped back. Thankfully it was too thick for him to penetrate. But that didn't stop him from furiously trying to break through and get at us.

After clawing at the thick glass for several seconds, he leaped over our enclosed walkway and started clawing at the glass from the other side. As he desperately tried to break the glass and kill us, Roisin commented, "He is from the swamps of the southeastern United States."

"I have camped throughout the south and never had any idea something like this was out there," I said.

"Have you ever been deep into a swampy area in the deep south where people don't normally go?" she asked.

I told her my father and I had been to some remote places in the swamps to go fishing.

"Were you out there at night?'

I told her we were. We camped out there.

"Well, we are very nearly positive this creature has all but died out, but I would be very cautious whenever you visit such a place in the future. People often mistake them for alligators, at first. They are certainly surprised when these creatures come strolling out of the water," she said.

Are we going to watch him eat anything?" I asked.

"No, he eats the fish we keep stocked in his little pool," she said.

The lizard man then suddenly stopped trying to break through the glass as he just stood and studied us with his head cocked to the side a little. We watched him watch us for a few minutes.

Roisin then finally said, "It is time to move on. I have more animals to show you. They live in darkness and are extremely dangerous, so we keep them down below. Get ready for a long descent."

As we began to walk out of the enclosure, the lizard man walked right along with us step by step, never taking his eyes off us. I could tell he badly wanted to devour us. He snapped and clawed at the glass one last time as we walked out of there. My impression was he was intelligent enough to know he was being held captive. I decided not to share that thought with Roisin.

We walked into a small dark room, and I realized my heart was beating a mile a minute. As I caught my breath, I noticed a metal circular stairwell going down. I thought about my crazy nightmare, and asked, "Roisin, is there any molten lava down in these caves?"

She gave me a crazy look and said, "NO! Why would we build an underground animal complex over an active volcano? That would be complete madness."

I suddenly felt very embarrassed.

"What would make you ask such an outlandish question? Are you some type of amateur volcanologist? Have you seen any evidence we might be over some type of volcano?" she asked.

I assured her I didn't know anything about volcanoes, and I apologized for bringing it up.

"Did you dream about molten lava last night?"

I told her I had.

"Are you certain you do not want to talk about it?" she asked.

I told her no, and we proceeded down the stairs. There were some small lights in the stairwell to give us some illumination, but it was still very dark. I could see light at the bottom of the stairs, but it was a long way down. I wish I had counted each stair because we descended for about five minutes.

When we finally got down there, we found a huge lighted tunnel made of steel, maybe about fifteen feet high. On either side of this tunnel was a giant concrete wall with a metal door. Each wall was about thirty feet or so away from the stairwell. Roisin was leading me over to the door to our right, but then the left door opened behind us, and we heard someone walking up.

A very frightened-looking man held out his hand to me and said, "Hello Buzz. It is nice to meet you." He already knew who I was, but he didn't give me his name. Before I could ask, he looked at Roisin and nervously said, "My lady, will all due respect, I was specifically told he would only see the first tier."

Roisin very calmly responded, "It's fine. I will take full responsibility for bringing him here. Please open the door."

"But my lady, your father gave me explicit instructions that only specific people would ever be allowed to see these lower-tier animals and only under specific circumstances. You must know what I am referring to. I would never want to offend you, but please, I can't disobey your father."

Roisin glared at him for a few seconds and quietly said, "It will be fine. Open the door. I won't say it again."

I felt awful for the guy. He had his original instructions from Lorcan, but when her father wasn't around, apparently Roisin's word was law. The man had no other choice than to begin unlocking and opening the massive steel door. As he was doing that, Roisin gave me a quick briefing as to what I was about to see.

"Buzz, Nigel was right. You were only supposed to see the first tier. But I do want to show you everything this wonderful island has to offer to give you a full understanding of the wonderful work we do here. This underground habitat was built by one of my father's companies that specializes in building underground bunkers, and escape is impossible. It must be. The animals upstairs would not stand a chance if any of these animals made it up to the upper tier—none of us would. Even the lizard man and the hellhound wouldn't stand a chance against these creatures. They were brought here when they were extremely young, and most animals are easy enough to handle when they are babies. But now they are fully grown, and their ferocity must be respected. This is why we must take so many precautions. But as I said last night, these animals should not be judged as evil due to the way they look or by their habits. Yes, they are extremely dangerous, but they are merely being what they are. Do you understand?"

I told her I did even though I didn't understand any of this.

"Just remember to stay with me and never try to interact with any of them in any way. Again, stay with me."

There was no need to have told me twice. Truthfully, I was not interested in seeing the animals down there. I wanted to tell her that, but I didn't want to show weakness. Nigel nervously opened the door and we slowly walked in. Once we were inside, he immediately closed the door and locked it behind us. It happened so fast that the door nearly hit me in the butt.

We walked down a fully lighted concrete tunnel for about a minute to another metal door not as big as the first one. Before we went in, Roisin asked, "Have you ever heard of a mythical creature called the White Thing? I thought you might have heard of it since you have traveled throughout the deep south."

"Yes, they have supposedly been seen in the north and central Alabama area for the past several years. But where I come from it is pronounced 'White Thang'."

Roisin rolled her eyes and said, "Yes, I have heard some of those backwoods bumpkins pronounce it that way. Well, you are about to see one, so prepare yourself."

In my entire life, I had only heard someone mention White Thang once. As I recall, my family and I heard an old man tell a story about it once at a canteen and bait shop in North Alabama. I believe his story went something like this:

"When I was a boy, we lived on a farm over in Etowah County. My pappy used to raise livestock to sell, and I helped out. One morning we went out to the chicken coop to feed the chickens and sometime during the night something had got in there and tore em all up. The mesh on the coop was all tore out, and there was white hair all over the place. I guess I must have been about ten or eleven years old. Anyways, pap and I figured it was some kind of big ole dog, but the crazy thing is we never heard nothin all night. We would have expected to hear the chickens raise a ruckus if a mean dog had got in there, but like I said, we never heard nothin. Whatever killed those chickens did it right good and quick. And all we found of them birds were some feathers and a whole lot of blood. When we had restocked the coup about a week later, pap and I got up in the loft of the barn that night with our rifles so we could watch from a high vantage point. Whatever had happened to that last bunch of chickens was not going to happen again if we could help it. Then, right about midnight, we saw this big old creature come out of the woods on all fours. It kind of acted like a bear, only it didn't look like no bear I ever seen. It was covered in white fur and had big sharp canine teeth and big ole red eyes. It slowly started moving towards the coop and I started crying a little cause I was getting all scared. I guess the thing heard me whimpering because it stopped dead in its tracks as it turned and looked right at me and pap. Pap grabbed my arm, which meant I needed to hush up. The thing then stood up on his hind legs like a man while it kept staring at us. I swear it was over seven feet tall. It then jumped in the air towards us and would have made it up into the loft, but pap shot him in the gut with the rifle. It let out a scream and fell back down on the ground. It looked dead and I wanted to run down there and look at it, but Pap told me to stay put. He wanted to watch it for a spell to make sure it was really and truly dead and not just wounded. After about thirty minutes or so he said we could finally go on down there and check it out. We got up slowly and went down the ladder. He made me walk behind him, and wouldn't you just know, it had got up and gone while we were coming down from the loft. Pap grabbed me and we ran inside the house. He got my ma and sister up and we went down to the storm shelter in the bottom of the house. We stayed down there with our guns until the next morning with the door shut. The next day we moved in with my granny who lived down in Jefferson County. Pap sold the farm about a week later, and we never went up there again. Well, that's the story."

The whole room erupted in laughter. The poor old man was visibly hurt and angry. People were accusing him of making it all up, but he immediately retorted, "No I did not neither. I did not." He then indignantly said, "Don't never say you weren't warned." He then stomped out the door and drove away in his pickup truck.

My father didn't say anything, but I could tell he was taking the man's story seriously. When I started imitating the way the old man talked, he told me to stop. We had planned to go bass fishing on the Tennessee River in Morgan County, which is not far from Etowah County. But we ended up changing our plans and going home instead. Dad never explained why.

I should also mention I was offended by Roisin's "backwoods bumpkins" remark. Just because someone is from a rural area and never had an opportunity to have the education that others do, does not mean that they are unintelligent–and I know that to be a fact. Some of the most intelligent people I have ever met came from remote rural areas. My parents and I encountered many of them on our travels, and I always learned a lot about camping, hunting, fishing, and life in general. But this was not the time to tell her that, and probably not ever.

The first thing that hit me when we walked into the enclosure was the smell. This creature liked to eat rotting flesh. The walkway went along the side of the pit, which was about twenty feet deep. There were lights in there, but they were low. Roisin explained this was a nocturnal creature and it didn't like bright lights. That was why these animals were never seen during the day. I was kind of disappointed at first to be up so high. But I changed my mind when the thing, or "thang" if you prefer, came out of his den located in the far wall.

He was on all fours at first, but when he noticed us, he stood up on his back feet like a man and I was able to get a good look at him. He must have been about seven feet tall, with red eyes, and white fur–just like the old man had described. His face was dark with no fur. He looked kind of like a bear, especially when he opened his mouth and showed us his extremely sharp teeth. After studying us for a second, he suddenly ran up to the wall and desperately started trying to climb up to us. I asked Roisin if there was any way he could get up the wall and she again assured me we were safe.

While we were watching him desperately try to climb up and kill us, she explained, "We believe this animal is a subspecies of the American bear. The white hair and red eyes would suggest it is merely a bear with albinism, but we have found it is much more than that. These animals have a much higher level of intelligence than their bear counterparts. They are smart enough to know they should avoid human beings and will quickly devour any humans unfortunate enough to happen upon them in the wild. In other words, they are sometimes seen, but the eyewitness rarely survives the experience."

I asked if this animal could be the explanation of the Rougarou sightings in Louisiana, and she reminded me those sightings are most likely attributed to large wolves like the one we had seen upstairs.

The animal desperately continued to try and claw his way up the wall as we were having our conversation, but it was no use. I looked down and saw the desperate frustration in its big red eyes. Just like the lizard man, this animal was smart enough to realize he was being held captive, and I couldn't help but feel sorry for him, as terrifying as he was.

Roisin directed my attention to his den as, yet another poor hapless goat came walking out of there and into the pit. There was a place in the back where they could drop in the live food for this beast. When White Thang heard the poor goat baaing behind him, he quickly turned and pounced on the poor creature. Roisin took my arm and led me out of that awful place while the White Thang tore his dinner apart. I saw nothing glorious about that creature and I wished she had not brought me there, but my experiences in the next two habitats would be far worse.

CHAPTER

THIRTY-TWO

We slowly walked to the end of the pit to another metal door. Roisin threw it open, and we were in another lighted tunnel like the first one. It took a few seconds for my eyes to adjust to the bright light as we walked down to another metal door. I expected us to walk right on in, but Roisin decided I needed another briefing.

"Buzz, by chance have you ever heard of the stories about the Dog Man sightings around Michigan?"

I told her I had never heard of the Dog Man.

"The stories are not well known, but we believe the creatures you are about to see are behind the Dog Man legends in Michigan, around Wexford County. It has also been called the Michigan Werewolf. The first reported encounters were in 1887, and these two have been with us since they were very young. As I said earlier, just remain with me, right up against the wall. Don't say anything, and please be careful about making any sudden movements."

She was nervous about this next viewing, and that concerned me—but I didn't ask any questions. I just wanted to get this part of the visit over with so we could leave.

I assumed this would be another habitat with a safe viewing area from a high vantage point with no way to access the creature (or creatures), but I was wrong. Roisin opened the metal door, and we walked down a flight of stairs into a dark pit that also smelled like rotting flesh.

When we got down there, I noticed there was no fence, glass, or anything. My assumption was we were going to walk out into the pit and access some kind of different room or area. But as I began to walk away from the wall and into the pit, Roisin grabbed me and pulled me back. I got the message. We were going to make our way across this room by inching along the bottom wall.

When we got to the middle of the enclosure, Roisin stopped and we waited, with our backs still up against the wall. There were low lights in this pit, just like the other one. My eyes finally adjusted, and I saw a very large opening across from us on the other side. We stood watching it with neither of us saying a word.

Have you ever walked into a friend's house who just happens to own a very ferocious breed of dog that doesn't like strangers? If so, then you probably couldn't help but feel a little put out with your friend for bringing you in there as the dog sits quietly growling at you. You want to make friends with the dog, so it won't see you as a threat, but your friend warns you to keep your hands to yourself. You assume you will be okay as long as your friend remains close by, but who knows? There is a very real assumption that if your friend gets up to visit the bathroom, you will probably get torn apart. And realizing that, you are scared for your friend to leave the room—even if it is only for a second. That experience would be just like this, except magnify the anxiety about a hundred times.

Roisin whispered in my ear, "Remember what I said. Do not try to interact with them in any way. Just stay here against the wall. And above all, don't try to run."

I didn't say anything. I just nodded. It was quiet for a few seconds and then two gigantic dogs slowly walked out of the opening on the other side. There was very little light in there, so it is hard to fully describe them. They looked like some kind of giant canines with a lot of sharp teeth, long pointed ears, dark fur, and claws that looked kind of like hands with single furry digits. One of them was pushing a little whitish ball with his nose.

And I would like to repeat, we were down in the pit with no apparent barrier between us. Looking back on it, I know full well the only way I was able to keep my sanity over the next few minutes was because of the water.

I began to wonder if maybe Roisin had given up on me for some reason and was ready to feed me to them, or maybe she had lost her mind. As I rolled those two possibilities around in my head, Roisin slowly walked away from the wall as she pushed on my chest ever so slightly as a reminder to stay put. Her reminder had not been necessary. I was pressed up against the wall so hard I almost felt like I was becoming part of it.

As she walked up to the Dogmen, she pulled something out of her purse. It was a small bag of dog treats. I couldn't believe it. She was giving them dog treats. They gladly accepted them in their teeth. They seemed to know who she was and were happy to see her. They had looked ferocious and terrifying at first, but now they were acting like regular domesticated dogs.

Then it got weird.

The two dogs stood up on their hind legs. Normally when dogs walk on their hind legs, they need to lean up on somebody. But these two dogs were standing up perfectly balanced like a man, and they were seven feet tall. As they happily took the treats from her, the one who had nudged the little ball with his nose, kicked it over to the side. That was when I saw it wasn't a ball after all.

It was a human skull!

I began to feel sick to my stomach. I wanted to run, but I knew I couldn't. As Roisin watched the Dogmen devour their after-meal snack, she happened to look over and see the skull on the ground. She looked back at me with a stunned and mortified look on her face. The Dogmen, meanwhile, didn't appreciate being ignored and started whimpering. She turned back to them and rubbed each of them on the stomach at the same time. They seemed to like that. This went on for a few minutes as they kept looking at me and then looking at her.

Finally, she began to slowly back towards me. The Dogmen seemed sorry for her and walked right up to us. They were so close I could smell their hot breaths, and it was horrible.

Roisin was on my left, and she ever so slowly began to nudge me towards the stairwell on the other side to my right. The Dogmen walked along the wall with us, maybe about three feet away. It was as if they knew precisely how close they could get without going any further like they had been trained somehow. Roisin and I proceeded to inch down the wall and then we slowly walked up the stairs. She quietly insisted I go first. When we got to the top, we looked down and the Dogmen were standing there at the bottom of the stairs looking very sad. It was as if they wanted to go with us, but they knew they couldn't. Roisin threw them a kiss goodbye, as she opened the big metal door. We walked back out into another lighted hallway. She closed the door behind us.

I slowly slid down the wall and sat on the floor while I caught my breath. Roisin sat down next to me. I think we maybe sat there for a half hour as I slowly came to grips with what I had just experienced.

"What were those things?" I asked.

"Truthfully, we are still trying to ascertain precisely what they are. They are maybe part bear or canine, but not completely. They appear to be a mix between one of those and maybe something else—but we are not sure what."

I saw no point in asking why one of them had a skull, and Roisin didn't bring it up. As we got ready to enter the next enclosure, I asked if we were going down into another open pit. Roisin laughed and said, "Oh no. You will be behind steel bars the entire time. You will be safe provided you do not try to enter their cage."

I told her I had no intention of entering any cage, and we proceeded. I was hoping this would be the last one because honestly, I was ready for this island adventure from hell to be over.

And as she described, we walked out to a viewing area that looked out into a giant metal cage. Roisin threw a switch, and some strategically placed lights came on in the rocks. She pointed to the ceiling of the cage, and I saw several vampire-like creatures about six to seven feet tall hanging upside down. Turning on the lights had gotten their attention.

They were bats, gigantic bats, bigger than any I had ever seen in my nightmares. They flew over to where we were standing, as I prayed for the metal cage to hold. Their teeth were long and sharp, and their red eyes glowed in the darkness. They looked terrifyingly demonic.

Roisin explained, "These animals were found over two hundred years ago in New Jersey. They are most likely the explanation for the Jersey Devil legend and possibly the recent Mothman sighting in West Virginia."

"You mean you found their ancestors two hundred years ago?" I asked.

"Oh Buzz, haven't you guessed? Our animals are kept alive by our wonderful water. Although we don't give it directly to the Kraken, we believe he has access to it. These animals all would have died out years ago if we had not taken them into captivity. This is the magic and wonder of this place and why I wanted you to come experience it with me. I just knew you could never say no to working for us if you could only see what we have here."

She then put her arms around my neck, looked me in the eye, and said, "Buzz, once you find the animal we so desperately need, I want you to stay here with me forever."

We were deep in the bowels of a cave with demonic-looking creatures flying around, and it felt like I was making a deal with the devil. But after my conversations with Otto, I knew this was not the place to tell her no.

"Roisin, can you and I live together on top of the mountain?" I asked.

"OH YES, WE WILL HAVE OUR WEDDING UP THERE," she shouted.

We kissed, and I guess we had gotten engaged in the middle of that dark and horrible place.

Roisin was elated to the point of euphoria—the kind that gives someone a false sense of invulnerability. I believe this is why she then had a temporary lapse of judgment, or sanity, depending on how you look at it.

She whispered to me, "Stay right here. And whatever you do, whatever happens, you are not to come out there with me."

She clapped her hands, and someone immediately appeared out of the darkness and handed her a bucket of dead animal parts, at least I hoped they were from animals. I couldn't tell exactly what they were, and I didn't want to know. She walked over to a metal gate I had not noticed before. My heart was pounding as she opened the gate and walked inside with those ugly giant bats. She then started offering each of them a piece of whatever she had. It looked extremely dangerous, but I assumed she knew what she was doing.

But just as she was tossing something to the last bat, the largest one (which was about a foot bigger than the others) got overzealous and flew right at her as it tried to take a bite out of her neck. She saw it coming at the last second and flinched as the horrible creature missed her jugular and sunk its teeth into the side of her shoulder. She screamed as the blood gushed into its mouth.

I immediately ran to her and punched the evil thing in the head as hard as I possibly could. It turned her loose and flew away as she turned pale and hit the ground. I picked her up and quickly carried her back into the safe area as I started screaming for help. I slammed the door closed with my foot and threw the latch as I put her down on the ground. She was bleeding profusely, and I was terrified I was about to lose her. It was at that moment I realized I had fallen in love with her.

I assumed the servant who had brought the dead animal parts would be the only one close by, but at least twenty people appeared out of the darkness and began working on her. I stood back expecting to see paramedic-type work, but that's not exactly what they were doing. They applied pressure to the wound and started cleaning up the blood, but they weren't doing much else. I ran over and yelled, "PLEASE, DO YOU HAVE ANY BANDAGES OR STICHES DOWN HERE? THAT DAMNED CREATURE FROM HELL NEARLY TORE HER APART! WE NEED TO DO SOMETHING NOW!"

They looked at me and smiled. Roisin then sat up and smiled.

"Is this some kind of sick joke?" I asked.

Roisin answered, "No Buzz, you just did a wonderful thing. You risked your life to save mine. I most certainly would have bled to death if you had not gotten that creature away from me in time. It might have even ripped me apart."

She showed me her shoulder and there was no evidence of any puncture marks. I blurted out, "But how did you heal so quickly? The water?"

"Yes, as long as a person doesn't lose too much blood, too quickly, the water enables the body to heal in a matter of seconds," she answered.

One of the servants said, "Oh my lady, after the way we lost your sister, it would have been so devastating to lose you the same……."

Roisin immediately got up, stood in her face, and said, "Silence you fool! GO!" The servants slowly faded back into the darkness without saying another word. Roisin turned to me and said, "Come, our visit here is done. It is time to return to the castle."

I had never been so happy to leave a place in my entire life.

She led me over to an industrial lift elevator installed up against the rocks. It slowly took us up to a pad with a helicopter. The sun was going down and as I realized we must have been in that place for over six hours, but it didn't seem like it.

All in all, I would have to say this had just been the strangest day of my life, and on this trip that was really saying something. As I thought about the lower-tier animals, I couldn't help but wonder which one of them would win if they were to get into a fight. It probably would have been a toss-up.

CHAPTER
THIRTY-THREE

I had never flown in a helicopter before, and it was a fun flight. Roisin put her head on my shoulder as we watched the sunset over the water. I was now getting married, whether I wanted to or not. My mother had always told me I should let a girl choose me, and to not allow myself to be snagged. At the time it seemed like I had been chosen. But as I look back on it, I was snagged.

As we flew across the water in the twilight of the day, a thought came to me, and I foolishly blurted out, "Roisin, have you ever considered letting the world know about these creatures and letting people study them? This place could make all kinds of money."

Roisin lifted her head off my shoulder and said, "Buzz, my family already has more money than we could spend in a hundred lifetimes. But if we were to let the world know about our animals and this special place, we would run the risk of revealing our most guarded secret. Remember what I said down in the cavern? It is the special water keeping these animals alive well past their normal life expectancies. And they are already being studied by experts within our organization. Maybe at some point we can share some of our discoveries with the world, but not yet."

She put her head back on my shoulder and I silently decided that in the future I would think before I made any suggestions about what this family should do.

We landed near the boat dock and took a Jeep back to the castle. Otto was waiting for us outside. He told us we were going to have our dinner in the private dining room in one hour. We raced upstairs to our rooms and kissed goodbye as we each went to get ready for the evening.

I took a shower and put on yet another nice suit that had been left for me sometime during the day. We met Otto downstairs an hour later, and the three of us proceeded to the private dining room. We had a spectacular dinner, while Roisin told Otto about our entire day and how I had "valiantly" saved her life. Otto had already been informed of the incident, and he thanked me repeatedly.

Roisin then looked over at me and said, "Buzz, because of your bravery throughout the day I have decided you are now ready to see our wondrous third island. I will take you there tomorrow, but it is much further away than the second one and can only be accessed by boat since there isn't a convenient place to land the helicopter. We will be spending the night there in a specially built compound, so you will need to pack some clothes. The accommodations are basic, but I believe you will be comfortable."

Hearing this threw Otto into an outrage. He jumped to his feet and screamed, "ROISIN, NO. HE MUST NOT SEE THE THIRD ISLAND RIGHT NOW. HE IS NOT READY."

Roisin gave him her trademark fierce glare, but this time he refused to back down.

"Roisin, I am begging you, please don't do this. Just thinking about that place makes my skin crawl," he pleaded.

Neither of them bothered to ask how I felt about this. But after the day I had just had, if Otto felt so strongly that I shouldn't see this third island, then I did not want to go—especially if it was going to be scarier than what I had just experienced.

But Roisin wasn't having it. She slowly stood up, got in his face, and told him to shut up or leave. He immediately sat back down as we quietly and awkwardly proceeded with dinner in silence.

We were quiet for several minutes as we looked down and ate our meals. Then it happened. We were done with the main course and waiting for dessert as Roisin looked over my shoulder and screamed.

I turned and Lorcan was standing in the door with his arms crossed. He was glaring at Roisin. We all jumped to our feet as he slowly walked over to Roisin and quietly, yet firmly, said, "You will go straight to my study and stay there. I will be there momentarily to speak with you about your deplorable actions and the way you have wronged this unfortunate young man. And Otto, I know about your involvement in this. You will go to our meeting room and stay there. I will be dealing with you as well."

Roisin put her face in her hands and started wailing, and I mean *wailing*. Otto looked like he was about to burst into tears himself as they slowly walked out of the room. Lorcan then closed the door and invited me to sit back down. We sat in silence as he appeared to be thinking about how he wanted to start the conversation.

He finally said, "Buzz, my boy. I believe Roisin, Otto, and the members of my organization who were involved in this horrible incident owe you and your company enormous reparation for the way you were all deceived. I am honestly so mortified right now I can barely speak."

We sat in silence for a few more seconds as he contemplated what else to say. He was shaking with anger and was having difficulty finding the words.

"Buzz.....................I have been dealing with this situation for the past twenty-four hours and the best I have been able to do is maybe keep it from getting worse. It was obviously a signal to your supervisors when you told Roisin they needed to take care of some fish named Juan, Pal, and Bongo—or something like that. I can't precisely remember the names."

I raised an eyebrow, and he quickly responded, "Buzz, I don't blame you for sending that veiled message. You were merely following the orders of your superior and I would have done the same. It was a very resourceful idea because sending the message did get their attention. The next morning someone from your company named Sam showed up at our place of business in Hong Kong and demanded to speak to you immediately. He became incensed when they informed him you were not there, and they couldn't tell him anything else. My people at the company were never informed about where you were going and why, so they were in an awkward position, to say the least. Sam came back a few days later with the owner of your company. By then they had called the FBI, INTERPOL, the government in Hong Kong, the American Embassy, and The Red Cross."

"The owner is very protective of his employees," I said.

"Buzz, that is an understatement. The man went as far as to bribe numerous people at the airport and the dock. He was finally able to piece together that you were put on a ship, and he has come very close to obtaining the ship's manifest. I truly believe if he had been able to determine where you had been taken, he would have arrived here with a large group of mercenaries on a rescue mission to find you."

"Oh, I'm not sure he would go that far," I said in disbelief.

"Buzz, we have learned he was inquiring about where he could find work for hire assassins."

A frightening thought entered my mind and I asked, "Lorcan, you keep referring to the owner in the past tense. You didn't have my friends killed...did you?"

"Oh no, that surely would have started an uproar. Our primary objective is to run our enterprises in a quiet and dignified manner, and to keep our amazing home peacefully away from outside interference. No, your friends have gone home safe and sound. And you will soon be joining them, I assure you."

He sounded sincere, but I knew he was lying. I had seen way too much. He wasn't going to just let me leave, but I let him keep talking.

"Buzz, I am also aware Roisin had you put you in chains. I can only imagine how horrible that must have been for you. We have no right to ask for your forgiveness, but I do want you to know how sorry I am."

I thought about how I should respond. I knew I had to be extremely careful. Since I was probably speaking to the most powerful man in the world, it made sense to tell him something he would want to hear.

"Lorcan, I want you to know that because Roisin brought me here, I have seen fantastic things I never dreamed existed. And I understand why you love this place and want to preserve it. And truthfully, I have come to love it as well. Since I have been allowed to experience these wonderful things most people never will, I am now eternally grateful to Roisin for bringing me here."

Lorcan seemed happy with that response, but I did see a hint of skepticism on his face. I believe he knew I was just blowing smoke because he responded by saying something I wasn't expecting.

"Buzz, you are either a changed man with a new outlook, or it is just the water talking."

He knew I had tasted the water. But how? If he didn't already know I knew the source of the water, then I sure didn't want to tell him.

"What's wrong with the water? Is something wrong with the water here?" I innocently asked. I was still able to lie without getting nervous.

"Buzz, I am aware Roisin invited you to her room on your first night here, and you stayed with her all night. I am also aware you were a very changed man when you walked out of her room the next morning. She showed you the source of our amazing water sometime during the night, didn't she?"

"I don't know what you are talking about," I answered.

Even with the influence of the water, this was still the most awkward conversation of my life, but I held on. He took a deep breath and said, "What if I were to tell you I know for a fact she showed you the source of the water? Would you dare to continue to lie to my face in my own home?"

I still wouldn't back down. I looked him in the eye and said, "She took me to her room and gave me some water because I told her I was thirsty. We then talked all night. That's all."

He leaned over with a terrifyingly fierce look in his eyes and whispered, "If I find out you are lying to me, I will kill you myself."

I didn't break eye contact, and I didn't lose my cool, even though I had just lied to the most dangerous man in the world.

After a few seconds of staring, he finally said, "Alright Buzz. You've convinced me, for the moment."

I nodded, relieved to know I was probably not going to be killed, at least not right then. But I was still wondering what was going to happen to Roisin, and I wanted to help her if I could. Plus, it was an opportunity to change the subject.

"Sir, please don't hurt Roisin for bringing me here. She was just trying to….."

He interrupted me mid-sentence and said, "Buzz, as disappointed as I am with my daughter, I would never do anything to harm her. Yes, I will need to address her deplorable behavior, and that conversation will not be pleasant. But just know I love her dearly and I would never allow harm to come to her."

I decided I needed to say a word for Otto as well.

"Lorcan, I would also like to point out that Otto was only trying to help when he….." He cut me off mid-sentence.

"Do not dare to speak to me about Otto," he snapped.

That was jarring. I sat quietly waiting for him to say something else.

After a few minutes he finally huffed and said, "Oh, I might as well tell you the story. You deserve that I suppose. On this island is a secret man-made passageway that leads to a well with special healing properties in the water. We are not sure who originally discovered the water, built the well, or created the passageway, but many years ago I was part of a group exploring this part of the world. We had heard legends that the fabled fountain of youth existed on one of these islands and we finally found it. We all expected to live forever, but as time passed, we discovered the water only retards the aging process. It doesn't stop it completely. We also learned the hard way I might add, that it does not make you invincible to physical attacks or freak accidents. So, if someone loses a limb, an eye, an ear, or something such as that, they will not miraculously grow another one. However, the water does have miraculous healing properties. If one is cut, even severely, the wound will most likely close and heal before there is a fatal loss of blood. But a person can still die if the cut is extremely deep, and the blood flow is not stopped. And yes, I heard about what happened with you and Roisin today. I do believe you saved my foolish daughter's life. If that creature had not turned loose of her, I don't think she would have survived."

He was quiet for a few seconds as he collected himself, and then he continued, "That well is a great treasure, and we have kept its location secret for centuries. Then, over the course of time, everyone in our group passed away. Eventually, my older brother and I were the only ones left.

We made the most of the extra years given to us. We told no one of the well's existence and we traveled back here once a year to drink from its life-giving waters. Just out of curiosity, how old do you think I am?"

I gave Lorcan an honest answer. I told him he looked like he was in his early to mid-fifties. He threw his head back and laughed as he said, "Buzz my boy, I am twelve hundred seventy-two years old."

I didn't know what to say. I just sat there with my mouth open. He continued with his story.

"For centuries my older brother and I made long-term, stable investments all over the world that paid off handsomely over time and we established numerous business ventures on a global scale. Within a century we had amassed a great fortune and considerable influence. My brother passed away a hundred years ago, and I became the sole leader of our vast empire."

"Why haven't people realized you never seem to age?" I asked.

"No one deals with me directly anymore, and we rotate family members to give the illusion that our people are retiring after a few years and turning things over to a younger family member. Only select members of our family and the people on our island know I am still alive."

A thought came to me while Lorcan was telling me all this. Dad had always said the most powerful and dangerous people in the world are completely unknown to the rest of us. I guess he was right.

Lorcan continued, "I have had numerous wives and children all over the world. They have had children of their own and so on. My brother's descendants are also part of the organization. Otto is my brother's oldest son and my favorite nephew, at least up until today. He is here to keep Roisin out of trouble, but it would seem he is only enabling her foolish behavior. Something will need to be done about that," he said menacingly.

Otto was clearly in hot water. I was pretty sure Roisin was going to skate, but I wasn't sure about Otto. I was worried for him, but I had my own problems. If he wasn't okay with me staying here with Roisin, then I was in big trouble. I decided to go for broke.

"Lorcan, today Roisin invited me to stay here with her and I accepted. In the beginning I didn't like being kidnapped, but I am now grateful to be here. And I don't want to leave your daughter."

Lorcan did not react to that, and that was a bad sign. Roisin had been ecstatic when I told her I wanted to stay, but I could tell he wasn't sold on the idea. I needed to prove myself.

"Lorcan, I know there is a creature you want me to find. If you give me a chance, you have my word I will find it and bring it here," I said.

He again threw his head back, laughed sarcastically, and said, "Buzz, my boy, you don't even know what the animal is. How can you be so sure you will find something when so many others have tried and failed?"

My heart sank, but I persisted. There was no other choice.

"Lorcan, my father was the greatest hunter, tracker, and outdoorsman I ever knew, and he taught me everything. If the animal you want truly exists, then I will either find it, or I will be able to tell you why it can't be found. Now please tell me, what is the animal you want me to find?"

Lorcan looked me in the eye and said, "Buzz, I never wanted you to find anything. Roisin became fascinated with you, so she lured you to the Hong Kong airport so she could bring you here. Frankly, her whole plan sounds like something a ten-year-old would have devised. But since you are here, I will give you the opportunity you are now demanding. I want you to return to the United States and find us a Sasquatch."

CHAPTER
THIRTY-FOUR

My father had always been adamant that Bigfoot did not exist. He would laugh hysterically whenever someone tried to bring it up in serious conversation. The strange thing is he was open to the idea there might be unknown types of animals to explain sightings of giant snakes, the Loch Ness Monster, Mokele-Mbembe, and even the White Thang. But Bigfoot? No way. He had always insisted the Bigfoot sightings could all be attributed to large mountain men who happened to be covered in bearskin or diseased hairless bears with mange. And once he had offered up those explanations, he was through talking about it.

I had never taken the Bigfoot legends seriously either. But here was an opportunity to get off this God-forsaken island and possibly make a break for it. I responded, "Sir, if you have reason to believe a Sasquatch is in a given area, then please take me there. If it truly exists, then you will have one."

Lorcan looked at me thoughtfully for a moment and said, "Alright. You will get your chance. We owe you that. Your training will begin first thing tomorrow morning. Now if you will please return to your room for the evening, I have some difficult matters to attend to. Good night."

I turned and left. No one escorted me, but there was no point in trying to go anywhere else since the guards were everywhere. They quietly stood and watched me walk straight up to my room. The guard stationed there closed the door behind me and locked it.

I sat in the sitting area for a few minutes, wondering what was going on downstairs. I then heard voices coming up through the old dumbwaiter. Fortunately, Lorcan and Otto had forgotten how easily sound can travel up the shaft and into my room. I crept over, but I didn't need to open the dumbwaiter doors. My hearing was still well above normal.

"Otto, how could you have let this happen? You are supposed to keep watch over her when I am not here."

"I had no idea what she was doing until right before she arrived with that unfortunate young man."

"But Otto, you weren't supposed to let her travel to the mainland. She is the keeper of the well now. Why did you let her get on the ship?"

"I didn't know she had left until after she was gone. The ship departed in the middle of the night and the next morning I was told she wanted to take one last trip to Hong Kong. I immediately started trying to contact you the minute I heard she had left us, but you are nearly impossible to reach while you are traveling."

"I wish you had been able to reach me. I would have met her in Hong Kong and put a stop to this madness. Buzz would have been paid the money he was owed, told he was no longer needed, and then he would have been sent home with a first-class ticket. He never would have seen any of this. But instead, I come home for a much-needed retreat, and within an hour I learn Ivan has sneaked back onto the island so he can come here and make a complete ass out of himself. And if that wasn't jarring enough, I also learned Roisin has brought another potential suitor into my home without my knowledge or permission. Two days later I learned his presence here is compromising our privacy and security. Otto, I am now wondering why you didn't tell me the circumstances as to how he was brought here two nights ago when he first arrived. I am sure you can imagine my anger and frustration with you right now."

Otto nervously responded, "Lorcan, I know I should have told you everything the first chance I had, but honestly, I was scared to cross Roisin and ruin her plan. She terrifies me and everyone else. She has gotten so demanding, and I don't know how to handle her anymore. No one does. Everyone gives her whatever she wants. That is how she was able to arrange all of this with just a few telephone calls before she arrived here. We all know she will be in a position of authority when you leave us, and no one wants to cross her in the meantime. There is no simple way to rein in a ruthless two-hundred-year-old woman who can have anything she wants, knows she is not going to face any consequences for her actions, and is fully aware she will one day have power over all of us."

It was quiet for several seconds. At first, I thought they had left the room. I then heard Lorcan say, "Anytime I have sent any of my offspring into the world to do real labor, they have always returned better for the experience. I believed Roisin would return with a newfound sense of restraint and humility. This has not been the case."

"But Lorcan, she wasn't away very long," Otto replied.

"Yes, I had planned for her stay at the camp to be longer. But after I lost Leela so tragically, I needed Roisin back here with me post haste. Otto, you know I have had numerous offspring over these many years. But Leela and Roisin were always my favorites out of all of them, and I loved their mother in a way I have never loved any other woman. The problem with living as long as I have, you experience an unbearable amount of tragedy–enough for twenty lifetimes. And after losing her mother and sister, I can't risk sending Roisin away again. Yes, she has become a problem, but now I believe the right man in her life who can properly handle her is the answer."

It was quiet for a few seconds and then Lorcan changed the subject.

"I hear the giant behemoth she loves so much was roaming around right before they arrived."

Otto seemed happy to talk about something else and quickly responded, "Yes, they had to delay their arrival so we could corral the giant ape and get him into the reinforced enclosure we had originally built for the Sasquatch. It seems to be holding him...for now. Buzz was told the delay in their voyage was caused by a violent thunderstorm, but I'm sure he knew otherwise when he arrived and saw the terrain was completely dry."

I had just heard the thing in the enclosure referred to as a "giant ape." If possible, I knew I had to see inside there before I left this place.

Lorcan hastily responded, "I've had it with him. He is far more trouble than he is worth. I wish you would all dispose of him. We have a much better specimen on the third island."

"But Lorcan, Roisin thinks he can be tamed again, and you know how she loves old fairy tales. It means so much to her to have him here."

I had never heard of a fairy tale with a giant ape. As I wondered what they were talking about I heard Otto nervously ask, "What do you plan to do with Buzz?"

I then learned what kind of man Lorcan truly was when I heard him say, "I've been working on that. I just got through telling him I was going to send him out on a hunt to find Bigfoot, but that isn't true. His situation has become much too volatile, so regrettably he must be dealt with. He will be escorted from his room at midnight tonight and told he is being taken to our training facility in the Pacific Northwest by ship. He will believe that especially since there are numerous stories of Sasquatches in that area. Buzz will then be quickly disposed of once he is on the ship. I have left detailed instructions as to how I want his body to be mutilated. I have also left instructions with my subordinates in Hong Kong. His mutilated body will be found in a seedy side of town and his employer will be told he must have been kidnapped and later killed by a common street gang. The employer and his entourage will take his body and leave once they believe the mystery is solved. My company will offer them generous reparations, and they will never be aware we are responsible for his death. Roisin will be told Buzz was taken to the area with the supposed Sasquatch activity and later found torn apart just like all the others. I will send Ivan to comfort her, and maybe he can win her back if he can just stop acting like a damnable buffoon."

"Lorcan, there must be another way. I don't know if you've heard, but he saved her life today. If he had not reached her in time, I believe those demonic bats would have torn her all to pieces."

"Yes, I know all about that. And if I find out Nigel allowed them to go in there, I will have him thrown to the dogs. I gave specific instructions...."

Otto interrupted, "Lorcan, I know for a fact Nigel had nothing to do with it. Roisin sneaked Buzz in there while Nigel was feeding the hydra on the other side, and you know how dangerous that can be. Now about Buzz, can't he be spared?"

"I deeply regret what must be done. Buzz is a resourceful and intelligent young man, and I am aware of what he has had to overcome in his life. I know he is brave in his heart, despite his near mental breakdown on the ship.

Being kidnapped in another country and waking up chained in the hold of a ship would have been enough to unravel anyone. But his employer has come dangerously close to learning the location of our island, and I have no doubt he will soon come for Buzz if we don't do something post haste. The world is changing, and I fear we have become far more vulnerable here than we would like to admit to ourselves."

"Lorcan, maybe if Buzz were to speak to his employer on the telephone, assure him that he is okay, and formally resign," pleaded Otto.

"No, that is far far too risky. Besides, even if his employer didn't care about him one way or the other, I do not believe Buzz will ever be a proper suitor for Roisin. When I am gone, she will need a man by her side who can fiercely protect her and keep her in line, and I do not believe Buzz would be capable of that—at least not anytime soon. Compared to the rest of us, at only twenty-five years old, he is practically a child. Ivan is the ideal suitor for her. I know there is a side of her that still loves him. I have heard she will often weep whenever she is reminded of him. I believe Roisin will gravitate back into his arms once Buzz is neatly out of the way."

Otto then asked, "Where is Roisin right now? Is she still in the castle? She might interfere if she sees him being taken away."

Lorcan responded, "I have already thought of that. Roisin has been banished from the castle for the moment and taken to the beach house on the west end of the island, so she won't be able to interfere. I also took her amulet away from her. By midnight she should be asleep and not have any idea of what we are doing, but I have stationed guards to keep an eye on her just in case."

That was all I needed to hear. I somehow had to get out of that nut house and off that island of the damned. Walking out the front door wasn't an option. And Roisin couldn't help because she had lost her amulet, whatever the fool that meant. The only idea I had was to see if I could climb out the window and scale down the wall since it was only about twenty feet up. Once I was on the ground, I figured I could try getting across that God-forsaken place and back to Mr. Terrible's boat. I had no idea where I might be sailing to, but it was going to be away from there. Maybe I could avoid them out on the open water long enough to get picked up by a ship or something. My plan wasn't perfect, but anything was better than just sitting there and waiting to be slaughtered.

I still had elevated strength all over my body down to my fingertips, and it wasn't hard to scale down the outside rock wall to the ground. I was worried someone would see me, but there wasn't anyone outside. I looked in a window and the entire house was standing outside the room where Lorcan and Otto were having their conversation, listening at the door. The conversation was still going strong. I would like to have heard the whole thing, but I had to get out of there. Fast!

I believe I could have gotten to the boat on foot if I had had all night, but I didn't have that much time. It was about eight o'clock, so I figured I maybe had four hours at the most before they realized I was gone.

I sneaked over to the stables, and I took one of the horses. I had not ridden bareback since I was a kid, but fortunately, he was wearing a bridle. I was glad the road wasn't paved because we didn't make as much noise as I would have thought. We broke into a gallop once we were a good distance away from the castle.

We raced to the mountain, and by then I could tell the horse was getting tired. It was time to take it easy, and it was just as well because I had some trouble looking for the road that went around. The foliage around the turn-off made it extremely hard to find in the dark, but I did find it. I was done with the horse, so I sent him on his way as he started trotting back down the road in the direction of the castle. With any luck he would trot back to his stable and no one would figure out I had borrowed him. I cautiously walked around the mountain and stayed off the road as I slowly walked toward the enclosures. As I crept up to the little street, I looked around and couldn't see anyone in the darkness.

There was a small cruise ship at the dock. I heard music and assumed everyone on this side of the mountain was at a party. I couldn't believe my luck as I walked down the center of the street and was ready to run down the hill to the boat. But I stopped at those last two enclosures I was not allowed to see.

I looked out into the ocean, and I saw the lights of a large ocean liner off in the distance. It was a perfect chance for escape. I could possibly sail to the ocean liner and beg for help. But my curiosity was getting the better of me because I couldn't tear myself away from seeing what was in those last two enclosures. I guess it was the courage effect of the water, or maybe I am just too nosey.

I thought it would probably be okay to just poke my head in for a minute or two, and then I would be off to freedom—with a story, no one will ever believe. I went inside the enclosure on the right, and it was a giant aquarium, like the other ones. Only I didn't have to climb up any stairs to see into it. The whole side of the aquarium was visible from the ground.

The lights were on, and in the water were six beautiful naked women kneeling on some rocks—but then I took a closer look. Although they looked like perfectly normal women from the waist up, from the waist down they were like giant fish. They were mermaids—six beautiful mermaids with long hair flowing in the water, and this time there was nothing reptilian or amphibian about them. They were the real thing.

I was stunned as I watched them sitting peacefully in the water. I walked over to the glass to see if I could get their attention. When one of them noticed me, she rose from the rock and swam towards me. She remained motionless bobbing in the water as she stared right at me. The others noticed, and they began to slowly swim over to me.

They all looked too beautiful to be human, but their looks of innocence slowly changed to fury. Their teeth were sharp with large fangs, and it was obvious they didn't appreciate me being there as they started clawing at the glass with their long sharp fingernails. I now understood why Roisin didn't want me to see them. These poor mermaids weren't your typical animals in captivity. Just like the lizard man, White Fang, and the Dog Men, they were intelligent enough to realize they were being held captive.

I turned and left, wishing there was some way I could help them get back into the ocean, or wherever they came from. I carefully crept back out into the street, and it was still deserted. The ocean liner was slowly passing by, and I knew I was running out of time, but I had to see what was in the final enclosure. If a giant ape was in there, I had to see it— even if it was just for a few seconds. I opened the door and slowly walked inside.

This enclosure was like a giant fort. The walls appeared to be six feet thick, but there was no roof, and the trees and plants were extremely dense. I slowly walked through the brush, looking for some kind of observation area. But I didn't find anything like that. It was all forest, and nothing else.

I was about fifty yards in, not believing the size of this place, when I began to smell smoke. Someone was cooking something up ahead. I crawled through the brush for another twenty yards, and about a hundred yards away was a big someone sitting next to a fire. He had his back to me, but I could tell his shoulders were abnormally broad. He didn't appear to be very tall, but that was an optical illusion because he was sitting in a pit.

I walked up and got a better look at him. He had a huge, bald head. He probably wasn't an ape, whatever he was. I began to think about the ocean liner and decided there wasn't much to see here. I turned to leave and accidentally stepped on a branch. It got his attention, as he turned around and stood up.

Standing before me was a giant, maybe about thirty feet tall, grinning with a rotten tooth smile, and wearing a fur-covered moo moo that went down to his knees with a single strap over one shoulder. He looked like a typical giant out of a fairy tale.

I don't think I have ever screamed so loud in my entire life. Yes, the water had given me courage, but apparently, it had its limits. I turned and ran for dear life, as the thing came after me screaming, "WAIT!!! WAIT!!!"

But I didn't wait. I ran like the house was on fire. I looked over my shoulder and saw he was having trouble moving, like maybe his knees were giving out. If he had been at full strength, I believe he could have caught me in two strides, but he was clearly in great physical pain.

I had no desire to try and interact with this thing. My curiosity was satisfied, and it was time to sail away. But then something unexpected happened. The poor giant sat down on the ground and started crying as he wailed, "I want mama. I want papa. I want to go home. I want to go home."

I didn't know what to do. I wanted to get away, but I couldn't leave him like that. I walked over and said, "Hey, I'm sorry I ran away. My name is Buzz."

He looked up and smiled at me through his tears as he uttered, "I am Nye. Can you help me to go home?"

"I will help if I can. How long have you been here?"

He held up all of his fingers and flashed them many times as he said, "This many. I been here long time, very long time. I now want to go home. I tried to walk home, but I got all wet and had to turn around. Water went up the holes in my nose and it stung. I came back on land, but now I am in this place and can't get out. You let me out?"

I could tell he had the mental capacity of a small child, which made his situation all the more tragic. He might not have understood the complexity of his situation, but he understood he was imprisoned. I wished more than anything I could have taken the big fella out of there and back to wherever he came from, but I had no way to do that. I decided to let him down easily, which was a mistake.

"Nye, I will help you, but first I need to go get some help and then I will see if I can help you get home. Okay?"

He angrily looked at me and said, "Why not I go now?" He slowly stood up on his feet and firmly said, "I. GO. HOME. NOW!"

There was no point in trying to reason with him, so I turned and ran towards the door of the enclosure. He was right behind me as I ran out into the street. The small door was just big enough for me, but not near big enough for him. As I ran towards the boat he started banging on the walls and screaming his head off like he had done the day before. I now recognized the emotional pain in his wails, and it broke my heart.

I ran down to the water and the boat was still docked right there. I felt such relief when I first began to unite it. That was when a tranquilizer dart hit me right in the butt, and I was out like a light.

CHAPTER
THIRTY-FIVE

So, there I was. It was early morning, and I was lying on the ground. I was wearing clothes made of burlap, which I guess made me look like a medieval peasant. I was on my side with my hands tied behind my back. I thought I was alone, at first.

Somebody cleared his throat behind me, and I recognized Lorcan's voice in the cough. I rolled over and saw a semicircle of about a hundred people standing around me not saying a word. Most of them were wearing peasant garb like me. A few of the guards were on horses and dressed like knights in shining armor in the bright sun. Roisin was sitting on the unicorn and dressed like a princess with a tall, pointed hat with silk wrapped around it. Her eyes were red like she had been crying. Otto was in a court jester outfit, but he did not look at all happy. And there was Lorcan, dressed in white tights, red velour pantaloons, a red velour coat, and a gold crown on his head.

He looked ridiculous. They ALL looked ridiculous.

I would love to tell you this was another one of my stupid stress dreams, but not this time. This was happening, and I was in big trouble. Standing in the middle of this giant semi-circle crowd was an old-fashioned guillotine with two big guys dressed in black standing next to it. They had hoods over their faces, with eye holes. They walked over to me, took each of my arms, dragged me over to the device, and stuck my neck in it. They bolted me in and with one pull of the rope, I would be dead. This must have been what Otto was talking about when he said this nut had moved on from using the drawn and quartered.

I closed my eyes, waiting for the blade to drop. I could have pleaded for my life, but I didn't see the point. Plus, I was fully expecting to be reunited with my parents.

After several excruciating seconds, Lorcan casually strolled over and said, "Buzz my boy, aren't you going to beg for your sad and miserable life?"

"Would it do any good?" I asked.

"Absolutely not. It is my responsibility to my minions and to all of my offspring to be a strong and capable leader. Although a strong leader can do much damage, a weak leader can destroy everything."

"What's that supposed to mean?" I asked.

"It means I will never let you leave here and expose what we have to anyone. But I so enjoy hearing those who have betrayed me beg for mercy as I kill them mid-sentence. You are not going to give me the satisfaction, are you?"

"No. No, I am not. My soul is prepared, I miss my parents, and this is a quick method of execution. If the blade is sharp, I probably won't feel much—if anything. And I did not betray you. You were about to betray me. I heard you tell Otto you were going to kill me on the ship after you and I had just agreed I was going to find Bigfoot for you. If you had been in my situation, wouldn't you have tried to get away if you could? You are not a man of integrity and killing me in front of your precious minions and offspring is not going to change that. You are only disgracing yourself right now, not me."

I am pretty positive Lorcan was not used to being spoken to like that. His eyes looked like they were about to bulge out of his head, but I was about to die anyway, so I didn't care. He then seemed to calm himself as he thought about what he had just heard, and said, "Yes, my boy, you are absolutely right. A guillotine is much too quick and painless. I will summon my knights to bring the chains and cuffs. We will do the drawn and quarter. I haven't enjoyed seeing that for quite a good while. Or maybe we could just tie you to a stake and burn you alive. I'll bet then you would beg for mercy."

"Sure, you could do that. But before you kill me, I should point out that right now I am your best option for finding a Sasquatch," I smugly said.

He sarcastically responded, "We already have one giant smelly ape of a man on this island. Why do we need another?"

I had one last card to play.

"Lorcan, if you torture and kill me, Roisin will secretly hate and resent you until the day she dies. She will never love you again."

I had a point, and he knew it, but he was through listening to me. He took a deep breath and yelled at the top of his lungs, "ENOUGH!!! OFF WITH HIS….."

He didn't get to finish that sentence. Roisin shrieked, "NOOOOOOOOO!!!" She leaped off the unicorn, ran over to me, and unfastened the guillotine as she pulled me out of it. As I kneeled there on the ground, she put her arms around me and started screaming through her tears, "OH DADDY, PLEASE DON'T KILL HIM. HE SAVED MY LIFE. AND HE WAS ONLY TRYING TO SAVE HIS LIFE SO HE COULD COME BACK TO ME. IF YOU KILL HIM, THEN I SWEAR I WILL ALSO THROW MYSELF TO THE MERMAIDS. I LOVE HIM!!!"

Lorcan looked thoroughly disgusted as she started weeping uncontrollably. Everyone in the crowd looked terrified, but no one dared say anything. Otto walked over to Lorcan, took off his jester cap, and said, "Lorcan, this is no good. Why don't we put Buzz in the cell, and then we can go back to the castle and think this over?"

Lorcan turned around in disgust and stomped away. Otto, and most of the party, went back with him not saying a word. When their backs were turned, Roisin smiled and winked at me, and I silently thanked her. She turned and rode the unicorn in the direction of its enclosure. The two goons stayed with me.

When everyone had left, they took off their masks and one of them said, "Hello Buzz, I'm Declan. First, let me say we are very glad we didn't have to kill you. Truthfully, we all believe you're a decent guy, and we would be happy for you to stay here with us. We like you much better than that maniac Ivan, but we didn't have a choice. We had to follow Lorcan's gruesome orders. On this island his word is law."

"Does he typically make everyone dress like they're in a Robin Hood movie?" I asked.

"No, dressing up like a medieval king is something new. Lately, he's been doing strange things like that when he is highly agitated. We're all worried," he answered.

"What's this about a cell? Am I going to a dungeon or something?" I asked.

"You are not going to the dungeon. That's in the bottom of the castle. Lorcan keeps his collection of authentic medieval torture devices in there, so you are much better off in our jail cell. It's over in the dormitory near the animal complex. We've never had a use for it until now, and I'm not sure why we ever had it to start with. The accommodations are basic, but for now, you will be much safer with us," he said.

We walked over to a Jeep hidden in the trees and they took me to the dormitory building. Although the outside of the building looked bland, the inside looked like a five-star hotel. I started thinking this was not going to be so bad, but then they took me to the basement where the cell was located. And "cell" was a good name for it. It consisted of a concrete slab with a thin mattress, a sink, and a toilet—all in one room. There were fluorescent lights overhead I couldn't control and no windows. The guys apologized, but they were given instructions to lock me up or it would be off with *their* heads if they let me escape. I knew that wasn't an idle threat and I assured them they would have my full cooperation. I asked for something to read, and they brought me *The Island of Dr. Moreau*, which seemed appropriate.

I read for a while, but I guess I was still dealing with the after-effects of being tranquilized. I fell asleep, even with the bright lights completely on. The bed wasn't much, but it was better than sleeping on the ground. That's all I can say about it.

Otto woke me up sometime later. He had all my suitcases from the castle. They took up most of the cell, but I was happy to have my things back. I was still wearing that stupid peasant costume and I was glad to have something else to wear. All my clothes were there except for the suits they had left for me, and it was just as well.

Once Otto had given me a chance to change, he came back in and pulled up the chair. I tried sitting up, but my head was killing me. Otto advised me to lie down while we visited. He wanted the first word and I let him have it.

"Well Buzz, you very nearly got away from us last night. You should know we are not affiliated with the ship that was passing through at the time, and it was sailing to an English-speaking country we have not been able to infiltrate. You most likely would have gotten clean away if you had left those last two enclosures alone. Our poor giant certainly raised a ruckus, but you were spotted while you were viewing those mermaids you weren't supposed to see."

"Why wasn't I supposed to see the mermaids?" I asked.

"I might as well go ahead and tell you. Lorcan knows his time is running short. He is aware he is not as sharp as he used to be, and he is not sure how much longer he will be able to effectively lead his vast organization. For the past few months, he has been dividing the responsibilities of his empire among his most able heirs. As you have probably surmised, the most coveted position is the overseer of this island, and thus the eternal well. Only Lorcan, and that chosen person, are supposed to know where the well is located and how to access it. It is best to do it this way to maintain its integrity, and to keep people from abusing it."

I nodded and he continued.

"Our problem is the water level in the well is ever so slowly beginning to decrease. It used to take two or three seconds for the bucket to hit, but as you must have observed the other night, it now takes several seconds. We are not sure why this is happening or if anything can be done about it. Since we are not sure how much longer we will have this wonderful resource, only the family members in our organization who have proven themselves most loyal are allowed to partake. Every month a group of these special members are brought to the island to have their yearly drink. That was the party you might have seen on the ship last night. One bucket of water from the well, diluted between twenty pitchers, is enough for about sixty visitors, and they remain on the ship while we bring it to them. Roisin's older sister, Keela, was originally chosen to be the keeper of the well, but then something horrible happened."

Otto stopped for a few seconds to collect himself, and he continued.

"She loved those beautiful mermaids more than anything and she thought they loved her back. She would throw them fish, sing to them, and watch them swim in various formations for hours. Then one day she must have slipped and fallen into the tank with them. The mermaids immediately tore her apart."

"Did you have any idea they were so vicious?" I asked.

"Oh yes, we were aware of how dangerous they are, but they deceptively seemed to love Keela and had never acted aggressively towards her. It would now seem they were just waiting for their chance to end her. Roisin now refuses to go in there and there have been some frank discussions concerning what we are going to do with them. It's a real conundrum. We have the only zoo in the world with real live mermaids, which is beyond all comprehension. But these particular mermaids killed a beloved family member most horrifically. My guess is they will end up in various private trophy rooms, but not here on the island. And Buzz, do not ever mention any of this to Roisin. I believe she will be coming to terms with what happened to her dear sister for the rest of her life. I also believe that is why she bonded with you so quickly. Her sister was her closest friend and she desperately needed someone else in her life, especially since Ivan has started acting so horribly to her."

"Doesn't she have a multitude of brothers and sisters to be close to?" I asked.

"She has numerous half-siblings, but they have always hated her and her sister since Lorcan favored them above everyone else. Lorcan loved their mother more than any other woman he ever married or fathered children with, and that is why he spoiled Roisin and Keela so terribly after their mother died. After being raised that way, Roisin has become terribly demanding and potentially dangerous if she doesn't get what she wants. I had hoped she would mellow, but over the years I believe she has only gotten worse."

I was ready to change the subject.

"What's the situation with the giant?" I asked.

"That's another story. Nye has been on the island for hundreds of years. He was found in Europe and brought here by another man in Lorcan's group. Lorcan was never comfortable with him being here. But he tolerated him since Nye was so childlike and emotionally helpless. Up until recently, Nye loved it here and never caused any trouble. He had his own giant home built into a nearby mountain, which you were not allowed to see. He helped us build that home and many of our enclosures, including the one he is in now."

"What set him off?" I asked.

"When Roisin recently returned to the island to assume her sister's responsibilities, she mistakenly read a book to him about a father, a mother, and a child. Something clicked in his head, and he decided he wanted to see his parents again. The obvious problem is his parents surely must have died some time ago and there is now a sprawling city where we believe he was originally found. I think it is safe to assume he does not have any living relatives in the vicinity. We're not even sure his parents or any of his kinfolk were alive when our people found him. With his mental capacity being what it is, he was never able to tell us much about his previous life. We gently tried to explain it was best for him to remain with us, but he threw a tantrum, which for him is tantamount to a deadly rampage. He flung two Jeeps in the air, and then he stormed towards the shoreline. We assumed he was going down to the beach to sit and pout, but he had it in his head he was going to walk home through the ocean. Only he can't swim, and he nearly drowned. But he was somehow able to make his way back out of the water. He was shaken, but still very upset. We tried to lure him into his present enclosure where we could contain him, but he ran off into the island interior the day before you arrived. We later found a new set of his giant footprints leading into the water and assumed he had tried to walk home again and drowned on the second attempt. But it was night, and we couldn't be sure he had not come back out of the water and was lurking around somewhere in an agitated state. That was why Roisin, and the entire crew were being so cautious when they were taking you to the castle. Until we found his body, we had to assume he might be out there getting ready to go berserk again. He was found right after you arrived, drugged with over fifty tranquilizer darts, and placed into what will hopefully be the Bigfoot enclosure. He was dragged in there with several Jeeps through a hidden gate on the far side. Thank heavens we got him in there before he woke up. Someone might have gotten killed."

"Where are you going to put Bigfoot if Nye is already in there? Are they going to live together?" I asked.

"Well, Nye has been here for a very long time, and he is no longer responding to the eternal water. It happens that way. The water can delay the aging process for centuries, but eventually, it does cease to have any effect. The poor fellow is now aging quite rapidly, and we don't think he will live much longer. This is going to break Roisin's heart. She grew up playing with him and she loves him dearly."

"So, I guess he's the last giant on earth?" I asked.

"No, he is not. On the third island, the one Roisin was going to show you today, we have a two-headed giant that is slightly bigger. We must be extremely cautious with him. The giant on this island is simple, but the other one is highly intelligent and pure evil. He loves the taste of human flesh and is adept at winning someone's confidence as lures them into his reach. Truthfully, the third island should not exist, and I believe we should take those creatures back to where they came from. I never plan to go there again if I can help it."

"That two-headed giant is not the only animal in your collection that eats human beings, is he?"

Otto looked at the floor for a second, like he tends to do when I ask him about something I was not supposed to know. He responded, "Yes, you are correct. Lorcan has been known to throw his enemies to one of those creatures in the lower tier of the second island. Our people down there were afraid you might see some evidence of that, which is one reason why Nigel did not want you to go through there. That, and Lorcan had ordered only specific people could ever go down there. But just know Roisin abhors this practice, and she plans to put a stop to it when she can."

I was ready to change the subject again and said, "If you built an enclosure that big for a Sasquatch, then you must believe one exists and can be found."

"You are correct. Despite what Lorcan said to you earlier, he does want at least one, but he would rather have an entire colony so we can observe their habits and learn more about them. This afternoon Roisin thoroughly convinced him you can help us obtain that goal, otherwise you would probably be dead by now."

"What do I get if I find you one?" I asked.

Otto told me to sit up, and he said, "Buzz, if you can bring us a Sasquatch, Lorcan will allow you to come back and be with Roisin. You will never want for anything ever again. But after ten days, if you are not successful, you will be terminated. I'm sorry to put it so bluntly, but you need to understand the gravity of your situation."

"Otto, I distinctly heard him say he didn't think I was right for Roisin, and he did not want me here under any circumstances because at twenty-five years old he thinks I'm still a child. Has he had a change of heart?

I asked him that, knowing I was about to get lied to.

"Oh yes, Buzz. I am happy to say he has had a complete change of heart about you. He was very impressed with the way you stood up to him in front of everyone."

Otto was lying, and I knew it, but I had to get off that island somehow. I continued to play along.

"How am I supposed to catch a live one? If they do exist, I could most likely track one down and bring back a dead carcass, or at least tell you where you can find them. But I have no idea how I could bring back one alive if they are as big as people say they are."

"All you will need to do is shoot one with a tranquilizer gun. After that, you will fire up a flare. Our crew members will quickly arrive to collect the creature. In the meantime, you shouldn't speak to anyone on the outside about our island or about what you have seen here. Most of the people you will encounter in the next few days already know about our island, which is why Lorcan has consented to let you go.

But not everyone knows about those monstrosities on the second island, so please be careful of what you say. I understand you did an excellent job of not letting it slip to Lorcan you know the location of the well. If he knew the truth, then you would already be dead."

He let all that sink in for a minute and he continued.

"You also shouldn't ask anyone where you are going. You are now a flight risk, and Lorcan doesn't want you to know where you are at any given time. Be assured you will be closely watched throughout your entire trip."

"And what about my employer coming to look for me?" I asked.

"You shouldn't worry about that right now. You have your concerns to address. You will remain here for tonight. Tomorrow morning you will be taken off the island by ship. Your voyage will be long, and most likely, uneventful. Don't expect to have much interaction with anyone and do not make any demands. You will be provided with necessities. That's all. Your handlers are there to transport you, and nothing else. Once you reach the mainland you will be taken to the site where we believe the Sasquatches gather. And Buzz, you must not try to escape again. Your handlers have been told to terminate you immediately if you are caught trying to leave. Truthfully, you are going to be so far away from any kind of populated area, there won't be any point in trying to leave. Then, you will be safely returned here where you can stay with Roisin for a millennium....provided you find us a Sasquatch."

"Sounds good to me," I said, even though I was lying. None of this sounded good to me. And regardless of what happened, it didn't sound like I was ever going to have an opportunity to live a normal life away from these people. I thought we were done, but he had to belabor the point.

"Buzz, I know I am repeating myself, but I just want to make sure you understand. There won't be any way for you to hide if you do manage to temporarily get away from us. Lorcan may not be connected everywhere, but he is well-connected in the United States and Canada. Once you are found, you will be killed, and there will be no way to negotiate out of it. Do you understand?"

I nodded.

"And do remember what I told you about the well. You are going to interact with several different people in our organization over the next few days in various places. In our very vast organization, some want only to come here and destroy our island if they could just get to that well and take control of it for their selfish purposes. The fate of the world hinges on the secrecy of that well."

"How do you figure that?" I asked.

"With that well and his vast resources, Lorcan could have taken control of the entire world many years ago. But he knows it is foolish to want that kind of power. He realizes he would be overthrown immediately, along with everyone closest to him since keeping that kind of power indefinitely is impossible. All he has ever wanted is to protect his interests and remain behind the scenes. As for the rest of the world, he just steps back and allows everyone else to settle things among themselves. So, you see, it is far better for someone like him to be the keeper of the well and this organization, rather than someone else who is bent on world domination. I know you must not think much of Lorcan right now, but just know that Roisin will also assuredly be killed if you let the secret out. Do you understand?"

I told him I understood. I also thanked him for talking Lorcan out of killing me.

"Buzz, I know you are a good man, and no one, besides Lorcan, blames you for trying to get away. I know hearing our conversation must have been jarring for you."

"Yes, it was, but I was relieved to hear you weren't in as much trouble as I thought," I said.

"Lorcan was frustrated and upset with me, but that was all. Roisin got off easy as well, even though she had to leave the castle for the night. All he did was walk into his study and say, 'Roisin, how could you?' and then he left her to talk to me."

I asked Otto if there was anything else, and he said no. I assured him I would follow my instructions to the letter, and we said goodbye. He walked out and locked the door behind him. I lied back down and thought about our conversation for the next several hours. I was about to fall asleep, and then I heard another familiar voice.

"Buzz?"

It was Roisin. At first, I thought I was dreaming. I sat up and she said, "Get dressed and meet me outside. I have something for you." She opened the door, walked out, and left it open for me. Once I had gotten dressed, I walked out of the cell and upstairs. Declan and the others were partying at a bar in the dining area, and they nearly fell over when they saw me.

"HOW DID YOU GET OUT?" he screamed.

"Roisin was just here, and she told me to meet her outside," I said.

"That's impossible. Roisin was never here. She's back at the castle under guard. Get your butt back downstairs," he ordered.

I ignored him and walked out the door into the street.

Roisin was out there waiting for me. She walked over and said, "Here, put your arms around me." We embraced and she touched some kind of charm around her neck. Declan and the others came running out in a mad panic. They ran all around us, but they couldn't see us.

Declan quickly organized search parties and they frantically ventured out in every direction. When they were all gone, Roisin said with a giggle, "Okay, let's go back in. I will tell them later I was behind all of this."

We went back downstairs and into my cell. Roisin took off an amulet from around her neck and said, "Buzz, this is an ancient and valuable talisman. Father has taken mine for the moment, but this one belonged to my sister. We thought it was lost, but I recently found it hidden in my room, which used to be her room. I now want you to have it. It makes the wearer temporarily invisible."

"Does this involve some kind of sorcery or magic?" I asked.

"Oh no, there is no magic here. This is a long-forgotten science dating back to the ancient world. It involves interdimensional transport. That's where all of our specimens on the third island came from, but you will learn more about that place when you return," she said.

"Am I going to get lost in some dimension or something if I use this thing the wrong way?" I asked.

"Oh no. We do have amulets that can allow you to travel to different dimensions, but this amulet is not near as strong. It only makes you unseen for a short time and then you gradually come back. You are still there, but you are not there. It's difficult to explain. But again, we will have time to discuss it when you return," she said.

She showed me how it worked. Lightly pressing down on the small jewel in the amulet would cause a person to be unseen for a short time. The amount of time you were invisible depended on how much power was in the jewel. Although the jewel was self-charging, it needed time to recharge itself. Using the jewel once a day would give you the longest time of invisibility. But using it in succession would give you less time of invisibility with each try until it completely stopped working. At that point, it would need to charge for a few days before it could work again."

"Why are you giving me this?" I asked.

She started to cry as she explained, "Buzz, we have an enormous amount of evidence that Sasquatches do exist. But everyone we have dispatched to find one has never returned, and we don't know why."

She was quiet for a few seconds and then she continued, "I did not bring you here to find Sasquatch. I wanted you to find a Chinese unicorn. The way you were able to track the hoof prints of a deer, I believed you would be perfect for that assignment. But father is insisting you do this, and I want you to have this extra advantage. So, Buzz, if your situation becomes dire, I want you to run. Just run as hard as you possibly can and use this talisman to get away. I do want you to return to me, but above all, I want you to live. And I will understand if you need to get away from the entourage for your safety. But if you do take your leave from the group, you should not try to contact me or attempt to reach out to anyone in our organization. I promise that I will be able to locate you when the time is right. In the meantime, try not to show this talisman to anyone. They won't know what it is, but I still don't want anyone to know you have it. Just tell them it belonged to your mother or something if they happen to see it."

She then put her arms around my neck and gave me a long kiss. She put the amulet (or talisman) around my neck, tucked it under my shirt, and walked out of the cell crying quietly. She left the door open as she walked away, but I had no intention of leaving. I lay back down on the bed and wondered if I was ever going to see her again.

She suddenly walked back in, took a deep breath, and said, "Buzz, there is something else I must tell you. We've lost track of Ivan. He's disappeared, and we don't know where he is. I believe he may be coming for you…"

It was all she could do to finish saying that before she broke down again. I held her while she cried profusely for several minutes. When she finally caught her breath, I looked her in the eye and said, "I will be fine. Thanks to you my hearing, sight, smell, and strength are well above normal. Plus, I can now get away if I need to."

"Make sure you do. And remember, I don't want you to stand and fight. I want you to run. Just keep on running and never stop until I find you."

I was not about to run from a fight and was going to tell her so, but she put her index finger on my mouth and said, "Don't argue. Just run. Get as far away as you can. I promise I will find you one day, and we will be together again. But for now, stay alive in the meantime. That's all I ask."

She turned and walked out of the room.

CHAPTER
THIRTY-SIX

Declan woke me up the next morning. I thought he would be mad about my disappearing act the night before, but he didn't mention it. He and a couple of guys escorted me upstairs to the dining area and we had an excellent breakfast. We sat around and talked for a few minutes and then I got up to visit the restroom.

Everyone in the entire dining room was on their feet in a second as Declan asked where I was going. I told them I needed to use the restroom and they all followed me, including the women. I was mortified to think we were all going in there together, but fortunately, everyone waited outside. Yes, I was a flight risk, but that was ridiculous.

Once I was done in the restroom, Declan and a large group of men took me out to the dock where a small cargo ship was waiting for us. I asked if I was going to be chained up in the hold again and Declan said I was going to be locked in a small state room with no windows. That didn't sound like much fun, but what choice did I have? I asked if he was going with me and he said, "No, normally my job on this island is to look after the mammoth since I am an elephant expert. My duties as your would-be executioner, and later your babysitter, were assigned on the spur of the moment. But good luck with your mission. We are all cheering for you. I'm sure one day we'll have a good laugh about all this."

It has been over twenty years, and I am still not laughing.

As I was about to leave, he stopped me and said, "Hey Buzz, I don't know if anyone has said anything to you, but I believe you should know Ivan is on the loose. Roisin insisted we do a thorough search of the ship before you boarded. We are reasonably sure he is not stowed away waiting for you. But once the boat arrives at your destination, you had better be on your toes."

I made the mistake of asking, "Can you tell me what happened with those two?"

"Well, Ivan was becoming way too territorial and possessive of Roisin. It got to the point where they couldn't go anywhere without him getting into a near-lethal fight with someone. He once nearly killed a guy just for giving Roisin a wink as they walked by. The guy later claimed he had something in his eye and was not trying to wink at her. I believe he was telling the truth. For Roisin that was the final straw and they got into a terrible argument. Lorcan decided to intervene. He thought it might do them good to be separated for a while, so he sent Ivan out on an assignment and Roisin was sent to run the hunting camp you visited. But come to find out, Ivan never followed through with his assignment. He followed Roisin to the hunting camp and stalked her the entire time. They have guards around the place, but Ivan intimidated them into secretly letting him come and go as he pleased. Then you and Roisin met, and shortly thereafter she officially ended her engagement with him. That was fine with us because no one ever wants Ivan to come back here. But you are now in grave danger. So much so, that several of us volunteered to go with you with guns, but Lorcan said that wouldn't be necessary. I don't know what else to tell you other than be careful, and above all, remain vigilant. We suspect Ivan has gone insane. The water does that to people sometimes after several years."

I thanked him and I boarded the ship. I decided it was best not to ask him anything else.

There isn't much to say about the voyage. My stateroom was adequate, but nothing special. It consisted of a small bedroom and bathroom with no windows. There was a small desk where I ate my meals three times a day. I asked if I could walk around on deck and was told I needed to stay where I was, by order from Lorcan himself. I asked if I could have a book and they brought me an old copy of *Treasure Island*. I was getting sick of reading about islands, but it was all I had.

I had plenty of time to think as I sat alone in my room day after day, and I thought about what my next move should be. I didn't see how a successful hunt was going to be possible since any fool knows Bigfoot doesn't exist. And since I had the amulet, I was thinking I could bolt as soon as we docked. But where could I go? If what Otto said was true, Lorcan and his people would probably find me eventually.

After giving it a lot of thought, I decided I would just play along and see where this adventure was going to take me. I could always disappear and run for my life if the heat got too hot. And with this amulet, I could possibly stay away from Lorcan and his people long enough to find a corner of this world where I could hide and live out my life.

It was late at night when we finally docked. A couple of crew members came to my room and told me I was going to receive my briefing while I was still on the ship. I asked how that was going to work, and they said I would be meeting with someone the next morning in another room.

They woke me up early the next day and I was taken down the hall to a small meeting room. Sitting at a table was a burly mountain man with a big smile. He extended his hand without standing up and said, "Howdy, I'm Jake. I am here to tell you everything I know about Bigfoot. Are you ready to learn?"

I told him I was ready to hear what he had to say. This was the first time anyone had been nice to me on this voyage, so I was happy to talk with this guy even though I believed he was probably out of his mind.

He started the discussion with a question I wish he hadn't asked.

"Buzz, I want you to be honest with me, and this is a yes or no question. Do you believe in Bigfoot?"

As I have said before, I was raised to believe the Bigfoot legends were nothing but foolishness, and a densely populated country like the United States could never have a colony of apes living in its borders without everyone knowing. On the other hand, I had just seen all kinds of strange creatures that weren't supposed to exist. So, I said, "Jake, I am open to the idea of its existence."

Jake responded, "That's not a yes or no answer. I will ask you again. Do you believe in Bigfoot, yes or no?"

I wanted to get things going so I told him yes, even though I was lying.

"Why?" he asked.

He wasn't making this easy. I couldn't tell him about everything I had just seen on the islands, so I gave him a safe answer and said, "There have been reports of large hairy bipedal animals living in North America for years. I believe the stories first started with the American Indians." (Yeah, I know. The proper name is now "Native Americans", but it was the late 60s.)

"There have been reports of mermaids and unicorns for centuries as well. Do you believe in them too?" he asked belligerently.

I was getting frustrated, and it was exacerbated by the fact I desperately wanted to get off this rotten ship.

I responded, "Sir, there haven't been any sightings of unicorns or mermaids in the modern era. Those animals are pure fantasy. But I know about what happened at Ape Canyon in 1924, and I believe those miners were telling the truth."

Dad and I never believed those miners saw Bigfoot. Our theory was they were being harassed by a group of crazy mountain men dressed in bearskin or ape costumes. But my answer seemed to satisfy Jake as he said, "Good. I can't work with someone who doesn't believe what they are about to do is worthwhile. Since it sounds like you will be receptive to what I am about to say, I can help you. First, let me say I know for a fact these Night People exist, and that's what they are. In other parts of the world, apes are apes. Although the creatures you are about to encounter could also be classified as apes, I know they are closer to being human than any other member of the ape family. The Wenatchee Tribe has always called them the Choanito, which means Night People, and I call them that, even though they are sometimes seen during the day. But mainly they only come out at night. That's one reason why they are rarely ever seen.

I still wasn't sure if this man was incredibly brilliant or completely out of his mind. But I could tell he was studying my reactions as he was telling me this, so I made sure to sit up and act like I was eating this up.

"It is my understanding you are not being hired to kill one of these Night People. You are merely trying to bring one back to prove their existence by hunting with a tranquilizer gun and then firing up a flare so they can come and properly collect it. Am I correct?"

I told him he was correct, and I would not be part of this if their goal was to kill one. It then dawned on me this guy sounded far more qualified to do this than me. I asked him if he had ever been out to find one, and he pulled away from the table to show me he was in a wheelchair. His right leg was gone.

He explained, "I lost this leg in the Second World War. But I know a thing or two about wildlife in this area, including the Night People. When I was ten years old, I once caught a glimpse of one that was off in the distance. I would love nothing more than to go out there and bring one back to prove their existence to the world before we completely wreck their beautiful natural habitat, but I would never make it in this chair since they stay so far away from civilization. So now I am happy to help others who can go out there and possibly find us one. I do want to see that happen before I die."

"Can you tell me where I might be going?" I asked.

"No, they never tell me where you guys will be going. They told me you won't know either. I guess they don't want you to come back later with another group of hunters. And for some crazy reason, I am not even supposed to tell you where you are now. By the way, they wanted me to tell them if you asked where you are going like you just did. But don't worry. I won't say anything. You know, I'm starting to get the impression you're not here of your own free will. Normally they bring the hunters out to my home. This is the first time I have been brought to the hunter, and on a ship no less. Tell me, are you being held captive?"

This man was perceptive. I could have told him I was in trouble and asked for him to contact the authorities on my behalf. But I knew that would put him in jeopardy, and probably wouldn't work anyway. My chance would come, but this wasn't it. I lied and said I was not being held by these people. I then asked him to tell me everything he believed I needed to know, and he did.

"They have an incredibly foul odor. And that's one reason why I say they are close to being like humans. If a human being were to live outside all his life and never bathe, you can imagine the incredibly foul odor he would emit. Well, it's the same thing here. You will always know they are near when you smell an odor ten times more pungent than a skunk. You know, on the Indian reservations, whenever the men smell that odor, they will not allow the women to go out alone, no matter if it is day or night. That should tell you something right there."

I asked what else I should look for.

"They will sometimes communicate over long distances by letting out a long howl. We don't know why they do that, but obviously, they are telling each other something. My guess is they are letting others know there are human beings in the area, and they need to beware. That might be another good reason why they are rarely seen. I believe they have the intelligence to realize they need to stay the fool away from us. They will also look out for and avenge each other. They are especially protective of their little ones.

I believe hunters shoot them all the time. But I also believe others in the area will descend on anyone who hurts one of their own in a matter of seconds, and no trace of the hunter will ever be found except for maybe a rusty gun years later. So, if you do happen to take one down with a tranquilizer dart, you need to be extremely vigilant because others will be nearby. I can promise you that. Just fire the flare immediately and stay on your toes until help arrives. Don't try to go and study it first. I think that's where your predecessors messed up."

I still wouldn't go as far as to say I was ready to believe in Bigfoot at that point, but something was going on with these hunters. More than ever, I was glad Roisin had given me the invisibility amulet. As I was rolling that around in my mind, Jake studied me for a second and said, "You either don't believe a word I'm saying, or you are the bravest man alive. Normally when I tell a prospective hunter about all this, they freeze up in terror, but you just sit there with no emotion."

"I don't scare easily sir. Please continue," I said.

"How much do you know about tracking animals?" he asked.

I told him my father was part Cherokee and had taught me how to track any animal found in the woods. I also had extensive knowledge about hunting and fishing. Jake tested me on that. I will spare you the next couple of hours, but he finally said, "I must say you are the most experienced outdoorsman I have ever seen them send out there. I honestly believe you have the skills to track down one of these Night People–but it will not be easy."

I asked him why and he explained, "They will leave tracks when they are walking in mud and plaster casts are sometimes made from those tracks when they are found. But Night People are smart enough to realize when they are leaving too many tracks and will go out of their way to take another path to avoid doing that over a long distance. You can bet they won't leave tracks straight to their homes. They are way too smart for that. Some have speculated their tracks end abruptly because they have stepped into a different dimension or something, but that is nothing but pure bull. Whenever you see their tracks have stopped, look around closely in every direction. That's a sure sign they have realized what they were doing and changed their path. Man, are they smart."

"I have heard stories where they were very docile, almost shy. And I have heard other stories where they were brutally attacked for getting too close. Why are some different than others?" I asked.

"Each Night Person will have his or her own personality, like a human being. And just like humans, some are sensitive and non-confrontive, and others will tear you apart just for looking at them the wrong way. You just never know."

"Is there anything else?" I asked.

"Yes, as much as it troubles me to see one of these Night People taken from their home, I realize it is necessary to prove their existence to modern science. Just try not to get a small one. Even though a little one would be the easiest kind to bring back, I believe it would be best to bring in an older adult if you can."

I told him I would try, but I could not guarantee. We said our goodbyes and he left. I wished I could have gone with him.

CHAPTER THIRTY-SEVEN

Jake left the room, and I sat waiting for someone to come get me. Two large crew members walked in, and they did not look happy. The biggest one shook his finger in my face and said, "You were told not to ask anyone where you are going. Don't do that again if you value your life." I was so mad I wanted to stand up and knock their heads together, but I kept my cool.

There was a mirror on the wall and my guess is it was two-way. It was a good thing I didn't tell the mountain man to call the cops since I probably could have gotten us both killed. They left me sitting there alone for another few minutes and then someone else came in with a bowl of cold soup. I hadn't eaten yet and was glad to get it even though it was probably straight out of the can.

After I finished my pathetic meal, another (less confronting) crewmember came in and sat down. I could tell he had something on his mind. I asked him what was wrong, and he said, "Buzz, we just received word from the island that a close friend of Roisin's passed away suddenly last night, and she is beside herself." I asked him who it was, and he said, "It was someone named Nye. Do you remember meeting him?" I told him no.

"Otto has suggested it would be a good idea for her to speak to you through our short-wave radio for a few minutes," he said.

I told him I would be happy to, and they took me to their radio room. He tried for about an hour, but he couldn't get back in touch with them. They took me back to my room and I was told I would be leaving the ship in a few minutes.

I gathered my stuff and waited. Two crewmembers came in and put a hood over my head so I couldn't see. I didn't like that, but they said it was either that, or I was getting drugged again. I put on the hood.

I was led outside and put in the back of a moving van with no windows. Once I was in there, they immediately closed and locked the door. I took off the mask. It was fortunately clean, but there was nothing to sit on. I made myself comfortable sitting on my luggage. It felt good to be back on solid ground again, even though I had no idea where I was.

The van ride took three hours, and I never saw any of it. It was a good thing I had gone to the bathroom on the ship before we left because we never stopped. Towards the end of the trip, I could tell we were traveling to a higher elevation, a much higher elevation.

We arrived at our location, and they opened the door. I jumped out and the two guys who had brought me unloaded my stuff. As I looked around, the first thing I saw made me sick.

I was standing in front of a hunting cabin that looked like the one at the camp from a few months earlier, but this one was maybe one-third or one-fourth the size. I would have no problem believing they were designed by the same architect. There was a front porch filled with a bunch of mountain men, just like last time. I half expected "Big Jim" to come walking out, but this time a clean-shaven man about six foot two came walking down the steps.

He extended his hand, and said, "Hey, I'm Adler. I'm in charge here." He seemed decent enough, and he looked vaguely familiar even though I was sure we had never met.

The van driver walked over and said, "Okay Addie, he's all yours. Don't. Let. Him. Get. Away." The men got back in the van and drove away. I wanted to break the ice, so I asked, "Can I call you Addie?" He said no.

The other men came down from the porch and began collecting my suitcases. I was about to follow them, but Adler informed me I wouldn't be going inside just yet. He quietly spoke to one of his men while I noticed the surrounding terrain.

We were in the mountains, but they didn't look like the mountains I was used to in the southern Appalachians. The area looked like pictures I had seen of the Pacific Northwest, and that made sense. These days Bigfoot sightings have been reported all around the country, but they seem to have started in the northwest part of the country. Plus, Lorcan had told me I would be coming to this region anyway.

We were on the plateau of a mountain and surrounding us were mountains and trees as far as I could see. My original plan had been to bolt if they ever brought me back to the mainland, but I had no idea where I could possibly go from here. It was, without a doubt, true Bigfoot country.

As I was checking out the terrain, Adler walked over and said, "We'd like to take you out and show you some of the area before we have dinner."

That was fine with me. For the past few weeks, I had either been on a creepy island or enduring a mysterious boat ride. But here I was in my element.

Adler led me to a small gravel parking lot behind the cabin. There were no Jeeps here, just three four-wheel drive Chevrolet Suburbans, and a one-ton Ford pickup truck with a giant cage made of iron bars sitting on a flatbed and a big wench on the back. Adler pointed to the truck and said, "This is how we plan to haul a Sasquatch out of here when we finally get one." About fifty feet beyond the parking lot was a small helicopter pad. Adler pointed to it and said, "If an emergency comes up, we can call in a helicopter that will arrive in minutes. Otherwise, it's a long drive and a near-impossible walk. We are not anywhere near civilization, and you would be wise to remember that."

We got in one of the Suburbans, and he drove us around to the front of the cabin. A couple of the guys jumped in, and we took off down a dirt road. I enjoyed the scenery as Adler explained what was going to happen over the next few days.

"We acquired this property and built this compound a few years ago. This area has always been known as a hotbed for Sasquatch activity. We have seen evidence of them and even caught a glimpse once or twice, but no one has ever successfully brought one in. We normally send one of you guys out stalk hunting with a tranquilizer gun and a flare gun to get our attention when you bag one. The problem is by the time we get there after seeing the flare, the hunter and any evidence of a downed Sasquatch are typically gone. We occasionally find the tranquilizer gun or the flare gun, but that's it. Buzz, we don't want that to happen to you. So instead of sending you out alone to track one down, we have a couple of stands you will hunt from. It will be like deer hunting, and we know you have experience with that."

That didn't sound right. Otto and Jake were clear about how I would do this, and they did not mention hunting from a stand.

"Adler, my instructions were to track the animal and then get your attention by firing a flare after I knock it out with a tranquilizer gun. I know it has been dangerous for the other hunters, but I promise I will be fine until you arrive," I said.

"No, that's not how we do it anymore. The sudden light of the flare gun seems to attract them for miles," he answered.

"That doesn't sound right. I would think a sudden burst of sparks from a flare would scare them off," I said.

Adler didn't respond, but I could tell he was getting hot. The guys in the Suburban were twitching and appeared uncomfortable. They were keeping something from me. But I didn't want to start on the wrong foot, so I let it drop. We drove along in silence as he took us up to the crest of a mountain. We got out and I saw one of the most spectacular mountain views I had ever seen. It made me wish I could have brought my camera.

Adler and the guys had probably seen this view any number of times, but I could tell they were in awe of it as well. "I thought this would be a good introduction to this place," he said.

I agreed and thanked him for bringing me here, and that's when I saw it.

"HEY, I THINK A BIGFOOT HAS BEEN THROUGH HERE. LOOK AT THAT PARTIAL PRINT ON THE GROUND!" I screamed.

You could barely see it, but there in the soft earth was a partial print of an enormous heel. Adler and the guys stood right up behind me as we all crouched down and examined it. Adler wasn't convinced. "That could be anything. I don't think that's a Sasquatch print," he said.

I pointed ahead a few feet and said, "Yes, it is. Here, look at how the small grasses have been slightly disturbed as he walked this way."

"I don't see anything but grass," said one of the guys.

But I wouldn't give up. I pointed a few more feet ahead and said, "No, look how he turned in this direction. I followed the very subtle prints made by the creature in the grass until we walked up to a small patch of mud, and that's where we found the proof. Before us was the biggest barefoot print I had ever seen in my life. It was about a foot and a half long, and it was fresh. Adler and the guys looked stunned as I triumphantly pointed out my find. I thought they would be impressed, but they all looked nervous. One of the guys whispered, "I heard this one is different, but I had no idea he was this good."

Right at that moment, someone or something let out the scariest howl I had ever heard in my life. It was loud, high-pitched, and probably about half a mile away. I am no expert on Bigfoot howls, but it sounded agitated. I looked at the guys and said, "That howl came from the same direction where these prints are leading. If you can go get me a tranquilizer gun, I'll bet we can bag one right now."

That was when the smell hit me. It was like a mixture of skunk, extreme body odor, and pungent feces. "Do you smell that?" I whispered. "There is one close by. Hurry, somebody needs to get a tranquilizer gun now. Please tell me you have one in the Suburban."

Adler quietly said, "Sorry, but we don't have one with us and there is no way we can leave you here while we go get one."

"I assure you I will be safe while you are gone. Just go get a tranquilizer gun now." I quietly snapped.

"What are you planning to do? Turn invisible?" asked Adler.

I was disgusted, but I wasn't about to admit I could do that. I decided there was no point in arguing as we quietly walked back to the Suburban. I was now convinced these creatures were here and I was going to find one if I could get some cooperation. For all intents and purposes, I had just become a believer in Bigfoot.

CHAPTER THIRTY-EIGHT

I t was silent on the way back. I began to wonder if they really wanted me to find them a Bigfoot after all. Adler had cooled off by the time we got back to the cabin. He apologized and assured me we would always have a tranquilizer gun with us in the future as we went into the cabin.

The first floor consisted of a large sitting area with an old radio, like the big ones they had before televisions. Behind that was the dining area, and behind that was the kitchen. On the left side of the cabin was a staircase that led upstairs. Adler informed me dinner would be served in about an hour, and he asked if I wanted to see my room. I said sure, and he took me upstairs. My room wasn't much. It basically looked like my room at the other hunting lodge with a bed, chest of drawers, and a small private bathroom. He asked if I wanted to wait in my room until dinner or come downstairs with him and the guys. I opted to go back downstairs.

We sat around near the radio listening to some old country and western station while we talked about fishing until it was time to eat. I tried to steer the conversation towards tracking Bigfoot a couple of times, but no one wanted to talk about it for some reason. Instead, they asked me my opinions about fishing for trout, catfish, and large-mouth bass, and they offered some of their opinions as well. We had gotten off to a rocky start earlier, but I was starting to enjoy myself.

Adler came out of the kitchen with a big pot of stew, and he told us to come and get it. The stew wasn't nearly as good as Roisin's, but it was okay. It was much better than the ship food, and I was starting to feel better about being there. After dinner, we drank coffee and visited some more. I asked if they all lived here throughout the year, and the room went silent. They all looked at Adler as he answered the question.

"I stay here through most of the year. I'm kind of like a caretaker. These other guys only come up here when we are hosting a hunter. They all have other jobs in the organization they normally do."

Adler then said, "Men, I have no doubt Buzz is the one we have been waiting for."

The entire room jumped to their feet and started applauding. I felt so awkward I didn't know what to do other than sit there and smile. The conversation went dead after that and everyone began to slowly walk towards the stairs, giving me the impression it was time to turn in. I didn't feel like sleeping, so I grabbed a book from an old bookcase in the sitting area. It was *Call of the Wild* by Jack London, and I was glad to not be reading about an island. I took it to my room and read it for about an hour before I fell asleep.

I learned the next morning why everyone got tired so quickly the night before. Adler started pounding on my door at 5:00 am. "Are you ready to go find us a Bigfoot?" he screamed. That got my attention, and I told him I would be ready in a few minutes. He told me to hurry up. I wasn't sure if he heard the expletive I called him, and I didn't care.

When I got downstairs the whole room was having a breakfast of bacon and eggs. I noticed Adler was letting someone else cook this time and I was told everyone took turns cooking. I offered to help, but they said I just needed to concentrate on the hunting. After breakfast, Adler took me outside and showed me how to load and fire a tranquilizer gun. It felt good to be on the other side of one of these things. He asked if I had any familiarity with tranquilizer darts and I said, "Intimately." He smirked as if he knew what I was talking about.

Once the training was done, he drove me to a plot with a deer hunting stand. I decided to plead my case again and I said, "Look Adler, the best way for me to find a Bigfoot is to go find one. Stand hunting is probably going to be a waste of time unless you have some kind of bait. Look, just give me the flare gun and I will find you one of these things, even if it takes all day and night."

But Adler responded, "Buzz, I know they said you would be stalk hunting, but as I said last night that is way too dangerous and Roisin will have us all strung up if we let anything happen to you. Stand hunting will be safe, but effective. I promise. Here, let me show you something."

We walked about twenty yards away from the stand and in the dirt were some gigantic footprints. That put me at ease. I asked him if we were going to use bait, and he said that he was about to put out some unwrapped Hershey Bars near where we saw the prints. I walked back to the stand and climbed inside. Adler came back a few minutes later and he put the unwrapped chocolate out in the field. He also gave me a sandwich and a Thermos full of water. He left without giving me the flare gun, and I forgot to ask.

I sat there all day but never saw anything. I got out of the stand a couple of times to relieve myself, but otherwise, I just sat and waited. No Bigfoots ever showed up and I never once smelled the rotten smell.

A couple of the guys came to pick me up at dusk. It's been so long that I have forgotten their names. I'll just call them Larry and Fred.

Larry said, "I'll bet it was nice out here today."

I answered, "Yeah, I suppose so. But something dawned on me while I was out there. No one gave me a flare gun. So, if I had shot one of those things with a dart, how was I to contact you to come get it? Was I supposed to run several miles back to the cabin and get you? Or was I supposed to wait here until you finally came to get me and chance having him wake up in the meantime?"

Larry looked at his watch and said, "You know what? It's time for dinner and we're late. And I don't like being out here after dark. Let's head back. We'll take the shortcut."

If there was a shortcut back to the cabin, I wondered why Adler didn't take it earlier. But there was no point in bringing it up. I was hungry, thirsty, and ready for dinner. I had finished the water and the sandwich by mid-morning.

The alternate road back was steep, but it was a much shorter trip. I was checking out the terrain, and when we were almost at the cabin, I looked up on a hill we were passing and saw something strange. There was a small cabin with a huge television antenna on the roof. As we passed by, I asked, "Who lives in that cabin up on the hill?" Larry and Fred both sat up very straight in the front seat. They were stunned with embarrassment as Fred barked to Larry, "YOU IDIOT! WE WEREN'T SUPPOSED TO GO THIS WAY! REMEMBER?"

Larry quickly pointed out, "Well, you should have said something when I told you we were going this way. You had no problem with it at the time." Fred told him to shut up and nothing else was said.

Something was off here. I wanted to know why I couldn't stalk hunt and I especially wanted to know why I wasn't supposed to see the small cabin with the giant antenna. I decided that later in the evening I would try out the amulet and listen in on some conversations.

I planned to have dinner with everyone and act like I wasn't suspicious. Afterward, I would turn in early and go up to my room. Once I had stayed in there long enough for everyone to believe I had gone to sleep, I was going to come back down and listen.

CHAPTER
THIRTY-NINE

They were sitting down to dinner when we returned to the cabin, and I noticed Adler wasn't there. I asked where he was, and they told me he had gone to town for provisions and would be gone until the next day. We visited like we had done the night before, except for Larry and Fred who were quiet the entire meal.

When we were done eating, I announced to the room I was tired after a long day of hunting and I was ready to turn in. They all looked surprised. I guess because it was so early, but no one said anything. I said goodnight and I went upstairs. I don't know how much they could hear from the ground floor, but I decided it was best to let them hear me take a shower and then get into bed. After lying there for a few minutes, I touched the amulet and got back up. I found I was able to walk right through the closed door and down the stairs without making a sound. With the power to do this, and the added health benefits of the water, I felt like a superhero. I was also ready to kick myself for not trying this thing out on the ship. But maybe it's better I didn't. They checked on me frequently. If they had come in and I wasn't there, it probably would have been lights out when they found me.

Everyone at the table was listening to Fred as Larry sat there with his head in his hands. "I just can't believe we forgot and took the short way back. Buzz noticed the cabin right off. We need to figure out what we are going to tell Adler," Fred nervously said.

"No, YOU TWO need to figure out what you are going to tell Adler. You are the ones who made the stupid mistake," one of them responded.

The oldest one in the group walked in from the kitchen and said, "I just called Adler and told him what happened. His instructions are to tell Buzz the cabin is a radio shack for our ham radio. But we should not bring it up if he doesn't."

Larry and Fred breathed a sigh of relief but then the older man glared at them and said, "Adler wants to speak with both of you when he returns later tonight and that you should wait for him down here. The rest of us now need to go to our rooms and stay there. It'll be bedtime in an hour anyway."

Without saying a word, the rest of the house got up and went upstairs while Larry and Fred looked horrified. When everyone else had gone, Larry said to Fred, "I say we leave right now. Our supervisor said we could leave at any time if Adler started flaking out again."

Fred agreed and suggested they should let everyone fall asleep before they crept upstairs to get their things. I was going to stay and watch the events unfold since I was invisible, but then I happened to glance down at my hand. I could faintly see it coming back into view. This amulet was only going to give me about thirty minutes or so of invisibility when it was fully charged.

I needed to get back to my room fast, and I quickly walked towards the stairs. Since I was slowly coming back into view, I could faintly hear my footsteps on the wood floor. When I was at the top of the stairs, I heard Fred ask Larry, "Did you see that?"

"Yes, I did. A faintly transparent man just went up the stairs. I knew this creepy place was haunted. With all the hunters they have done away with over the years, I knew it had to be haunted by one of them—maybe all of them," answered Larry.

"I'm not staying here another second. Let's go get our things and leave now," whispered Fred.

I went to my room and closed the door. I could hear Larry and Fred quietly, but quickly, race up the stairs to their room, and then I heard them run back down the stairs and outside. Two seconds later I heard one of the Suburbans peeling out of there. I stayed in my bed, but the others were immediately out in the hall as the older man ran back downstairs and outside. He came back and announced, "Well, they're gone, but they won't get far if they keep the Suburban. Everyone, this is not our fault. Adler never told us to restrain them or watch them, but I'm sure he will wish he had. I now need to call him again and I am not looking forward to it. The rest of you go back to bed and please make sure that for the rest of this trip you follow your orders to the letter. This plan can still work, but Adler is going to be in an extremely foul mood tomorrow. So do be careful and watch your step with him. And above all, everyone please keep an eye on Buzz until we are ready to deal with him."

One of them said, "Hey, Buzz must be a pretty heavy sleeper. None of this commotion seems to have woken him up."

I was lying in bed when they knocked on the door. I sleepily asked, "Is it time to get up already?" Someone said, "No, we are just checking on you. Good night."

They all went to bed, but I was wide awake. I was worried for Larry and Fred, but I had my own problems. I now had no other choice than to follow Roisin's instructions and get away from this place if I was part of some kind of crazy plan I didn't know about, not to mention the fact they were in the habit of disposing of their hunters when they were done with them. This place was way more screwed up than I had originally thought.

I began to think about how I could get away. Stealing a Suburban would draw too much attention and they would be after me in a heartbeat. Plus, I had no idea where I was, and I didn't know the roads. Another idea would be to turn invisible and kill them all in their sleep before leaving. Although that would probably give me plenty of time to find my way out of here, my conscience and belief system wouldn't let me do that. Plus, it would be a very awkward thing to explain once Roisin and Lorcan tracked me down.

I prayed for another solution and a thought came to me. Even though they had told me we were miles from civilization, it had not dawned on these geniuses I could just follow the access road for the power lines right on out of here. It had to lead to a main road. And being able to temporarily turn invisible would make it possible to get a head start. I guess I could have left as soon as the amulet was charged, but I decided I wanted to stay a while longer. I had become convinced that Bigfoot existed, and I wanted to see one.

Normally I kept my amulet on the nightstand when I was sleeping or in the shower, but I decided I now needed to keep it on all the time. I fell asleep a few minutes later.

CHAPTER FORTY

A dler woke me up at six am. I sat up and asked, "So, is it time to take another crack at it?" I was cheerful and I think that caught him off guard.

"Yes, I'm taking you somewhere else today," he said suspiciously.

"Okay, I will be downstairs as soon as I can," I happily responded.

They were all eating their breakfast and listening to country music playing softly on the old radio. Yesterday everyone was happy and upbeat, but today the room was sullen. I didn't ask questions; I just ate my bacon and eggs without saying a word. When I was finished, I asked Adler if I could take some more food and water with me. He apologized about the day before and told me that Larry and Fred should have provided provisions throughout the day and periodically checked in on me, but they had forgotten all about it. My thinking is that Larry and Fred weren't the brightest bulbs in the box. My mother would have shaken her head and said, "Bless their hearts."

We got in the Suburban and Adler drove faster than he did the day before. He was agitated and it was coming out in his driving. When we got to the new stand, I got out, grabbed the tranquilizer gun out of the back, and got in the shooting house without saying a word. Before I closed the door, he handed me two big thermoses. One had hot coffee and the other had cold water. He also handed me a lunch box full of food. I thanked him and he left without saying much else.

He again left me without a flare gun, and I didn't bother to ask. I had a feeling I wasn't going to need it.

This house looked out on a meadow, but Adler didn't put out any bait, and I didn't expect him to. It was obvious we were just going through the motions. They had something else in mind for me, and I sat there all day wondering what it might be.

The day before I had not bothered to look around when it was time to relieve myself. But on that day, I discreetly looked around when it became necessary to step out of the shooting house. Out of the corner of my eye, I did see a Suburban on the next hill, and my suspicions were confirmed. I was not alone.

Around five o'clock I was met by two of the men and they were probably the ones who had been watching me all day. I decided to stir the pot a little and I asked if we could stop by the radio shack because I wanted to see if I could get in touch with the island and say hello to Roisin. They asked me how I knew it was a radio shack for a ham radio. I responded, "What else could it be? So can I call my girlfriend?" I wanted to drop these people a hint that if they messed with me, they would end up messing with her. They nervously looked at each other for a second and said no in unison. We got in the Suburban and rode back to the cabin. We didn't take the steep road with the radio shack.

When we got inside, I noticed Adler was gone again. I asked where he was and was told that he had gone to get more provisions. I asked why we needed even more provisions, and one of them snapped, "Just shut up and don't worry about it."

We sat down to eat dinner. No one said much of anything as we again listened to country music on the old radio. During the commercial break, we heard a news update. It was reported that two recently charred bodies were found in the woods. I perked up when I heard that, but one of the guys walked over and turned the radio off.

Once everyone had finished their meals, I announced I was going to bed early since I had been up since six am. This was becoming a pattern for me, so no one seemed surprised. I went to my room and took a shower. I then plopped down loudly on the bed so they would be sure to hear me lie down. I turned myself invisible.

I went back downstairs, and the mood was lighter. A few of the guys were playing cards and telling dirty jokes. I listened to their conversation for a few minutes, but no one said anything about me or the hunt.

I decided to take a look at the little cabin with the big antenna. If the amulet wore off while I was gone, I could just wait in the cabin or the woods until it had self-charged. I walked through the front door with no problem. I didn't see anyone outside. I also noticed that none of the Suburbans were missing. The one Larry and Fred had taken was back, and Adler had not taken one of these vehicles when he left.

Someone had either picked him up, or maybe he was still here, and the provisions story was a ruse.

I stealthily walked up to the cabin. It was extremely small inside, and there was no ham radio or anything else in there. I let my eyes adjust to the dark and then it hit me, the horrible Bigfoot smell was coming from somewhere. I went back outside, and the smell faded away. I went back in, and the smell was back, which didn't make any sense. I began to wonder if maybe there was a dead skunk under the cabin. I looked around and noticed a small handle on the floor. I pulled it up and found it was attached to a trap door.

I opened the door, and the smell was so pungent I almost fainted. I was about to close it and leave, but then I heard something. It sounded like some kind of symphonic music. I could also hear a series of yips and howls as if someone or something was reacting to what they were hearing. There was a ladder leading down into the hole, and I decided to investigate. In my haste to find out what was going on, I forgot my time of invisibility was running short.

The ladder went down about twenty feet. I slowly climbed down as the smell got more intense. At the bottom was a small cave room, and about ten feet in front of me was an opening to the area where the game was being watched. I crept up to the opening and slowly glanced around the corner. And what I saw will stay with me until the day I die.

They were watching a symphonic concert on a twenty-five-inch Zenith color television. So, the big antenna was not for a ham radio. It was for TV watching in this cave. And watching the game were twelve gigantic hairy people sitting in enormous chairs that must have been specially made. And sitting in the middle of these giant people on a very sturdy couch was Adler. He had a big clothespin on his nose, holding it shut.

I stayed off to the side and examined these enormous creatures. I couldn't get over how human they looked in their faces, but otherwise they were covered in fur from head to toe. They were also extremely muscular. They watched the concert as if they understood what was happening and they all seemed to be enjoying it. A smaller female, about five feet tall, walked in and sat down on the couch with Adler. She leaned over and put her head in his lap, as he slowly started to stroke the fur on her head.

It was all coming together. Adler had become a member of their small society, and it would be safe to assume he would not want any of them to be killed or taken away. I foolishly decided to walk out into the room to take a closer look at them. But as I slowly strolled in, one of the female Sasquatches made eye contact with me as she let out a giant howl. I was no longer invisible.

Adler turned purple with rage. He jumped to his feet and screamed, "GET HIM!" I turned and started running towards the ladder. I think I made it up about ten feet when a gigantic hand wrapped around my ankle, and I was angrily yanked back down to the floor where I was hit with a hard thud. If I had not had the extra strength benefit of the water, I believe he would have broken my back. He picked me up and threw me over his shoulder as he firmly held me in place. It was like being in a giant vice. He took me back into the room and threw me down at Adler's feet. Adler made a motion for the creature to turn me over. Once I was on my stomach, Adler jammed a tranquilizer dart right into my butt while the giant hairy man held me down. Man, I was getting sick of people doing that. Wouldn't you know it was the same cheek every stinking time? Just thinking about it makes me want to stand up.

CHAPTER
FORTY-ONE

I don't know how long I was out, but I don't think it was very long. Normally a hit from one of those darts was enough to knock me out until the next morning, but I am thinking I was only out for an hour or two. Adler had either given me a smaller dose or maybe I was developing a tolerance.

I was handcuffed with my hands behind my back and lying on the ground near a campfire. I sat up and Adler walked out of the trees. I was on my feet in a second and felt like I was still strong enough to break the cuffs. But then he pointed a .357 Magnum right at my heart, so I froze. A large contingent of Night People came out of the woods and surrounded us. There was a log behind me, and Adler motioned silently with the gun for me to sit down. He slowly sat down on a log facing me with the fire between us. He carefully put the gun down next to him.

We sat looking at each other for a couple of minutes. He finally said, "I guess I owe you an explanation."

"Okay," I said, not knowing what else to say.

"Buzz, there is no way I will ever let one of these Sasquatches ever be taken away from this place. They are my family, and I will do whatever it takes to protect them," he said.

"That explains why you wouldn't let me stalk hunt like I was supposed to. But what was the point of making me sit in a stand all day for no reason?" I asked.

"At the end of the ten days, after you had failed miserably, we thought you would be so scared for your life that you would be only too happy to tell us what we need to know," he responded.

"And what is that?" I asked.

"We are aware of your complete personality change while you were on the island. We also know Roisin took you into her room for several hours, and the next morning you were completely different," he said.

"I have no idea what you are talking about," I said.

"I believe you do, and I'm not in the mood for games. Okay fine, the guards in the castle who were watching your floor said you went into her room right before bedtime and you didn't come out until the next morning. During that time her handmaiden went in there to check on her, and you were both gone. The next morning you were different. Everyone noticed."

"How was I different?" I asked.

He huffed and said, "You went from being a crying little coward to some kind of superhero. We believe she showed you the source of the eternal water and you are now going to tell us where it is."

"Us?" I asked.

He took a deep breath and said, "I am a direct descendant of Otto. Maybe you see the resemblance. When his father died, Lorcan assumed control and the direct line of succession is now with his descendants. But that is not how it is supposed to be. Control should have been passed to Otto, but for some reason, he was never given the location of the water source. Lorcan was the only one who knew where it was at the time, so he took command. But Lorcan is slowly going senile. I heard about the way you were almost beheaded. Does dressing up like King Arthur and expecting people to take you seriously sound like something a normal person would do?"

"No, I thought it was downright crazy," I said.

"Precisely. He is the most powerful man in the world, and he is losing his mind. Did you also hear he sometimes dresses up like a Samurai warrior, and other times he likes to pretend he is a sheriff in the old west?"

"Are you sure he's not just being eccentric?" I asked.

"He has always been ruthless and evil, but playing dress up is something new. And I'll tell you something else, we suspect Roisin is losing it too. I know about the way she kidnapped you and then tortured you psychologically," he said.

"Well, it wasn't exactly like that," I said. We were getting off subject, so Adler continued his pitch.

"For years only Lorcan and one other person knew the location of the well, and that doesn't make any sense. If something were to happen to both of them at the same time, then the source of the water would be lost forever. If you did get a sip of that water, you should feel very privileged. It is not shared with everyone in the organization. Normally you have to be declared worthy of it by completing several accomplishments and passing a complicated interview process. I was told if I could play a hand in bringing a Sasquatch to their psychotic zoo, I would be guaranteed access to the water for a millennium. But as I have said, I will never let any of them be taken away. And yes, I know you were told that you would be killed if you didn't bring one back in ten days. But it doesn't have to come to that. If you could just tell me where the water is located and how to get to it, I promise nothing bad will happen to you. You can even go back to your old life like nothing ever happened if that's what you want. Lorcan will be overthrown, and he will no longer be able to hurt you."

"If you think the source of the water is at the castle, then why don't you just overthrow them and demolish the place until you find it?" I asked.

"We've considered that, and we could easily bring enough people to overthrow all of their loyalists since there are some on the island who agree with us and see that a change in leadership is needed, but it's too risky. As crazy as this might sound, we are not sure the source of the water is necessarily at the castle or even on the island itself. We have strong reason to believe they may have discovered a method of interdimensional travel through a secret portal at the castle and maybe the water comes from another universe altogether," he said.

I laughed out loud and said, "That has got to be the stupidest thing I ever heard. Yes, I drank some water during my stay on the island. I also drank tea and coffee. All of it made me feel like a new man."

He leaned over and said, "Buzz, Papa Otto told me to tell you that you needed to tell me where to find that water."

"Well, Otto told me not to trust anyone who said something like that," I smugly said.

That pushed him over the edge. He jumped to his feet, put the gun right in my face, and screamed," TELL ME THE SOURCE OF THAT WATER NOW OR I SWEAR I WILL BLOW YOUR HEAD RIGHT OFF!"

I cooly responded, "I am no good to you dead."

It was quiet for a few seconds, and then off in the trees, I heard a familiar voice say, "Adler, how about putting the gun down and letting me talk to him for a little bit? You're not getting anywhere."

It was Big Butt Jim from the camp. I was so shocked to see him that I blurted out, "Jim, you're alive."

"Yes, no thanks to you. When you blabbed to Roisin that I never told you about their ridiculous deal, she put out an order to have me killed. But a close friend sent word I was in trouble. I immediately left the camp and have been part of the resistance to overthrow Lorcan and Roisin ever since," he said.

He looked over at Adler and said, "Go back to the cabin and pull yourself together. My friend and I will talk to him. He will listen to us......if he knows what's good for him."

Adler stormed off and Jim sat down across from me. He seemed calm, but I had been around him enough to know when he was quietly seething. I decided to take the first word.

"Jim, when I told Roisin that you did not tell me about their deal, I was chained in the cargo hold of a ship with rats running around all over the place in the dark. I was scared out of my mind, and I said it by accident," I said.

"Buzz, if my friend had not warned me that Roisin was sending her father's secret security to kill me, my truck would have blown up the second I turned the key. They do things like that, and you will never know they were ever there. They know how to dispose of people. And let me tell you, their numbers are vast, all over the world. Did you hear about what happened to Larry and Fred? They didn't get far, and the vehicle they stole was returned within hours. Adler and his men didn't do that. Lorcan's secret security handled the whole thing within a couple of hours."

"Haven't they drawn the attention of local law enforcement or the government?" I asked.

"Buzz, they are in all areas of law enforcement and government. You can't get away from them, not by traveling conventionally. They are in bus stations, train stations, and airports. They are in all major cities. You may be able to run for a while, but you won't be able to run forever. If I had not joined the resistance and started living underground, away from society, I am sure I would be dead by now. My advice is for you to do the right thing and tell us where to find the secret well. If you do that, I promise you will always be protected. Helping us is the right thing to do, especially since this whole mess is all your fault," he said.

"How is any of this madness my fault?"

"Remember when you wouldn't listen to any of us when we tried to tell you the buck that sorry kid shot was lost? You wouldn't be sitting here right now if you had just listened to us. But you wanted to kiss up to your boss and be a big shot in front of all your stupid irresponsible friends who had no business hunting or using guns. And that's another thing. Weren't you the one who supposedly taught all those idiots about gun safety? Those rotten, spoiled little brats played army battle with real rifles and then a gun went off in the cabin. It's a miracle no one was killed. Here's the bottom line. Roisin never would have become obsessed with you if had just minded your own business and you never would have heard from her again."

I was quiet for a minute as I gathered my thoughts.

I finally responded, "As I recall you were supposed to have activities for those kids in the middle of the day. That was part of the deal, wasn't it? But you were so ticked off about us getting there late the night before and sleeping in the next morning, that you didn't want to fool with it. Those kids didn't have anything constructive to do, so they went outside and got into trouble. And as for the gun going off in the cabin, it was your job to make sure everyone had unloaded their guns after the hunt, not mine. I don't remember you or your men reminding anyone of that when the hunt was over. You were only thinking about dinner and going to bed since you had been up since 5:00 am. And as for that deer, if your man had just climbed down the hill and done a better job of looking around, he probably would have found it on his own. But he gave up on it too quickly because he was also ready to call it a day, even though Cecil was heartbroken. So, the way I see it, I was doing your job for you even though I was only a guest. But if you had done your job and supervised your men like you were supposed to, Roisin never would have had a reason to notice me. So, as far as I'm concerned, this is all your stupid fault."

The whole forest went silent. It was as if all the animals could sense the tension in the air. I think even the crickets stopped chirping. But regardless, I was right, and he knew it.

He then, very slowly, said, "Buzz, a few minutes ago I mentioned my good friend who saved my life and told me Roisin had sent her father's goons after me. You are now

388

going to talk with him, and I highly suggest you cooperate if you want to survive this next conversation."

With an evil smile, he gestured to his left as Ivan arrogantly walked out of the darkness.

CHAPTER FORTY-TWO

I knew I was going to cross paths with Mr. Terrible at some point on this Godforsaken trip. You had to see it coming. But I wasn't as concerned about this recent development as you might think. Throughout the previous two conversations, I felt confident I could break the cuffs, touch my invisibility amulet, and get away from this rotten place when the time was right. Honestly, I was just hanging around to hear what these idiots had to say.

Ivan asked me why I was holding my hands behind my back as if he didn't know.

I told him that I was in handcuffs, and he said, "Jim, hasn't this man suffered enough? Remove those cuffs this instant. He deserves better."

"Are you sure it's safe?" Jim asked.

Ivan very smugly said, "I'm sure, you coward. Take the cuffs off and leave us."

Jim removed the cuffs and left. I put my hands on my knees. My right hand was ready to reach for the amulet.

Once he was settled on the log, Ivan took a deep breath and said, "Buzz, I just heard your previous conversation and I agree with you. Jim and his staff did a poor job of management during your stay with them. You had every right to step in and take charge for the good of your friends, and I commend you for doing so. I also believe it is deplorable the way Roisin manipulated your superiors into sending you to an unfamiliar land where you could easily be snatched away against your will. And as if that wasn't horrible enough, that madman Lorcan sends you out here to find a Wildman, or else he was going to have you killed. It is all a complete disgrace, and I believe you have handled yourself honorably throughout this entire debacle. Again, I commend you, my friend."

Ivan's accent wasn't as pronounced when he was speaking calmly. But even though I was seeing another side of him, I wasn't fooled. This man was evil incarnate.

I replied, "Ivan, I never intended to take anything from you or anyone else. I was just trying to be a good employee on that ill-fated hunting trip, and by taking that foreign assignment."

He nodded and said, "Yes, my friend. I agree you have done nothing wrong, and I now want to help you. I feel a responsibility to make this right and give you the opportunity you so richly deserve. But first, there is something you must know. Roisin is not aware of this, but Lorcan sent me here to watch over you and to make sure you do not get away from us. He also gave instructions to finish you once you had completed your task and brought in a Wildman. One reason you are still alive is because Roisin convinced him you are fully capable of accomplishing this, and he desperately wants to find one."

"It sounds like Lorcan trusts you a great deal," I said.

"Yes, he does. After this, he is planning to send me after other animals, and he also wants me to help him recruit hunters to find other animals."

It was quiet for a few seconds and then he said, "Buzz, it is with deep regret I must also tell you he does not think you are a proper suitor for Roisin."

"Yeah, I know."

"I should also tell you how things happen here. Lorcan acquired this property since it has always been a hive for Wildman activity. It consists of thousands of acres, and for many years there have been footprints, howls, smells, and the occasional glimpse from a long distance. Adler was sent here first, and for months he reported there were no Wildmen—but that wasn't true. Adler somehow encountered the Wildmen and they became close. And unknown to Lorcan, Adler became their protector. Lorcan sent several hunters to comb the area at once, but Adler always kept the Wildmen safely away in a vast cavern system underneath our feet. Lorcan surmised he had sent too many hunters here at once, and maybe the Wildmen were being scared away. So, he decided to send contract hunters here one at a time under Adler's supervision with the promise of great fortune whether they found the creature or not. But Lorcan is such a fool he could never see what was happening. Adler killed the hunters and disposed of their bodies not long after they arrived. I know it's barbaric, but I must admit I agree with Adler. Those creatures should never be put in a zoo. That would be wrongly sentencing them to a life of imprisonment–just like those vindictive mermaids who deeply resent their confinement."

"Doesn't Lorcan ever ask what happened to the hunters?" I asked.

"Adler tells Lorcan that when the hunter fires up the flare, he and his men go out, but there is no hunter or Wildman. All they find is an empty field. Lorcan foolishly assumes the hunter and the body of the Wildman are being carried off by other Wildmen."

"That's pretty gruesome for Adler to kill people in cold blood," I said.

"Well, my friend, the hunters never would have survived anyway. Lorcan always has his contract hunters who happen to be outsiders killed at the end of their hunt, whether they are successful or not."

"Does he not want to pay them?" I asked.

"It's not that. He easily has the resources to pay them. Once Lorcan no longer has use of an outsider, he disposes of them in the name of secrecy. He has no conscience. That is how he has become the most powerful man in the world."

Ivan let that sink in for a moment.

He continued, "The other reason you are still alive is because we believe you have important information. You see my friend, although I am close with Lorcan, I am also part of the resistance. He and Roisin are too ruthless to be left in charge of such a vast worldwide network. The world must be free of his evil, but we are all kept in place because they are the only ones who know the location of the eternal water. And Adler is wrong. Otto is not a good replacement for Lorcan. He is content to be his lackey and does not desire to be in control or even to know the great secret."

"Then who is the right one to take control?" I asked.

Ivan gave me a big grin and said, "Why me, of course. If you will only tell me the secret location of the water, we can easily take control from that madman. You could be my right hand. You could be my Otto. Tell me, my friend, will you be my Otto?"

I had to agree with Ivan on a couple of points. First, the Bigfoots did not belong in any kind of zoo. It was easy to see they were much too intelligent for that. And second, I agreed that Lorcan was a madman, and the world would likely be a better place if he was gone. But I was also positive this world would not be any better off with this fool Ivan in charge. I thought about the leaders throughout history who had been deposed, only to be replaced by someone far worse.

It was time to bolt, but before leaving I had to say, "Even if I did know the location of the water you speak of, I would never tell a crazed maniac like you where to find it. Roisin was right to leave you. She doesn't love you anymore and I doubt she ever will again. Regardless of what her father might want, Roisin loves me now. And you are powerless to change it."

Ivan gave me an incensed look of rage as he slowly stood up. It was time to leave, so I reached into my shirt to touch the amulet, but it wasn't there. It was gone!

"Are you looking for this you little fool?" he asked as he triumphantly held it up.

I then began to rethink everything I had just said in the previous few minutes. Man, I must have the most rotten luck in the entire world. He studied the amulet for a few seconds and said, "I do believe this amulet belonged to her horrible sister. It would have been so much easier if you had just told me the location of the water, but I will learn the secret with this. I will return to the island and covertly follow Roisin to the legendary place. Once I know how to access the well, I will kill Roisin, Otto, and Lorcan. The island and then the world will be mine. I can't believe the irony of being able to do this with her sister's special amulet since I am the one who caused her to die."

"You did what?" I asked in shock.

"One day when she thought she was alone watching those evil mermaids, I saw my opportunity and pushed her into the tank with them. It was so satisfying to watch her die slowly and painfully."

"How could you do such a horrific thing?" I gasped.

He shrugged and said, "She never liked me anyway. And it was all part of my plan to get Roisin away from the camp and back to the island where she wouldn't be distracted by other men. Roisin was next in line to be the keeper of the well, and I knew Lorcan would summon her back immediately if her sister were to meet an untimely demise. After the night I saw Roisin with you looking for that blasted deer and then later at the cabin in front of the fire, I secretly returned to the island and waited for the right opportunity to kill her sister."

He said all of that with no emotion at all, like an unfeeling monster. As I thought about what he had just said, I had to know how he was able to secretly get on the island and do that horrible thing.

"You returned to the island without anyone knowing you were there? And without the help of an invisibility amulet?" I asked.

"Oh, I had help on the island. Everyone who works there loves me and wants me to rule someday," he boasted.

I knew full well that was a lie. If anyone helped him while he was hiding out on that trip, it was out of intimidation. But I just let him talk. I needed for him to be briefly distracted.

"After I dealt with her sister, I immediately left to avoid any suspicion. To my knowledge, no one knows what actually happened to her or that I had anything to do with it. I proceeded to my assignment in Mongolia to find that ridiculous death worm, which I am now reasonably sure doesn't exist. Thereafter, I was going to return and offer comfort to Roisin over the horrible and sudden demise of her dear sister. She would then take me back and finally become my bride. And once we were married, she was going to submit to my authority and show me the location of that well."

There were so many things wrong with that, I didn't know where to begin. But I continued to let him keep talking. I was almost ready.

"I thought surely Roisin would be done with you once she had returned to the island, but then she hatched that foolish plan to bring you to her. My operatives in the organization informed me she had summoned you, and I immediately traveled to your city to warn you."

I couldn't let that one go, and I blurted out, "You weren't there to warn me. You showed up to kill me because I had inadvertently gotten in your way. You gave me the cutthroat sign."

"If you had just come over and spoken to me like a man when we were out in the street that day, I would have warned you not to take the offer. But you ran away like a child, so I decided talking to you man-to-man was not going to be possible. Then that fool Lorcan tracked me down and sent word he wanted me to go find a thunderbird in the American West. And I can tell you with certainty those things do not exist. I wandered around in the steaming heat until I was told Roisin was in the process of bringing you to the island."

"Why didn't you just walk up to me that day in the street, introduce yourself, and talk to me like a normal human being? Why did you have to follow me around and act creepy like that? I thought I was about to get mugged. Then, when I was taken against my will to the island, you had to show up and be pathetic about it. Did you think acting so foolish was going to win Roisin back? I wish you could have heard yourself. It was an embarrassment. And I know for a fact the people on that island do not want you to ever return. They like me better. They told me so," I said.

He stared at me for a second, shook his head, and said, "I still can't believe she cast me aside for a fool like you. Don't you realize you could have been free long before now? You could have walked away the moment you stepped off the ship. But you do not know how to use this precious device because you are weak and lack the courage to do what needs to be done when the moment arrives."

He then looked down to study the amulet and didn't notice I was discreetly reaching for a big piece of wood sticking out of the fire. Once I had a good grip on it, I jumped to my feet and went upside his face with the lit end as hard as I could. The burning tip caught him right in the eyeball. He grabbed the side of his face and let out a loud wail of pain as he dropped the amulet and fell to the ground.

I don't know what the Night People thought he was saying to them, but they were still standing around in the trees and responded with a collective wail of their own. It was the loudest unified sound I had ever heard in my life and my ears rang so bad I started getting dizzy. But I still had the presence of mind to pick up the amulet and put it on. I had used it up earlier and it had not yet fully charged, but I was hoping it had built up enough juice to turn me invisible for a few minutes at least. Adler and Jim came running to see what the commotion was. As they were watching Ivan roll around on the ground in intense pain, I stealthily walked over and punched each of them in the side of the head as hard as I could. I don't think I killed them, but I am sure I gave them each a skull fracture and a concussion since I felt bone cracking in my knuckles upon impact.

I didn't mean to hit them so hard. I guess I was still getting used to having increased strength. When Ivan and Jim had fallen, the Night People just stood around looking very concerned. But when Adler hit the ground, they went into hysterics. They ran around in different directions trying to figure out what was happening, making all kinds of strange sounds. I had to get out of there fast.

I went in the direction Adler and Jim had come from and found we were not far from the cabin. The rest of the men were running towards me with guns, but they ran right past me since they couldn't see me. I ran up to the power lines and down the clean-cut access road to sweet freedom.

CHAPTER
FORTY-THREE

I followed the access road for several miles in the dark, knowing it had to lead to a main road at some point, making it the most likely route to civilization. The invisibility amulet gave out after about ten minutes, but that was enough time. For the first time in several weeks, I was free. I didn't know precisely where I was and I had no idea how to call for help, but I was finally free.

I didn't bother with my luggage at the cabin, but I didn't leave anything that couldn't be replaced. My wallet and passport had been taken before I woke up on the first ship and I never bothered to ask for them back. But the passport and the contents of my wallet could also be replaced.

I knew going back to the city was a bad idea since that would be the first place they would look for me. But I had left some pictures of my parents in the storage facility, and I wanted to get them if I could. My backpack and some of my clothes were in there as well. I had the key to the storage facility hidden in one of my shoes, and fortunately, they never found it. I also had a hundred-dollar bill hidden under the sole of each shoe.

After what happened to Larry and Fred, I knew traveling by conventional means was not an option, at least not around here. But before I could come up with a travel plan, I first needed to know where I was. When I found the main road, I looked to my left and saw nothing but darkness, the kind of darkness that eats up any kind of light. I looked to my right and saw the very faint lights of a city off in the distance. I went in that direction. I stayed on the side of the road and off in the trees as much as I could. I hit the ground whenever some kind of vehicle went by, which wasn't often.

About four hours later I finally arrived at a small town that was completely deserted. I saw the town clock and it was just after midnight. I found a newspaper box and learned precisely where I was. I now needed to travel two thousand miles east without drawing any attention, but I didn't know how I was going to do that. I considered stealing a motorcycle or a car, but I didn't feel right about doing that.

That was when I heard a train whistle off in the distance, and it fortunately turned out to be a cargo train. I found the tracks right off the main square and I waited for it. It slowed down as it traveled through town, and I jumped into one of the open box cars. I didn't know precisely where I was going, but it was heading east, and that was what I wanted. The box car was empty, and I quickly fell asleep.

When I woke up, it was morning and the train had stopped. At some point, four other passengers joined me. It was jarring to find I wasn't alone, but they told me to take it easy. They didn't want any trouble, and they turned out to be helpful. I told them where I needed to go, and they had some good advice as to how I could get there by riding the rails. They also explained how to avoid the railroad security, but I was planning to use the amulet if I ever ran into any of those guys. They told me their life stories, but they didn't ask any questions about my situation.

I rode the rails for the next few months, and it was a rough and dirty trip. Sometimes I would get on a train and later find it had taken me hundreds of miles further from my destination than where I had been the day before. I was wearing durable hunting clothes, which was good because that was all I had. I was later able to pick up a cheap coat at a second-hand store. It smelled like moth balls, but it was warm. My money eventually ran out and I had to panhandle a few times so I could eat.

I got lucky towards the end of my journey when I came across two elderly women whose car wouldn't start. They had corroded battery terminals and I asked if they had a bottle of soda. They did, and I was able to partially clear some of the corrosion. They were so grateful when the car started, they gave me fifty dollars. I explained it was only a temporary fix and that they needed to find a mechanic who could properly clean the terminals, but they were just glad to not be stranded anymore. I'm sure they felt sorry for me as well.

Since I hadn't showered or shaved in a while, I became too embarrassed to go into any kind of eating place when I had money, even a cheap diner. I would often grab a small bite to eat from a street vendor in the middle of the day. I think they also felt sorry for me because they often wouldn't let me pay if I didn't order much. I didn't think anyone from Lorcan's security detail could track me under those circumstances, but I was glad to have a full beard and mustache with hair down to my shoulders.

A few times I jumped on a railcar and was spotted by the railroad security. They were shocked when they climbed in and found no one in there. Then there was the time three big guys climbed in the car with me. They were quiet at first. But after we were moving, they told me to give them all my money. When they moved in to collect, they became hilariously terrified when I faded away right before their eyes. They immediately took their chances and jumped out of the car, even though we were moving kind of fast. Hopefully, that scare made them give up a life of crime, provided they survived the jump.

It was about two a.m. when I finally reached the city. As I walked through those deserted streets, it felt like I had been away for years even though it had only been about seven months. I was about to give out when I made it to the owner's building with the basement storage facility. It had a secluded door at ground level that could be accessed from the alley behind the building.

The place was climate-controlled, and it was comfortable in there. I collapsed on my old couch, and it felt good. Even though this place wasn't a home, at the time it sure felt like one. I fell asleep as my head hit the throw pillow. I used my old coat as a blanket.

CHAPTER
FORTY-FOUR

The next morning, I knew I needed to go by the company and attempt to explain what had happened to me, even though they were probably going to have me hospitalized for possible brain trauma after telling such a ridiculous story. Maybe I didn't have to tell them everything, but I at least needed to let them know I was alive. The owner did promise to put me up in a five-star hotel, and that would have been nice while I was trying to figure out what to do next.

I packed some clothes and the pictures in my backpack. I still had my mother's gold jewelry I had planned to give to my future wife, but now I was thinking it was best to sell it. I hated to part with it, but I desperately needed money. I walked down the street to a pawn shop and sold it all for a fraction of what it was worth. I then headed towards work.

The front doors were locked when I got there. I looked inside and the place was deserted. Every bit of furniture was gone, and the lights were out. This scared me. Where was everybody? Surely, they didn't have the whole company killed.

I walked down to the local YMCA that I had stayed in when I first got here and explained I was hitchhiking and camping across the US. Having a backpack helped sell the story. They let me in on one condition. I had to immediately take a shower, which I was happy to do. After that was done, I left my backpack in my small room, where they promised it would be safe. I decided the next thing to do was ask the Y if I could use their phone and borrow a phone book.

First, I tried to call the owner, but the line was disconnected. I then called my supervisor, Sam, and everyone else I could think of. The numbers were either disconnected or they just rang and rang without an answer.

It dawned on me there was a small sandwich shop across the street from the job where several people in the company used to eat all the time. I headed over to get a sandwich. It was the first time I had eaten like a normal person at a table in a real restaurant in months. There was hardly any lunch crowd, so the cook wasn't busy. I asked him what had happened to the business across the street, and he explained, "They were bought out by some foreign company several months ago. The way I heard it, the owner was in the Orient on some kind of emergency trip when he died suddenly. They think it might have been a heart attack due to extreme stress. Within a week of the funeral, some foreign investors contacted his family and made a generous offer to buy the company. His heirs were only too happy to accept, and they moved away. But then something strange happened. Once the transfer of ownership had been finalized, the company was immediately shut down, and all those poor people lost their jobs. I guess by now they have all scattered to the wind, and I sure hate it. Business hasn't been the same. I wish somebody would move in there."

I thanked him for the information, and he went back to the kitchen. I sat and ate my sandwich as I let that sink in. Lorcan could have had him killed, but the owner did have a lot of health problems. He didn't take good care of himself, and the doctor had been warning him to lose weight and stop smoking for years. He may well have had a real heart attack, but who knows? I wasn't even sure the owner's family still owned the building where my stuff had been stored. It's a good thing the key still worked, and my things were still in there undisturbed.

That afternoon I went back to the Y and shot some pool by myself in the rec room. It was the most relaxing afternoon I had had in months, and it gave me some time to think about what my next move should be. Do I try to set up my life again, and then pray no one hunts me down and kills me in my sleep? Or do I just keep living as a transient laborer for the rest of my life and never use my real name and social security number? I considered the various scenarios.

If Lorcan remained in charge, I am sure he would still want me out of the way, providing he could keep Roisin from finding out he had put out the order to have me killed. If the resistance were to take charge, they would probably want to hunt me down and torture me until I revealed the secret location of the well. And assuming those three idiots could still lead normal lives after surviving my attack, I am sure they would each want me dead regardless of who was in charge.

And then there was Roisin. I had no way to warn her about Ivan. She needed to know what had really happened to her sister, and there was no way to tell her. It sounded like she wasn't even safe from the guards outside her room or her handmaid, whoever that was. Plus, Ivan was part of a secret plot to overthrow her father, while Lorcan is trying to set him up to be his son-in-law. The whole thing was mind-boggling. Maybe I should have stomped Ivan's head in at the camp when I had the chance, but the only thing I was thinking about at the time was getting away. That, and I am not sure it is in me to intentionally take the life of another human being, even when they want to kill me. Maybe I am pathetic.

I guess Roisin made a tactical error by not giving me some kind of private plan for reaching out to her if something went wrong. But I am sure she would be okay with everything I had done up until that point. Running away was precisely what she had wanted me to do, and I never told anyone where to find the water. I never even confirmed she had shown it to me.

I then started thinking about my crazy Aunt Nora who believed thunderstorms on a trip were a bad omen. She had once said the entire world was being controlled by a secret empire led by a crazed madman who lived on a private island out in the middle of the ocean. To my knowledge, no one in the family ever bothered to ask her where she got that from since they all thought she was crazy, but maybe she wasn't crazy after all. Maybe those little superstitious beliefs she used as an excuse for changing her trip plans were just a ruse so she could get away from an area she didn't think was safe. Maybe she was running away from this organization as well. It made me wish I could track her down and compare notes, but by now she was probably dead of old age if nothing else.

I also couldn't help but second-guess every decision I had made that led to me getting into this ridiculous mess. Jim said this was all my fault because I refused to let them give up on the deer, but that was wrong. Insisting I get a crack at finding the deer was the right thing to do. My co-worker and his kid were heartbroken, and the owner had paid a lot of money with the expectation everyone would have a good hunt.

I also considered maybe the company and I shouldn't have taken a deal with so many mysterious strings attached. But even if we had turned it down, I'm sure Roisin would have tried something else to have me taken away.

After much thought, I had to admit to myself my key mistake was when I didn't take Ivan's boat and sail out to freedom when I had the chance, but my curiosity about what was in those last two enclosures had gotten the best of me. I don't know where I would have ended up if I had made it to the ship, but Otto seemed to think it would have been a clean getaway. I guess the lesson here is when you are kidnapped and have even the remotest chance to escape, you should take it—as fast as you can and don't stop for anything.

As I bounced all of that around in my mind, I had another idea. Sam and I used to eat at a restaurant specializing in Hong Kong cuisine. He had grown up with the owner, and I was sure the guy would know where to find him. I knew where I now wanted to eat dinner.

And sure enough, the owner recognized me the second I walked in the door, even with the long hair, beard, and mustache. He asked me how I had been, and I had no idea how to answer that. He already knew what I was going to order, and it was the best meal I had eaten in months. While I was eating, he commented I had gotten way too skinny, and I didn't argue. After dinner, he came over and sat down, and I casually asked about Sam.

He explained that several months ago Sam was in Hong Kong on a special business trip when his supervisor, who happened to be with him, passed away suddenly of a heart attack. During the trip Sam decided to take a position with another company in London. He and his wife quickly relocated, and they were doing very well. That was all he knew.

It sounded like Sam was going to escape this debacle, and I was happy to know that. I went back to the Y and had a long night's sleep in a bed I normally would have found uncomfortable.

I had a revelation the next morning. I couldn't be sure anything Jim had told me was true, but he did say Lorcan's people were mainly in the big cities. So, I figured I might be safe in my hometown. It was the late 60s and back then it was easier to get away from people. I called my attorney friend and asked if he still had a job for me. He asked how soon I could get back.

I was sick of riding cargo trains as a stowaway. My appearance had changed so much I didn't think I would have any trouble traveling home by passenger train, and I was right. I got back to my hometown the next day. I went straight to my attorney's office, and he almost didn't recognize me as he commented I looked much older than when he last saw me. I was still young enough to take a comment like that as a compliment, but I guess the previous couple of years had taken their toll. He told me I could start work as soon as I got a shave and a haircut.

Six years went by, and I lived peacefully and frugally. My heightened senses and increased strength eventually went back to normal, but I had expected that. Working as a paralegal didn't pay much, but it paid the bills, and it was somewhat interesting. I rented a mobile home in a local trailer park right outside of town. It was an easy walk to my job, the grocery store, and anything else I needed.

I saved my money, and I was finally able to buy a Mustang. It was a few years old, and it had some engine problems. But I didn't pay much for it and I was happy to finally have one. I could get it to start, but it needed some work before I could take it out on the road. Since I was going to need to work on it outside, I decided to wait until the weather got warmer and I continued to walk to work. I maybe had it for about a month before I lost it.

One Saturday evening I went to visit with a buddy from high school who also lived in the park. When I walked in and sat down, he asked, "Hey Buzz, this afternoon I was talking to our neighbor Mr. Tillery. He was driving past your place around five am one day last week and he saw some hippie messing with your car. Did he ever say anything to you about it?"

I told him no and I was aggravated Mr. Tillery had not spoken to me about it. People in our little mobile home community never wanted to get involved. I figured this "hippie" must have been planning to steal it and decided not to fool with it, or maybe he was stealing some parts. Regardless, I was planning to give the car a good once-over the next morning in the daylight. The conversation went on to other things, and then about an hour later, we heard it.

BOOM!!!

I and the rest of the park ran outside. My Mustang was engulfed in flames. Some unfortunate man had been under the hood trying to hot wire it and another man was running away for dear life. We called the Sheriff, and they had no problem finding the guy. He was sitting on the side of the road crying about a mile away. Later that night a deputy picked me up and took me to the Sheriff's Office. After talking with him I knew my life as I knew it was over.

"Buzz, two men attempted to steal your car this evening. One was trying to hotwire it and the other was his lookout. The lookout man freely admitted this. But apparently someone else had rigged your car to explode when the ignition was started, and that's what I want to talk about. We spoke to some of your neighbors, and last week a couple of them saw a very large, dark-haired man with long hair, a full beard, and an eye patch lurking around near your home just before sunrise. I wish someone had called us because that description does not fit anyone who lives in your neighborhood. Do you know who the man might be?"

I told him no.

"Are you sure? I was hoping you would be able to identify him."

I again told him no.

"Are you sure?"

"Yes. I am sure."

"Do you know of anyone who would want to kill you?"

I again told him no, but I don't think he believed me.

"A car will patrol your neighborhood regularly for the next couple of nights. I think we should also find another place for you to stay while we try to apprehend this individual," he said.

I thanked him and said that I could probably stay at my supervisor's office. He had a small couch in the breakroom, and I was sure he would be okay with me sleeping on it temporarily. The Sheriff called my attorney friend, and he insisted I be taken to a motel in a nearby city for a few days while they were getting to the bottom of this. The attorney volunteered to pay for the motel. The Sheriff agreed that was a good idea and one of the deputies took me back to my place. He came in with me while I loaded my backpack with some clothes, some provisions, and the pictures of my parents. He asked if I was planning to take any more luggage or anything else. I told him the backpack was all I needed. He drove me to the motel.

I was constantly looking behind us the entire time and I was scared to get out of the car. He assured me a police officer would be outside my door all night. I went inside and turned off the light so they would think I had gone to sleep.

Around three in the morning, I heard a train whistle off in the distance. I sneaked out the back bathroom window and ran over to the railroad tracks with my backpack. I waited for it to pass by, and I took it right out of there. I didn't know where I was going, but it didn't matter. I just needed to get as far as I could from that place, and never stop. I have been a transient worker who never gives his real name or social security number ever since.

My guess is Ivan was able to track me down because I was foolish enough to return to my hometown, use my social security number, and live under my real name. And I would also guess Lorcan must have sent him after me, but who knows? Ivan might have just been trying to settle the score. Plus, he had foolishly made me a serious loose end by bragging about killing Leela. Lorcan would surely change his opinion about him if he knew. I am sure Ivan would have ended up in that torture dungeon or fed to something. But even if I could contact Lorcan and let him know, would he even believe me? Roisin would, but Lorcan might not.

But it was all a moot point. There was no way for me to contact them directly. The only thing I knew to do was to keep running for dear life and pray no one close to me ends up becoming collateral damage.

I wish there was some way to make them believe I'm dead, but I don't know how I would pull that off short of killing someone and leaving a burnt corpse where they thought I was staying. And there is no way I would ever do that.

I now live my life constantly looking over my shoulder, and I never stay in one place long. I don't even visit my parents' graves because I wouldn't put it past them to keep a watch on the place twenty-four hours a day, seven days a week. I sometimes think about Roisin and I do wish I knew what happened to her, but I guess I will never know. Since she never tracked me down like she promised, I fear she was killed. But on the other hand, I have no idea how she would find me. I've become a master at living off the grid. I also sometimes wonder what the third island was all about, and why Otto didn't want me to go there. But I guess I will never know about that either.

In the years since I have slept under bridges, in back alleys, and in condemned buildings. The little cabin where I now live is luxurious compared to what I am used to. And every morning when I wake up, wherever I am, I pray, "Lord, help this poor soul."

CHAPTER FORTY-FIVE

Pap, Dad, and I sat there in stunned silence for several minutes. Had I not met Burt Russell or Ivan the Terrible, or whoever that maniac was, I would have thought Buzz was just another drifter with a wild imagination.

Dad finally broke the silence and asked, "Buzz, do you have any idea how the locals found out about Joey's meeting from the day before? And how they were able to get a few details completely right and other details completely wrong?"

Buzz explained, "Yes, I believe I know what happened there. While I was in the diner waiting for my monthly cheeseburger and fries, George Bailey came in and announced to the room that his wife had just heard something at the beauty parlor. According to her, one of the instructors from the junior college was getting his hair cut and told his hairdresser all about your secret hunting trip and all that money."

"Well, that's weird. How did he know about it?" I asked.

"I don't know. He never told us that part. But although the instructor knew about the trip and the money, he couldn't quite remember the name of the man you had met with. He said the last name was Russell, but he couldn't remember the first name. The hairdresser asked if it was Kurt Russell and the instructor mistakenly confirmed it was. Mrs. Bailey was eavesdropping in the next chair, and afterwards, she went home to tell her husband. Mr. Bailey decided he wanted in on it and convinced himself you owed him a shot at the opportunity. He was going to come over to your house and make his pitch, but he remembered you slept during the day until sometime after lunch, so he went by the diner to kill some time. While he was there, he started running his mouth about your good fortune. Then, as luck would have it, you just happened to come in for breakfast."

"So how did the mention of Ted Nugent become involved in this?" asked Dad.

Buzz explained, "The number one important detail about this story was the money. The name of the person Joey met with was beside the point. Kurt Russell and Ted Nugent are both famous entertainers who like to hunt. Someone must have confused them when they repeated the story. I believe that's what led to all those misguided teenagers roaming around town with those record albums and permanent markers."

"And Mrs. Banks had nothing to do with this?" I asked.

"Are you talking about Josie Banks who works up at your college? What would she have to do with any of this?" asked Buzz.

I told Buzz about what had taken place in Dr. Seavers' office. When I'd finished, I asked Buzz if he knew someone named "Burt Russell." He said no. Buzz asked me to describe Russell. I did, and he said, "If Ivan is still having to recruit hunters after all these years, I guess that means he never got control. I would love to know who is in control, but there is no way for me to find out without blowing my cover. Speaking of which, it's time for me to go."

As he walked towards the door, Pap grabbed his arm and said, "Sir, now that we know about all this, we promise we will never tell anyone your story. You can count on that."

Buzz responded, "You can write a book for all I care. You won't be seeing me around here again. No one will."

He turned and walked into the night without saying another word. We went to the door to watch him walk away, but he had already vanished without a trace once we got out there. We didn't even hear his footsteps in the darkness. For several seconds we stood there astonished as we listened and looked out into the night. But there was nothing there, just silence.

We went back inside. Pap shut the door behind us, took a deep breath, and said, "Well, I have heard some fool stories in my day, but that had to be the biggest bunch of malarkey I have ever heard. Mermaids? Giants? Dinosaurs? Bigfoots? People living forever by drinking funny water? What kind of fools does that old redneck think we are?"

I tried to respond, but Pap cut me off mid-sentence as he stuck his finger in my chest and said, "Boy, don't you ever think about leaving this town again without saying something to somebody. I don't care how mad you get at us. Understand?"

I told him I understood.

After a few seconds of awkward silence, I looked down at my watch and it was three in the morning. I wanted to go see what was left of my home, but it made sense to wait until daylight. There was also no point in going to bed since we were all too keyed up to sleep. We went up to Pap's place to wait for daylight.

We sat around his kitchen table drinking coffee for the next couple of hours. I had not eaten a real meal in a couple of days, so Dad cooked up some hot dogs.

The three of us then had a serious talk. First, Dad offered to let me stay in my old room while my home was being rebuilt, which was a huge relief. We also talked about our argument from the year before. Pap took the lead.

"Joey, your daddy and I didn't mean to hurt your feelings when we confronted you with the fact that you like to sleep all day. We also didn't mean to give you the wrong impression when we told you we wanted you to pursue a different type of career," he said.

"I thought you were ashamed of me because I work as a janitor," I said.

"No, nothing could be further from the truth. There is never any shame in honest work. We're proud of you. You never gave your teachers any trouble, and they always said your writing skills were superior to everyone else. Plus, you were not a difficult kid to raise. You always did what you were told, and we never had to tell you to do your homework."

Then Dad chimed in and said, "Joey, we know you work hard down at the college. Seavers told your grandfather you do the work of three people."

I looked at Pap and asked, "You know Dr. Seavers?"

"Yes, Joey. He and I went to high school together. I made better grades than he did. I used to help him with his homework. I don't think he would have aced twelfth-grade math if it hadn't been for me."

I was shocked. All this time I had no idea my grandfather and Dr. Seavers were friends. I also never knew my grandfather had such an interest in school, but I knew he was smart. He had started as a carpenter for a construction company and ten years later he was an independent building contractor.

Pap continued, "I could have gone to college. Seavers and I had talked about being roommates in the dormitory. Then your great grandfather died unexpectedly during my senior year of high school, and I had to quit to help support my mother and younger sisters. I now want you to do what I couldn't do. That's why I called Seavers and asked if he could find a place for you at the college during your senior year. He told me he would have someone contact you, but he misunderstood. He thought I was asking him to find you a job. But what I really wanted was for him to help you get started with classes."

Dad jumped in and said, "Joey, it's not too late. You haven't settled down with a wife, and you don't yet have a family to look after. Since you still have plenty of free time on your hands, we want you to at least think about starting in college and seeing how it goes."

As I sat back and thought about it, I noticed the sun was slowly beginning to rise over the mountain. I was ready to go see what was left of my home.

CHAPTER
FORTY-SIX

There wasn't much to see, just some smoldering embers. The air was still heavy with smoke and ash, making it hard to breathe when we got close. Everything I owned was gone. Even now I can't bring myself to list everything I lost. I started getting furious, so Pap and Dad gently guided me back to the car.

They wanted to take me back to my parent's place, but I asked if we could go find Buzz's cabin. I realized I never thanked him for calling the cops. We had to ask around before we found someone who knew where it was, and it was hard to find. But it was deserted when we finally found it. There were no personal items, just the bed, table, chair, and stove.

Buzz was never seen in town after that. For a while, a story floated around he was run over by a hit-and-run driver while walking on the side of the highway. Others heard he was wanted for murder and had been running from the police for years. He was finally picked up in a neighboring county and later killed in prison. I was hoping none of that was true, but there was no way of finding out for certain since none of us ever knew his real name. Those stories could have been about someone else who went by the same nickname, or maybe they were just stories made up by people who wanted to look like they were in the know. As time went by, he was eventually forgotten and never mentioned again.

We got back to my parents' place at 10:00 am. My feelings of anger over what had just happened were consuming me, but I was also being overtaken by exhaustion. I needed to sleep in a real bed. But first, I wanted to have words with Dr. Seavers. It was bugging me that the instructor knew all about our meeting and I wanted to know why. I called the office and Mrs. Banks answered.

"Honey are you okay?" she asked. I told her I was safe, but I was far from being okay. She told me she was sorry about what happened, and she would be praying for me. I thanked her and she patched me through to Seavers. I could hear the embarrassment in his voice as he explained what happened.

Dr. Seavers went to his scheduled monthly staff meeting with the instructors after we met with Mr. Russell. In his excitement, he couldn't resist telling them the college was about to receive five million dollars. That led to several questions, so he went ahead and told them about me and my proposed hunting trip. The agenda for the meeting was quickly abandoned as an argument ensued among the instructors and administrators over how the money should be allocated. The instructors who didn't need any supplies or equipment for their teaching wanted a raise across the board for everyone at the college, opportunities for sabbaticals, and better scholarship opportunities for the students.

That seemed like a logical plan, but there were instructors, such as Mr. Jones who taught the automotive courses, who desperately needed new materials and equipment. Jones, for example, needed a new lift and diagnostic equipment so he could better show his students how to do wheel alignments. He was told point blank he would not be getting that, and he stormed out of the room. The meeting broke up soon after. In all the excitement Seavers didn't think to tell anyone it was all confidential. The next morning Jones vented his frustration to his hairdresser, and the secret was out. He also told me Mr. Russell had called his office that morning right before I did and told him he was aware it was him who had let the secret out, and not me. Nevertheless, the offer was hastily withdrawn.

"So, Mrs. Banks knew nothing about it?" I asked.

"No, Mrs. Banks just happened to be pouring herself a cup of coffee from the coffeemaker next to my door. When she took a sip, some of it went down the wrong pipe and she coughed it up on the door frame. She was merely cleaning up her mess when I opened the door and had not heard anything. Joey, this was all my fault, and again, I am sorry."

If there was any truth to Buzz's story, then losing this deal was not the worst thing that could have happened. But I nonetheless was almost killed by the locals because Seavers had spilled the beans, and I pointed that out as I screamed, "THOSE MANIACS TRIED TO KILL ME, AND THEY DESTROYED EVERYTHING I OWNED."

I no longer cared if I offended him and lost my job. There is nothing like having an angry mob chase you through town with guns and knives to help you put things into perspective.

But Seavers didn't get mad. He was almost crying as he said, "Yes, Joey. I know. I thoughtlessly ruined an opportunity of a lifetime for you, and I nearly got you killed doing it. I wouldn't blame you if you were to quit right now. But before you do, I really would like to send you down to my beach house for a month. I also want to give you a fifteen percent raise."

I went ahead and accepted his offer. I still needed a job, and he didn't know the offer was probably going to get me killed–assuming Buzz was telling us the truth, and I believe he was. I could have told him all about Buzz, but Seavers had a big mouth, and if Russell, or Ivan the Terrible, or whoever that maniac was, was still hanging around and learned that we had spent time with Buzz, I figured we would all be in danger. I also knew I would get the royal treatment from Seavers for the rest of the time he was there if he believed he had blown a multimillion-dollar deal for me. I was about to fall asleep on my feet and ready to end the conversation, but then Seavers said something else.

"Joey, before Mr. Russell hung up, he asked me about some guy nicknamed Buzzcut or Buzzsaw or something like that. Do you know anyone around your little town who goes by that nickname?" he asked.

I was stunned. I didn't say anything at first, but then I pulled myself together enough to say, "No. I don't know anyone who goes by either of those names."

"Are you positive?" he persisted. "Apparently, he is a mountain man drifter or some such. Does the name not sound at all familiar to you?"

"No," I said.

"Well, that's a shame. Mr. Russell wants to find him."

"Why?" I asked.

"Well, when someone named Bailey burst into the diner to tell everyone about your special deal, it was told this mysterious mountain man muttered an expletive and blurted out something about a death trap. But no one heard exactly what he said."

"How did Russell find out about that?" I asked.

"Someone in the diner told the police about it. He also told me the local police wanted to help Mr. Russell find this man. Mr. Russell suspects he might be the man who caused him to lose his eye many years ago. He also said this man killed two of his friends in cold blood. You know, this might be a good way to get back in Mr. Russell's good graces. Are you sure you don't know him?"

I again said no, and I changed the subject by asking when I could come pick up the key to his beach place.

***

I went back to work when my four weeks at the beach were over. Seavers let me bring my parents, but my grandparents wanted to stay behind and supervise the building of my new home which was now going to be in proximity to my parents and grandparents. It would not have as many windows, and it was going to be made of brick and cinderblock. It was a good time to get away from town.

And on a side note, a friend told me what happened when Ivan the Terrible showed up at my place at midnight to pick me up. He was furious when he encountered a large group of people with lanterns begging to go on the trip. He immediately asked where I was and why my house was no longer there. Various people in the crowd hastily told him what happened, or at least their version of it. But it looks like he got the gist. They all mobbed him when he tried to leave, but he fired a gun in the air, and they all scattered. He sped off in a Bronco with a couple of very large men and that was the end of that.

As I walked into the custodian's area on my first day back, my supervisor told me Dr. Seavers wanted to see me first thing. I nodded and casually walked down to his office. Mrs. Banks smiled and sent me right in. Seavers again apologized all over himself and I didn't feel like a custodian speaking to the president. It felt like we were speaking to each other man to man as equals.

"Joey, I have been talking to your grandfather and he tells me you now want to get a college degree. I would like to help. You are entitled to a partial tuition break since you are a full-time employee, and I can arrange for some scholarship money since you are over twenty-five and a first-generation college student. Once you finish your associate degree here, I can see about getting you enrolled at the university down the road if you would like to continue and get a bachelor's degree."

I accepted his offer, and I will be starting a class this fall. It's called English Composition. It meets three times a week at 11:00 am, so I guess that's the end of my daytime sleeping. I'm planning to study and write my papers in the library between class and work. I'm excited and kind of scared at the same time. We'll see how it goes. I decided that writing this story was a good way to practice my writing skills. Up until now, I had not written anything since high school. The future lies ahead.

EPILOGUE

Twenty years have passed since I first started college, and my life is completely different. It was an enormous amount of work, and more than once I wanted to quit, but I did finally get my four-year bachelor's degree on my thirty-fourth birthday. I started with just one class every semester, but then I picked it up to two, then three, and eventually, I was going full-time–all while working as a second-shift custodian.

Most college courses are taught in the morning or early afternoon, so class scheduling was never a problem. In the evenings, after I had finished my custodial responsibilities, I found a quiet place to study instead of playing cards with the others. I also studied and completed my projects on the weekends.

Computers became more prevalent on college campuses during this time and, our junior college opened a computer lab. Dr. Seavers gave me access to it after hours and generously gave me a computer to use at home. It wasn't a loan from the college inventory. It was a personal gift from him.

I was married by the time I graduated with my bachelor's degree. My wife was from out west and had come here to play on the women's basketball team. The best way I can describe her is she is an athletic tomboy who grew up to be beautiful.

She graduated when I did, but she chose one of those fun majors that isn't marketable, at least not in the mountains. I guess she could have found a job somewhere if she had been single and relocated. I once made the mistake of referring to her major as an M.R.S. degree and ended up spending the night in the back of my truck. I'm glad it was summer. She was so furious I considered heading back to the bunker.

She was a stay-at-home wife and then later a stay-at-home mom when our twin daughters came along. That was okay since I had found a good job right after I finished my undergraduate degree. I was an older graduate and well familiar with the challenges faced by the students from the local population, so the university hired me as an academic coach and advisor. Ironically, I later ended up advising Jack Hawkins' daughter. She was nothing like her father and a brilliant student. He was in prison during her upbringing, and I believe that was better for her. She took over my advising job a few years later. By then I had a master's and a doctorate.

After I successfully defended my dissertation, I was offered a teaching position at a university out west—not far from where my wife grew up. My parents and grandparents lived long enough to see me get my undergraduate degree, but they have since passed away.

When we moved out here, I decided it was best to turn my land inheritance over to my older brother. I won't go into it, but he was never a family favorite and was left out of the will when it came time to divide the property after my parents died. I helped him get my old job as a custodian at the junior college, but he didn't go any further than that. He now lives the life I almost had—mopping floors in the evenings and hunting and fishing in his spare time. But since he now has a stable job with benefits and a free place to live, I don't have to worry about him so much.

It was also better for my wife and kids to get away from there. They never enjoyed living in the mountains, especially after they learned what had happened to me years earlier in the diner. I would have been content to never tell them about it, but you can't keep an incident like that quiet. My wife already knew a version of it before she and I ever met, and the girls heard about it at school. They both requested to be home-schooled since many of their classmates were related to various people from the diner, a few of which died in prison.

The story that's now passed around is I didn't really go to the beach for four weeks after the incident, and my dad and I did in fact go on the big game hunting trip to some "far flung place." I think this new rumor started when I did have the opportunity to meet Ted Nugent and get my picture with him. I thoughtlessly put a framed copy of it in my office at work and the story went from there.

This is how they think I got the money to rebuild my home and go to college for so many years. Obviously, these people have never heard of homeowners insurance, automobile insurance, tuition scholarships, and graduate stipends. And why would I continue pushing a mop and later work full-time as an academic advisor if I had all that money? It's not that people don't know the truth, it's that they don't want to know the truth—but that is no longer my problem.

For years I was furious over what had happened to me. I lost some special and personal things because of selfishness and cruelty. Plus, I never felt completely safe in my own home after that and for years there were nights when I couldn't sleep at all—even though I was closer to my family. We installed an alarm, but I would often get up and check it three or four times during the night. We talked about modifying the underground shelter into a permanent home for me, but that would have been like living in a prison.

Peacefully attending the church I had grown up in became an impossibility. Not long after the incident, a couple of the parishioners, who were assuming I did have a lot of money, got in my face after a Sunday morning service and started carrying on about how I should forgive my enemies and help them financially because that is what a real

Christian would do. I guess they were hoping I could be guilted into sharing some of my nonexistent bounty.

I responded by asking them if they had confronted my attackers for their behavior that day. They said no. I quickly pointed out that although they were confronting me because I was mad about what those people had done to me, it wasn't right they were not willing to also confront the people who had started the whole thing. They quickly responded that I was the one who had started it because I had told everyone to "stick it" when the others had politely asked for some desperately needed help.

I was about to respond with some choice words, but my grandfather spun me around and pulled me away from the conversation. I didn't attend church or even pick up a Bible for years afterward.

Many years later, with the help of my wife and a good therapist, I was finally able to forgive those people–as crazy as that might sound. As my wife later pointed out, those people were still controlling me even though we lived far away and many of them had long since died. But despite that, they still had a grip on me. And she was right. At my wife's urging, I went to see a therapist who happened to share our faith.

It was during one of the sessions I came to realize something. Even though I had had to endure running for my life, losing my truck, losing my home, and the complete loss of my inner peace, I was still able to overcome it all and become more successful than I would have been otherwise. When you think about it, if none of those horrible things had happened to me, I might still be a lonely bachelor in the mountains. The therapist pointed out a verse in Romans about everything working together for good. I don't remember the chapter and verse. You'll have to find it yourself, but it's there.

It was also during these sessions I had another revelation. I finally had to admit that if I had not lost my temper and left the diner when Buzz first advised me to go, a lot of that trouble might have been avoided. Even if they had still gotten violent, it would have been much tougher for them to justify their actions if I had controlled my anger and attempted to walk away peacefully from the onset.

I always thought forgiving those people would make me feel weak, but the opposite was true. It made me feel stronger. Years of anger and frustration were finally released.

Over time my sleeping habits improved, and several of my new friends and colleagues noticed a change in my personality. But true forgiveness can be elusive over the long haul. Now and then, when I think about a lost family heirloom I could have given to one of my daughters or a lost picture I would have wanted to show them, the fury starts creeping back. There are also people in that town who still believe the whole thing was my fault and that I deserved what I got that day. But as I start dwelling on that, I catch myself and ask for help. I never want my peace and happiness to be robbed by the actions of others ever again—not if I can help it.

I have also established a benevolence fund in the church in that town. The pastors can use those funds at their discretion to help anyone, whether they are members of the church or not. For all I know, some of the money might have gone to people who hurt me, or their relatives who were later cruel to me. The pastors never tell anyone where the money comes from. Remarkably, doing that has also helped me a great deal.

But the true hero of this story is Buzz. He had lost everything and would have been justified in leaving town immediately when he heard Ivan was in the vicinity recruiting a new hunter. But he instead stayed long enough to warn me.

My family and I are now happier than we have ever been. We have a home in a nice neighborhood and a multitude of good friends. We also live near my wife's family so the kids can see their grandparents, uncles, aunts, and cousins regularly. Last year I was promoted to a tenured position, so here is where we will stay.

I recently ran into Buzz. My wife and I were eating breakfast at a ski resort when I spotted him busing tables. The years had not been kind. His hair was long and it had turned white. His unshaven face was weather-beaten, and he was in the beginning stages of osteoporosis. I guess carrying that backpack around for so many years had taken its toll. I was elated because I guess that meant Lorcan's evil empire had never caught up with him. I wanted to see if I could help him. I had a few hundred dollars in my pocket and wanted to give him all of it. I also wanted to see if I could do anything else to help him. I made eye contact as he walked by my table. He paused for a second and gave me a confused look like he knew me from somewhere but couldn't quite place me. But when he recognized me a split second later, he immediately turned and went back in the kitchen. I didn't see him again for the rest of the meal. I later learned he walked out the back door without saying a word to anyone.

He was never heard from again.

www.ingramcontent.com/pod-product-compliance
Lightning Source LLC
Chambersburg PA
CBHW070859260626
47162CB00007B/2509